Beds in the East

ANTHONY BURGESS

Beds in the East

HEINEMANN : LONDON

William Heinemann Ltd
15 Queen Street, Mayfair, London W1X 8BE

LONDON MELBOURNE TORONTO
JOHANNESBURG AUCKLAND

First published in 1959
Reissued 1968
Reprinted 1973
© by Anthony Burgess 1959

434 09814 0

Printed Offset Litho and bound in Great Britain
by Cox & Wyman Ltd,
London, Fakenham and Reading

Allah is great, no doubt, and Juxtaposition his prophet (*Amours de Voyage*)

Good, too, Logic, of course; in itself, but not in fine weather. (*The Bothie of Tober-na-Vuolich*)

—ARTHUR HUGH CLOUGH

To Edward Jones, Esq., M.Sc.

I

Either side of the bed was the wrong side. True, it was possible to get out of it by inching slowly forward on one's fat brown rump to the foot, but that, for some reason, often woke both of them. It was better, far better, to risk waking only one. But, this lie-abed dawn of the Sabbath, which one?

Syed Omar lay for an instant debating, caught in an agony of indecision which was no grim pleasure. In common with the rest of the country, he had not absorbed all that much from the West. He could speak English, drive a car, distinguish blindfold between brands of brandy, run an office, smell out injustice a mile off, but no white official had ever spoken to him of those philosophies fashionable in post-war Europe. It was all too late now to complete the course; his elected rulers had not heard Toynbee warn of the danger of sipping, rather than draining, the West. And now the jungle, after its short doze, was ready to march coastward again.

On one side lay Maimunah, his wife; on the other lay Zainab, also his wife. He lay walled in by brown female flesh. And that was wrong, most irregular, uncleanly, contrary to the strict Islamic custom. But the house had only one bedroom and in that bedroom there was no inch of space for what was not purely functional. The Malay language was more exact than the English in calling it a sleep-room. And in his house Syed Omar did little more than sleep.

On other beds lay his children, the palpable record of his past virility, the breathing memoranda of his present responsibility. As the light came up, brown chubby limbs, careless in sleep, were defined, and innocent mouths open, as in the ecstasy of hearing music. All round the room brown blossomed in many shades—coffee of varying strengths, varying temperings of tinned milk, from the watery brew of Sin Chai's shop to the robust infusion of Ooi Boo Eng: many kinds of brown, flat and unsumptuous in the hard light, dredged from the unrecorded pasts of his own and his wives' families, and eighteen or so different sizes, denoting the harvests of eighteen or more years. Syed Hassan, the eldest, his sleeping mouth pouting as into a microphone, his delinquent hair tousled; Sharifah Khairun, only four, her sarong kicked off, her perm glossy on the pillow. All the boys Syeds, all the girls Sharifahs, proud little trumpets before their individual names, proclaiming them to be of the line of the Prophet.

Syed Omar, their father, felt again the prostatic twinges which he must now accept, at dawn or false dawn, as appropriate to his forty-seven years. True, he had been drinking the night before (and now the night before began to shape itself in his mind and he began to palpitate) but that made no difference. Every morning was the same. He swung his legs over the sleeping form of Maimunah. She breathed gently to the ceiling. But, as always with one or the other, his levering hand jabbed her thigh and she woke.

It was her custom to wake, when roused accidentally thus, in shock, as though the thieves, murderers, ravishers had at last arrived. Zaïnab's way was to resume, almost in mid-sentence, the monologue of the evening before. He had not done this, he had not done that, what was to happen to her children (*her* children)? Syed Omar pre-

2

ferred, on slight reflection, the more dramatic *aubade*.

"Go back to sleep."

"Eh? Eh? What?"

"Sleep." Incisive, firm, so that a ripple passed over the sleepers. Syed Omar surveyed them all, splay-foot and stubby, tying his sarong at the waist, surveyed them like a general surveying the carnage. "Sleep," he said more soothingly, like Titania or a mass-hypnotist, but it was too late. A small child (its name did not come automatically to mind) looked up at him from clear morning eyes, and Hassan called from his unconscious, in a loud adolescent voice:

"Dig that cat."

Syed Omar stared, wondering what this could mean, frightened, as hearing the voice of prophecy. But he padded through the wrack of stirring bodies and reached the bathroom, which was under water. It was the women of the house who were most inconvenienced, he reflected, by its being situated on an old paddy-field. He could stand, as he did now, on the top step, on the shore of the flood, and perform this first morning act with no trouble. As long as the wet season lasted, his wives would suffer from an excess of water in the wrong places, and in the dry they would suffer from no water at all. Still, the more elemental their sufferings the better: they could thus be distracted from those more sophisticated grievances which transcended season. But their grievances were nothing to his.

As he stood, long, on the step, Syed Omar reviewed the previous night. There had been a farewell dinner for Maniam. Cold curry and warm rice, toasts and speeches. Many speeches. The Chief Police Officer and the Officer Superintending Police Circle and the Officer Commanding Police District and the Officer in Charge of the Special Branch and various other officials had stood up and spoken,

3

some in Malay, some in English, some in both, about the good work Maniam had done. He had come for a brief time only as relief Chief Clerk, they said, but they were all sorry to see him return to Pahang, they were appreciative of the great work of reorganisation he had done, they revered him as a man and loved him as a friend. With men like him sitting organising in offices, a free Malaya had nothing to fear. Mr. Godsave, the last white man of the Police Department, said that he himself would soon, with many other of his fellow-countrymen, be leaving this land he had learned to love so well (hear, hear) and, in the rigours of an English winter, often look back nostalgically at happy days spent in the East. He might say that, not only in Malaya, but also in India, he had learned to respect the ability of the Jaffna Tamils, of which race Mr. Maniam was an undoubted ornament. (Here Mr. Maniam had shone, ornamentally, smugly.) Mr. Godsave said that the Jaffna Tamils had been brought up in a tradition of service to the State which might well be taken as a model by the other races. He concluded by saying that it was a great loss to the State Police Department that Mr. Maniam should be going, but that his work would long be remembered and be an inspiration to those who had had the good fortune to work with him.

Then Syed Omar, uncalled, unexpected, had stood and said, in English:

"Much time has been spent tonight in praising Maniam. I do not stand up to praise Maniam. I stand up to say the truth about Maniam. I know his race and I know him. I know his methods and I know the methods of his race. I would say this. If Maniam wants to get on, let him get on. But let him not get on by grinding the faces of others into the dust. If he wants to climb, let him climb, but let him not climb over me. I know that he has been telling others

4

that I am not good in my job. I know that he has been making a list of the days I have taken off. And I also know that his sister-in-law was brought specially from Kuala Lumpur so that she could meet the C.P.O. and waggle her bottom at him and show him her teeth and show how fast she could take down shorthand and how well she could type. I know I cannot take down shorthand fast, but I have never pretended to be able to take down shorthand fast. But my heart is pure and I am a man of integrity. I have always tried to do my work well. Now there comes a man to lie about me and try to have me kicked out. This is the man you have praised. I warn you, especially you Malays, that you have enemies in your midst, and this Maniam is one of them. The Jaffna Tamils will try to grind you in the dirt and snatch the rice from the mouths of your wives and children. They have no love for Malaya but only for themselves. They are a lot of bastards. Thank you."

Syed Omar completed his morning's libation, thoughtful, surveying the rest of that lively evening. There had been no fight. There had been many restraining arms which Maniam, for his part, had not needed, for he kept saying, over and over: "I forgive him. He is still my brother. It is proper to forgive those who revile us," somewhat like an unmuscular Christian. But Syed Omar had said: "I swear in the name of God that there are clerks and peons who will bear witness that I have, myself, restrained them from doing physical harm to Maniam. But Maniam has not gone yet. There is still time. His plane does not leave till twelve tomorrow." Friends had carried Syed Omar off to a coffee-shop, and there beer and adrenalin had flowed till midnight.

War, thought Syed Omar, adjusting his sarong. War, he thought, with an unholy thrill. The Malays against the world. But, entering the bare living-room he was chidden by a poster on the wall. It was a portrait of the Chief Minister, smiling benevolently and extending loving silk-clad arms. Beneath, in ornamental Arabic script, was the single legend *Keamanan:* Peace.

The children were rising, tuning up for the day The wives had started a whining canon about the price of dried fish, arranging the while each other's hair. Hassan was already at the radio, squeezing out a remote early-rising station. At the single table, over which presided a grave portrait of the Sultan, little Hashim was doing his homework. It was Geography, and, in a labour of neatness, the child wove the words of an essay.

"What is this?" asked his father, not unkindly. Hashim was his favourite, the hope of the family, the only child who wore glasses:

"Ceylon, Father."

"Ceylon? Ceylon? Who gave you Ceylon?"

"Mr. Parameswaran, Father."

Syed Omar breathed over the child's thin shoulders, reading: "Jaffna is the most important part of Ceylon. The Jaffna Tamils come from there. They are hard-working people and very clever. In Malaya are many Jaffna Tamils. They are in many government things. They help to run Malaya properly."

Syed Omar, enraged, clutched and crumpled the essay, uttering a stricken cry. Hashim, astonished, looked on and then began to wail. Syed Omar blindly clawed the child's atlas and crunched Ceylon and Jaffna with it, and all the encircling ocean. Soon the wives came and Hassan gave an adolescent guffaw.

Syed Omar cried: "It is for you I do this, for you! But no appreciation, no thought! I am nobody in this house, nobody! I am going out!"

He began to descend the house stairs to the flooded path, but found he was unshod and half-naked. He returned sheepishly and sulked in a corner. Hassan, having forgotten to switch off his grin, grinned at the radio dial and then produced from the set a sudden brassy blast which opened Syed Omar's sweat-ducts. He panted in the corner, his eyes misty.

Maimunah said: "Cannot afford to tear up books with the wage you bring in. A disgrace." Zainab comforted the snivelling Hashim: "There, there. Bad, bad Father."

Syed Omar said, sarcastically: "Enough of this nonsense. My breakfast, if you please. In four hours' time I must be at the airport."

At that moment, in profound crapula, the élite of the Jaffna Tamils of the town were already drinking coffee, black and bitter. After the Police party had come the party in Vythilingam's house. Vythilingam was the State Veterinary Officer and with him Maniam had been staying. Maniam was a nephew of Vythilingam, or perhaps an uncle or a cousin: relationship was not clearly defined, but relationship existed. Indeed, relationship existed between all the Jaffna Tamils who sat in their striped sarongs this Friday morning and day of Maniam's departure, silent and aching. Jaffna is a small community. The party that had just ended had been, in some measure, Hellenic, a black shining parody of the Symposium at which Socrates had spoken of the virtues of intellectual love and Alcibiades had come in tight, slobbering his admiration for the snub-nosed master. Alcibiades was Arumugam, the Air Control Officer, whose manly beauty was marred by a high squeaking voice with curious gargling undertones. Socrates was Sundralingam, the doctor. He, with flashing glasses, had spoken at length of the nugatory value of the heterosexual relationship: women were there solely to produce more Jaffna Tamils, the romantic poets had written nonsense, to place woman on a pedestal was a Western perversion. Arumugam had kept saying: "How right you are," his eunuch's voice somehow giving a sour-grapes quality to the agreement. But it was all really sour grapes. All close to, or in, the thirties, they had not yet found wives. Women there were in the town, but not women of the right sort. They wanted women of good caste and of the right colour, worthy of professional men. Kularatnam, the State Inspector of Motor Vehicles, had not come to the party. He was in disgrace, for it was known he was carrying on with a plump and well-favoured Malay princess who kept a bookshop.

Vythilingam knew that he too would soon be in disgrace. As his guests sucked at their coffee, he said tentatively: "Could anyone . . ." The word would not come out. He had not so much a slight stutter as a slight hesitation. He raised his mild face to the ceiling, as though the better to exhibit the glottal spasm. "Anyone . . ." If it was food he was going to suggest, they all thought not. "Not just yet," said Sockalingam, the dentist. "Anyone . . ." Their language was English, the language of professional men. ". . . eat some fried eggs with onions?"

After so much effort, "No" would seem an ungracious answer. They grunted and Vythilingam called his Siamese servant. Vythilingam glanced mildly round at the company, their faces creasing with pain as the sharp light from the window caught their hangovers. "We'll all feel . . ." Maniam shook his head with a sad smile. ". . . better . . ." But behind the mildness what tigers, what jungles. The speech hesitation was a symptom of the most complicated tensions. The hands that performed their veterinary duties with such tenderness and skill could cheerfully throttle

8

necks. Vythilingam knew how to hate. First, he hated the British. He had smarted from what he called British injustice ever since he could remember. He had seen ill-qualified tow-haired officials promoted over his head. In Kuala Lumpur once a British soldier had called him a nigger. A former white State Veterinary Officer had once said to him: "Of course, you've only got a colonial degree . . ." Another white man had once tried to take him into a white man's club, and the Chinese steward, lackey of the British, had ejected him. The white man had shrugged his shoulders, said: "Sorry, old boy," and then walked in on his own. But before that, before he was born even, his father, a clerk in Ceylon, had actually been struck on the face by an Englishman. Or, at least, that was a tradition in the family. Out of this hatred of the British stemmed hatred for his mother, for she had, after his father's death, married an Englishman, a tea-planter settled in Ceylon. And that was why he was going to spite his mother by marrying a woman she had not even met, let alone chosen. And yet in his choice of a wife there was something masochistic. Rosemary's reputation was known; he would, by obscure logic, become retrospectively a cuckold. Her caste, as her name, the name of a Christian, proclaimed, was of the lowest, and that hurt, and yet that would hurt his mother more, and yet perhaps it would not, because what had she done but marry a Christian? But it should not hurt him really, nor should the knowledge of her looseness, for he was a Communist and race and religion and caste did not matter, morality was a bourgeois device of oppression. And yet he kept his Communism quiet, because he was a Government officer. But if he was a Communist he should be in the jungle now, stinging the effete capitalist régime with odd bullets. But he did not really like the Chinese. And he was not really fighting the oppressive British, whatever he did, for they were leaving Malaya anyhow. And again, he was only really happy when injecting penicillin into ailing cows, or putting thermometers into the anuses of sick cats, and he would literally not hurt a fly, which all reeked of Hinduism, and his mother, though she had married a Christian, was still a devout Hindu.

The Siamese boy brought in plates containing wormy shreds of over-fried egg, seasoned with blackened bits of onion. Everyone languidly picked at this breakfast. The sun rose higher, the day warmed. Dr. Sundralingam spoke his first words of the day, and, as if, against his will, time had been wasting, he said urgently to Maniam:

"Do you think you can get Samy that job?" Samy was Kanikasamy, first cousin to Sundralingam. "You know the people down there; I don't."

"I think so," said Maniam. "The Malays just can't do the work. The fools won't see it, they won't accept it. But I think I can fix up a vacancy. The pay won't be much at first, but there are bound to be other vacancies, higher up the scale. Don't worry."

"And do you think it's going to be all right for Neelam?" asked Arumugam. His high voice smote wounded nerves like a fortissimo flute. Neelam was the sister-in-law of Maniam and a cousin or niece or aunt of everybody present.

"Yes. Syed Omar will be out. That's definite. If only you could have heard him last night . . ."

"You'll have to be careful. He is very hot-blooded."

"It is all talk," smiled Maniam. "They talk and talk and shout but they never do anything. Besides, it is too late for him to do anything."

"Be careful, just the same," warned Arumugam.

Vythilingam covertly looked at his watch. Soon it would

be time for him to shave, dress, and, his professional black bag on the seat beside him, drive to Rosemary's house. In that house there were several cats, eight or nine of them, all of them presents from Vythilingam. She had once complained of mice. This was the only way he could visit her, the professional way, solicitous for the cats' welfare, ready with Vitamin B injections, penicillin, tonic drops, for she was panicky about what the neighbours would say if they saw men visiting her purely socially. Supposing spiteful people wrote to her boy-friend in England, saying she was carrying on? Then her boy-friend would never marry her. But Vythilingam knew that her boy-friend would never marry her anyway. Once, at a dance, he had seen this boy-friend, proud and white in his dinner-jacket, circling in a waltz, Rosemary in his arms. This boy-friend, dancing, had caught the eye of a friend of his, a loutish ginger salesman of tobacco. He had made, taking his right hand from Rosemary's back to do it, an unmistakable ithyphallic sign and followed it with a wink. The British never kept their promises. And that Rosemary had been defiled by this Englishman gave Vythilingam a twinge of curious grim elation. His marriage to her would be a gesture of many kinds of revenge.

"I think, now," said Vythilingam, "we ought . . ."

"There is plenty of time," said Maniam. "My plane doesn't go till midday."

"Ought . . ."

Black but comely, Rosemary Michael sat in the full sunlight of her living-room, re-reading the last letter from Joe. Everywhere cats lolled, fought, played, stalked, washed: the many cats of a spinster, but Rosemary was only a spinster in the strict sense of denotation. She was eminently, eminently nubile.

The perfection of her beauty was absurd. The lack of flaw was a kind of deformity. It was not possible to say what racial type of beauty she exemplified: the eyes, black, were all East—houris, harems, beds scented with Biblical spices; nose and lips were pan-Mediterranean. Her body, clad now in a wide-skirted, crisp imported model, was that of the Shulamite and Italian film stars. The décolletage, with its promise of round, brown, infinitely smooth, vertiginous sensual treasure, was a torment to the blood. Yet only to the white man were these treasures revealed, for Rosemary could not stand the touch of brown fingers. The list of her lovers was formidable, ranging from the District Officer to the manager of the local Cold Storage. Many had promised marriage, but all had gone home, the promise unfulfilled. For Rosemary had little to offer, except her body, her fragments of training college learning, her ability to arrange flowers, and her quite considerable capacity for all kinds of sensuous pleasure. She desperately wanted marriage with a European, but she didn't want marriage without love. Love, of course, was the familiar hoarse entreaty after the evening's drinking, and Rosemary would quickly enough yield to the entreaty, hearing the love grow hoarser and more urgent and thinking too, 'How can he fail to go on wanting me for ever once he knows what I'm capable of giving?' And true, the men did go on wanting her for a long time, till the end of the tour or till transfer or till Rosemary's voice—inexpertly Sloane Square after much drinking—made them cringe with embarrassment. And other things got them down—her inordinate passion for Worcester sauce, her wanting to be wanted all the time, her tears, tears which didn't humanise her face by making it pathetically ugly but just made it not a face at all, her lack of 'reality-control' (she just didn't literally know whether she was lying or telling the truth). And now, all over Malaya, the white men were leaving—the brown sauce-stain spreading over the table-cloth—and time was getting short.

But Joe was still writing, and Joe had promised to send her an engagement ring, and Joe said he was still looking for a job, a good job, so that she wouldn't have to work once she was married. Rosemary believed him, and a proof of her faith was her three-months' fidelity, despite the occasional crying-out of her warm woman's blood. Again she read:

. . . I keep thinking of you and I all the time in bed together. Honestly, darling, on these long winter nights when I am lying on my own I want you more than ever. Yesterday I saw old Mac and we had a couple of drinks together, just like old times, and he introduced me to his sister who is really a smasher, but I wouldn't have anything to do with her, because I keep thinking of you. I do hope you are keeping yourself for me and not seeing other men. You can see Crabbe, of course, because Crabbe is by way of being your boss and there wouldn't be any funny business with Crabbe anyway, him being past all that. Well, darling, I am looking for a good job still, but there are not many cars being sold now, and who knows I may be back in good old Malaya before long if Mac can get me in with this new export firm. But I know you would want me to definitely try and fix something up here, you knowing England and liking it so much. Well now I have come to the end of the paper, these air-mail letter-forms are too small, aren't they, so close now with fondest love from your Joe.

That was really a lovely letter, much nicer than the one in which he had told her not to send any Christmas presents to his father and mother, as his family did not go in much for presents. He had been really rude about it, but he had at least added: "Save the money, darling, to help furnish our little house." Rosemary had a shrewd idea that Joe had not told his parents anything about her, and that perhaps was a bad sign. Perhaps they had this absurd colour prejudice.

And yet, she reflected, she had seen little enough of this absurd colour prejudice when she had been in Liverpool, doing her course of teacher training. How the men had been after her! She had been treated royally. Her story then had been that she was part Hawaiian and part Javanese, a romantic combination, and she had not denied the soft flattering suggestion that perhaps she was of princes' stock. The middle-class low-caste Christian Tamil family in Kuala Hantu had then ceased to exist. And the distinguished, grey-haired managing director who had asked for her hand (if she wished, they could have separate bedrooms) and the tall young men at Claridge's and the appearance on 'In Town Tonight' and in the *Daily Mirror* and modelling for Norman Hartnell. How graciously the Queen had bowed to her! But no, perhaps that hadn't really happened. Surely, though, the Secretary of State for the Colonies had pleaded with her not to return to Malaya, that night they were dancing among chandeliers and decorations-will-be-worn, massed flowers and champagne. It all happened, of course it all happened.

What happened now was that the front door of the small Education Department house was pushed open and massed flowers entered. Behind the massed flowers was Jalil, the Turk, a man who worked in the Town Board offices but had shares in a couple of rubber plantations. Emir Jalil, as he liked to be called, put the flowers rudely on the table and then, without invitation, sat down in the only other arm-chair. He was squat, short-necked, beady-eyed, strong-nosed, fifty, wore a cravat in his open shirt and breathed heavily, being asthmatic. The cats, knowing he hated cats, approached him with fascination, and one tough tom, with a face like Disraeli, tried to climb on to his knee. Emir Jalil brushed it off roughly.

"You shouldn't come here," said Rosemary excitedly in English. "You know you shouldn't. I gave the amah instructions not to let you in. Supposing somebody sees you, with all those flowers too? Supposing somebody writes him a letter? Ooooh!" (a pure round open Tamil O.) "Go now, please go now, please go!"

"Come eat," said Jalil. "Come drink. Come make jolly time." He coughed long and sighed after it.

"I can't," said Rosemary, agitated. "You know I can't. Oh, please go."

"He not marry you," said Jalil. "He never marry. He tell me he not marry you."

"No, he didn't," said Rosemary. "It's a lie, you're a liar. He's going to send me a ring."

Jalil indulged in comfortable, quiet, asthmatic laughter. Rosemary saw the flowers and walked briskly over to them on high heels. Her ankles were possibly, just possibly, not by any means at all certainly, a little too thin. She put the flowers in water, thinking that with Jalil it was a bit awkward making up one's mind whether one ought to shudder at the prospect of his touching one or not. She had read in a book that Turkey was really part of Europe, which meant that Jalil was a European. But how could he be? He was a Muslim and had three wives, and Europeans were Christians and had only one wife. But Jalil looked like a European. And he had money. And he could divorce his other wives. Yet he never said he loved her. If he panted at all, it was with asthma.

She brought the flowers back from the kitchen sink to

the living-room. Three cats jumped up on to the table to inspect them, one—a half-Siamese—trying to lap the water. Jali coughed and sighed again, his chest labouring, and, in a resigned sort of way, took from his shirt pocket a cigarette-case. His thick fingers, grasping the case, produced also a green card which, caught for a moment in the fresh breeze, fluttered to the floor by Rosemary's feet. Jalil wheezed up from his chair with some agility to retrieve the card, and Rosemary thought she saw guilt or anxiety, certainly a twinge of disconcertment. Rosemary herself snatched it rapidly from under a cat's hind paws and scanned it with appetite.

"I get yesterday from Postmaster," said Jalil. "I mean give as surprise."

"You disgusting, disgusting, horrible . . ." Rosemary stamped her foot as a substitute for the noun she could not find. "It's mine. It says there's a parcel for me. Oh, go away, get out. I never want to see . . ."

"I mean bring as surprise. Make happy." Jalil was seated again, recomposed.

"You didn't want me to see it. You wanted to keep it from me. Because you're jealous. Oooooh!" Suddenly Rosemary was alive with excitement. "It's the ring, it's the ring. He's sent it at last. It's in the Customs Office." She jerked from one emotion to the other. "And I could have had it yesterday. And you kept it from me. Oh, you horrible, horrible pig of a man." She kicked his right shin vigorously. Jalil gave a deep chesty chirp of laughter. "And today the Office is closed. And I can't get it. But he's sent it, he's sent it, it's here!" Her face all alight, she was not perhaps so beautiful as in vaccine repose; the features could not stand much of the humanising distortion which makes for a more civilised comeliness. But the teeth were all there, ridiculously white and even.

"Come drink," said Jalil. "Come make jolly time."

"Not with you, not if you were the last man in the world," she said, all pout and stormy eyes. And then she swung over. "Oh, I must celebrate, I must, I must."

"Be sure what in parcel first."

"It's the ring, it must be the ring!"

"We go see. We go on way to drink and make jolly."

"But it's closed. It's Friday. There's nobody there."

"We go. Is watchman there. He open for me. He give parcel. Me he owe money."

"Oh, Jalil, Jalil, can we? Oh, I could kiss you."

Jalil did not seem to want to be kissed. He sat still, quietly asthmatically chuckling almost with no sound.

"You go get ready," he said.

"Nothing matters now," said Rosemary. "They can say what they like. They can gossip all they want to. I'm engaged, engaged!" She pranced into her bedroom, singing horribly high, then pranced back again to the photograph, framed in silver, which stood on her Public Works Department escritoire. "Oh, my Joe, my Joe," she crooned, flattening her breasts with the hugged picture, then drawing it away, adoring it, then covering the mean mouth, the pale wavy hair and the knowing eyes with kisses. "My Joe, Joe, Joe, Joe." Then she pranced off again to her dressing-table. Jalil coughed, sighed and chuckled comfortably.

When she was ready, Vythilingam was standing shyly by the open door. Jalil was still in the arm-chair, breathing deeply and seeming to brood on the picture of Vythilingam hovering awkwardly, as though he were really a picture.

"Oh, Vy," cried Rosemary, "it's come, the ring's come, I'm engaged!" She had already begun to celebrate: too much lipstick, like too much drink, her hair pulled back stark—the style she favoured for dances—into a top-knot secured by a round silver grip.

Vythilingam exhibited his working larynx, his eyes up to the ceiling as though inspecting damp. His lips chewed. "I know, I know," sang Rosemary. "It's marvellous, isn't it? It's made me almost speechless, too. I'm going off to get it now, Vy. Oooooh, I can hardly wait."

Vythilingham began : "I . . ."

"Tigger," said Rosemary, "has been a bit off his food." She nodded at a great striped creature that sat like a hen, hatching malevolence. "Do give him something to make him eat, there's a dear. Oh, I'm so happy." She was off down the path, to Jalil's car. Jalil got up, as if with effort, and made a kind of warbling noise to Vythilingam, a throaty descending half-octave of chromatics, nodding not unpleasantly the while, and he lumbered out. The cats surveyed Vythilingam expectantly, without unease, as though he and they were opposing teams lined up.

In the airport stood Crabbe, leaning on the bar, the only white in a sea of brown. Malays were everywhere—on the bar-stools, drinking iced water or nothing, round the rattan tables, promenading up and down as in an opera interval, crouching miner-like, sitting tailor-wise, standing, leaning, surrounding Crabbe with a faint smell of warmth, a hint of musk. They had come from the town and the kampongs to watch the pilgrims return. They had come early, time being no object. Crabbe caught stern fishermen's faces, the resigned droop of poor farmers, the up-looking open-mouthed wonder of the children, perhaps seeing white skin for the first time but too polite to chatter about the prodigy. The women sailed along or sat in long patience. Hard light defined their clear flat features, the extravagant sarong-patterns, flowing in from the naked airstrip, accentuating the pallor that gazed back at Crabbe from the mirror behind the bar. Crabbe looked at himself: hair now riding back from his forehead, the beginnings of a jowl. He looked down at his paunch, pulled it in, flinched at the effort, let it out again. He thought it was perhaps better to be middle-aged, less trouble. That growing old was a matter of volition was a discovery he had only recently made, and it pleased him. It was infantile, of course, like the pleasure of controlling excretion, but transitional periods of history had always appealed to him most—Silver Ages, Hamlet eras, when past and future were equally palpable and, opposing, could produce current. Not that he wanted action. But, of course, that was true of the phase, and that was why the phase didn't last long. Imagine a Silver Age *Æneid*! And so let middle age come, him grow paunchy, no longer show his profile to women, stand at the Club bar rather than dance. He felt he wanted nothing further from women, anyway, his first wife dead, his second wife having left him. His state appealed to him—an Education Officer waiting to hand over to the brown man he was training, in the twilight of British rule. Suddenly, poking with a match the swollen cigarette-ends in the water of the ash-tray, he saw all this as romantic—the last legionary, his aloneness, the lost cause really lost—and instinctively he pulled in his paunch, stroked down his hair to cover the naked part of the scalp, and wiped the sweat off his cheeks. He caught the eye of a Malay girl in the mirror and smiled wanly, hiding his teeth. She moved out of the mirror, smiling though, and in something like good humour he ordered more beer.

Moving through the crowd towards him he recognised Syed Omar, plump, bothered, in a shirt with a newspaper pattern. Syed Omar nearly tripped over a child on the floor, apologised to the mother, greeted a Malay farmer with a false smile and then stood by Crabbe, saying:

"Where is the bastard? Has the bastard arrived yet?"

"Which particular one?"

"The Tamil bastard, Maniam, the one who has tried to have me kicked out."

"Have a drink, Omar."

"A large brandy. I'll get him, I promise you I'll get him. Last night was no opportunity. I know they have told you, and everyone else, that I am a coward, but I was prevented last night, you see, prevented from having my revenge." He gripped his left breast, on which rode the printed photograph of a Hollywood star, and said: "I swear to you in the name of God I will get him." Crabbe read, on the right sleeve of Syed Omar's shirt: "Thanksgiving dinner is an unalterably American tradition. It must include roast turkey, cranberry sauce, creamed onions, potatoes, pumpkin and mincemeat pies. Since Pilgrim times, housewives have seized upon the stuffing of the bird as the one ingredient in this time-honored menu upon which they can exercise their individuality." Then Syed Omar's hairless arm began. "Those creamed onions sound good," said Crabbe. He looked inside Syed Omar's sleeve to see if the article continued on the hem.

"Yes, there is muscle there," said Syed Omar, "enough muscle for that hairless bastard."

"Some Tamils went upstairs to the control tower," said Crabbe. "I don't know this Maniam, but I'm quite sure I heard Arumugam's voice. He must be on duty up there." Syed Omar's brandy came and he sucked at it impatiently. After the sucking came tilting and pouring. He put the glass down.

"I'm going up there," he said.

"Oh, look here, Omar," said Crabbe. "Don't start anything, not today. The pilgrims are coming back, you know.

It's not my job to start telling you all about peace on earth and what-not, but I do think you might let it rest. You can't do any good."

"To him it is not good I intend to do."

"Forget it. Have another drink."

"No. While I am hot, while I am angry I will go." He resisted the friendly restraining hand of Crabbe, which clutched the article on Thanksgiving Day stuffings, and went. Crabbe watched the swim-suited film star on his back disappear in the crowd. He heard Syed Omar's voice, arguing with the Chinese official at the Customs barrier. He heard the voice climbing the stair to the control tower. Then he heard the approaching plane. The Malays heard it too and some went out to the airfield fence and the car park, straining their eyes to the west, where Mecca lay, whence, logically, the aircraft must appear. But its noise soon began to fill the south.

It landed in the outfield and slowly, clumsily approached, on fat, flat tyres. And now the Malays began to unleash their excitement. They wanted to get at the pilgrims, to touch them, to receive a blessing. The fence was too high to climb, so they moved—excited but orderly—towards the open sliding door which led to the control tower, the Customs barrier, the aircraft itself. They had already seen a Malay go through that doorway.

A Chinese, thin, nervous, in whites and a peaked cap, barred their way, saying: "*Tidak di-benar masok*. You cannot come in here." They pressed on. The Chinese said: "Please go back. It is not allowed." He tried to slide the door shut. His voice held no authority, he was nervous of kampong Malays; some had already got through, the door could not be closed. And now Crabbe left the bar, nervous himself because the plane had brought back from Singapore what he believed to be a precious burden. Crabbe tried to cut his way through the crowd, which yielded softly, courteously enough. Taller than any member of that crowd, he could see quite clearly the Chinese official do a foolish thing: he feebly pushed at the foremost man; with pork-defiled paws he laid hands on a Muslim. The glory of Mecca already shone on these simple folk. They could see, the foremost of them, the loose Arab robes, the Bedouin head-dresses, the turbans of the pilgrims who were already coming from the aircraft, hands ready to greet and bless though clutching cooking-pans and parcels. The kampong people would have no infidel between them and the glory. The official went to the wall, in a posture of crucifixion. His fellow leaped the documentation counter to help, shouting: "Back! Back!" He was entangled in Malays, and one fisherman thrust him aside like a curtain. The bar-boy ran out for a policeman. Now Crabbe was among them, shouting too. Him they would not harm, Englishmen being, though infidel, yet the race of past District Officers, judges, doctors, men perhaps, in their time, more helpful than otherwise, powerful but mild. Yet the more eager of the kampong people were already approaching the pilgrims with loud religious greetings, the rest of the crowd was following, and, ahead of the pilgrims, was the Chinese boy with the brief-case whom Crabbe had come to meet. They would tear him out of the way, they would knock him down and trample on him and perhaps his brief-case would be kicked away, lost, stolen. Crabbe ran, panting with middle age, and pulled the Chinese boy from the pilgrims and those who greeted them and embraced them, dragging him to a safe nook at the foot of the control tower stairs. The boy was frightened, saying: "What is this? What is happening?" But Crabbe had no breath.

Clamour before them, fright and anger and joy, and

now clamour above and behind them. Syed Omar was being kicked down the stairs by Dr. Sundralingam, and Arumugam's voice was piping loud. One sees so much violence on the screen, in the papers, reads about it, accepts it as part of the pattern, but one is always shocked anew by the aspects which records can't catch: the smell of sweat, the blood moving on the face, the hoarse breathlessness, the cracked voices speaking strange words. Sundralingam was nearly shirtless, Syed Omar's hair spiky, one of his sandals missing. But the Hollywood actress still posed in smiling languor, and the Thanksgiving Day article was intact. Syed Omar lay, his hands over his head, like a camel-boy in a sandstorm. The pilgrims passed him, some smiling gravely at what they considered to be an extravagant posture of veneration. Sundralingam and Arumugam were back up the stairs, perhaps to tend Maniam's wounds, Arumugam squeaking, Sundralingam panting and rumbling.

The crowd was clearing. The police had arrived, Malay police, standing shyly, doing nothing. The Chinese officials were drinking brandy in the office, quacking clipped indignation. The incident—if it was an incident—was over. "But this won't do," said Crabbe, "this won't do at all." Syed Omar, groaning, sat up. His forehead was bruised and his lip swollen. He felt his teeth methodically, one after the other, with a vibrato movement of finger and thumb.

"It won't do, will it?" said Crabbe. Syed Omar made a throaty animal noise. "Come and have some more brandy."

The place was fast emptying of Malays: the pilgrims had arrived, it would soon be time for mosque. At the bar were a few passengers and also Emir Jalil, asthmatic but benign, and Rosemary Michael, pouting and unhappy. Crabbe,

23

his arm on the Chinese boy's elbow, gave greeting. Syed Omar followed, twisting an eye-tooth like a violin-peg.

"Was fight," said Jalil. "We miss big fight." Rosemary pouted. "She not very happy. She think he send ring, but he not send ring. He not send anything."

"Oh, shut up, Jalil. Shut up, shut up." Rosemary began to cry quietly into her gin. Jalil chuckled silently.

"How unhappy we all are," said Crabbe. But the Chinese boy seemed neither unhappy nor happy. He waited, courteous, his brief-case under his arm.

"The pig," said Rosemary in gargoyle anger, "the bloody pig. He wants to hurt me, that's all." She cried. "Look at it," she cried, "and I thought it was going to be the ring." She cried bitterly. Syed Omar handled his back in a rheumatism pose, groaning. Crabbe examined the object, rising jauntily from bunched brown paper. It was a ghastly metal model of Blackpool Tower, its silver paint chipped. The note said: "Thinking of you here, Rosemary. Having lovely time at college. The men will not leave me alone! Janet."

"Janet da Silva," said Crabbe. "That's nice of her."

"And two dollars Customs charge," wailed Rosemary. Suddenly she stopped wailing and looked at Crabbe in a kind of horror. "Oh," she said. "I mustn't stay here. People will talk. Take me home, Victor. It's all right for you to take me home. Joe said so." She cried again at the name. "And I thought I was engaged. It would have been all right if I was engaged."

"You stay here," said Crabbe soothingly. "You have a nice drink with Jalil and Omar. They'll look after you. Robert and I have things to talk about."

"Take me home, Victor!"

Some of the passengers began to look at Crabbe with curiosity and envy. Crabbe said: "No. You stay here. Jalil

24

will take you home. Come on, Robert, we'd better be going."

Jalil watched them go out together. He said: "He not like women any more. He like only boys."

"Oh, shut up, Jalil."

"He like Chinese boys. Me, women I like."

2

The violins carried their sawing figuration up to the last chord, while the viola hinted at a sort of parody of the main theme and the 'cello plunged right down to its dark bottom string. Then the tape wound to the end, broke free and swished round and round. Crabbe switched the machine off. The silence contained an image of the quartet as a whole, clear and yet as though seen from a distance, so that the shape was more apparent than the details. The first movement had seemed to suggest a programme, each instrument presenting in turn a national style—a gurgling Indian cantilena on the 'cello, a kampong tune on the viola, a pentatonic song on the second violin and some pure Western atonality on the first. And then a scherzo working all these out stridently, ending with no resolution. A slow movement suggesting a sort of tropical afternoon atmosphere. A brief finale, ironic variations on a somewhat vapid 'brotherhood of man' motif. It was a young work, boyish in many ways, but it held together, it was coherent, and it showed remarkable technical competence. Its composer had never heard a live quartet, knew the masterpieces only from broadcasts and gramophone records, and some of the orchestral works he studied—Mahler, Berg, Schönberg—he had never heard at all. And yet the score of the symphony Crabbe held on his knee—neat spidery dots and lines and curves, showing a kinship to Chinese calligraphy—seemed confident in its handling of orchestral forces on a perhaps too large scale, its use of unorthodox combinations—xylophone, harps, piccolo and three trumpets, for example—and its precise signals of dynamics and expression.

Crabbe looked at Robert Loo—Mozart, Beethoven, Brahms, Loo—and felt irritated that he showed no sign of either pride or humility, no excitement, not even a craftsman's dissatisfaction. He merely examined closely one of the parts of his quartet, saying: "The second violin played A natural instead of A flat. That was my fault. I made a mistake in copying it out."

Crabbe asked yet again: "What did they say about it?"

"As I told you, not very much. Mr. Crispin said that the violin writing was awkward in places, Mr. Sharpe said that one piece of treble stopping on the viola was impossible, Mr. Bodmin said he enjoyed the 'cello part."

"And what about Schwarz?"

"Oh, yes. Mr. Schwarz asked to be remembered to you. He said it was a pity that Mrs. Crabbe married, because she had a promising musical career. And he said he was sorry she died."

Just like that. Musicians could be inhuman, musicians were mere functions, themselves instruments played by music. But, after all, he was only eighteen with an eighteen-year-old's callousness; after all, English was only his second language and he was deaf to its harmonics. But Crabbe saw Robert Loo now as a rather dreary boy, not very intelligent, emotionally less mature than he should be, strapped to a talent which had, quite arbitrarily, chosen him, driving him to teach himself to read music at fourteen, pore over Stainer, Prout, Higgs, Forsyth at sixteen, at eighteen produce two works which, Crabbe thought, were probably works of genius. Crabbe felt sure that he did not really like Robert Loo. He was hurt at the lack of gratitude (surely it could not be shyness, when one saw the large confidence of the symphony?) for the trouble Crabbe had taken and the money he had spent—air fares to Singapore and back, pocket money, hotel expenses, the letters to Schwarz and to the people in Radio Malaya who had arranged the recording. Robert Loo took all this calmly, as he would take everything else Crabbe gave. And the things given would have to include a scholarship to England—wangled God knows how—and a performance of the symphony.

"What did Schwarz say about the symphony?"

"Very crude, he said. But he only seemed to be interested in the string parts. But he copied some of the themes out in a manuscript book. He said he would show them to his friends in England."

"Did he indeed? That means we can look forward to a tasteful little piece called *Oriental Sketchbook* or *Souvenir de Singapore* or something equally corny. Schwarz always did like other people's themes."

"It doesn't matter."

"Well, we don't seem to have got very far. I know we've got a recording of the quartet—that's something—but I thought Schwarz might have been willing to do more. He's got all the contacts. I haven't any. But minor musicians are never very generous, I suppose. Music's a corrupting art."

"I don't understand that."

"You don't have to. Just carry on composing, that's your line. Keep out of the world of action. I'll try the British Council and the Information Department and—oh, there are lots of things I can do. We'll get that symphony performed. We'll get you to Europe."

No thanks. Robert Loo said only: "I don't think my father will let me go to Europe. There is the business, you

28

see, and I am the eldest son. He wants me to take a course in accountancy."

"I'll have to speak to your father again. Doesn't he realise that you're the first real composer that Malaya's produced?" Crabbe took a cigarette from the box on the gin-table. "But I don't suppose it can mean very much to him. A lot of people think that music's just there, like bananas, and anyway it's not a thing you can write down on paper."

"He did not want me to go to Singapore. He said it was the wrong time, because it was the end of the month and it's then that we send out the bills. Now they will be late. But I told him that you insisted because the Schwarz Quartet would only be there for two days and it was a good idea for me to see Mr. Schwarz."

"And so your father blames me?"

"Oh, yes, to some extent." Robert Loo returned Crabbe's look calmly. "It makes it easier for me, you see. I don't want too much trouble. I cannot work if people are shouting all the time. But you are in the Government and my father thinks you can give orders to people, and you don't mind having trouble."

"Look here, Robert," said Crabbe in irritation, "what the hell do you want?"

"I want to have a quiet life and to go on writing music."

"Don't you want to study? You're clever, but you don't know everything. How can you at your age?"

"I can find things out in my own way. I've had to do that. The headmaster at school knew I was composing but he didn't help. Nobody wanted to help. And so I can help myself."

"I see. The white man let you down, did he?"

"I didn't say that. I meant that they thought what I was doing was mad. They left me alone and let me do it.

I suppose I should be grateful for that. But they didn't want to help."

"Haven't I helped?"

"Oh, yes." Robert Loo sounded neither convinced nor convincing. "Thank you," he added, formally. "I've heard my quartet. It has been a confirmation. I knew it would sound like that."

"But have you no curiosity? Don't you want to hear a live orchestra? There are fine ones in Europe, you know."

"Of course. I've heard them on records. I suppose it would be nice," he added, again without much conviction.

"Don't you want to hear your own symphony?"

"Oh, but I've heard it." Robert Loo smiled patiently. "I hear it every time I look at the score."

Crabbe got up from the arm-chair and walked the sitting-room. He entered a belt of sun from the window, gazed out for an instant on palms and Government houses, wondered dizzily for a moment what he was doing here anyway, and poured himself gin and water.

"So," said Crabbe to the boy's back—thin nape, plastered hair, white shirt soiled by travel—"you just write for yourself, is that it? You don't think other people might want to hear it. And you've no particular love for your country."

"My country?" The boy looked around, puzzled.

"Some day Malaya might be proud to have a major composer."

"Oh, I see." He giggled. "I don't think that will happen."

"Music can be a big thing to a country finding itself. Music presents a sort of image of unity."

"I don't see that."

"No, I suppose not. Your job, as I say, is just to compose. But even a composer has to have some sense of responsibility. The best composers have been patriotic."

"Elgar is not one of the best composers," said Robert

Loo, with a boy's smug dogmatism. "His music makes me feel sick."

"But look what Sibelius has done for Finland," said Crabbe. "And de Falla for Spain. And Bartok and Kodaly . . ."

"The people of Malaya only want American jazz and ronggeng music. I am not composing for Malaya. I am composing because I want to compose. Have to compose," he amended, and then looked embarrassed, because he had admitted to a dæmon, an obsession. He had very nearly been seen without his clothes.

"Well, I'm going to do my best anyway," said Crabbe. "For this." He pointed with his cigarette at the manuscript of the symphony. "And you're going to be made to study. I shan't rest till I see you on that boat." But, of course, he reflected, one never knew whether one was doing the right thing. He might go to London and, corrupted by a new ambience, produce music in the style of Rubbra or Herbert Howells. In Paris he might be emptied of what was peculiarly his own and filled with Nadia Boulanger. He needed advice, and the only person Crabbe could have trusted to give it was dead. Crabbe knew enough about music to be satisfied that Robert Loo's voice was his own and, at the same time, Malaya's. The waltz and the ländler were never far from Schönberg's music; similarly, Robert Loo had sucked in hundreds of polyglot street songs with his mother's milk, absorbed the rhythms of many Eastern languages and reproduced them on wind and strings. It was Malayan music, but would Malaya ever hear it?

"Tell me, Robert," said Crabbe roughly, "have you ever been with a woman?"

"No."

"Do you have any strong affection for anybody or anything, apart from music?"

31

The boy thought seriously for half a minute and then said: "I think I like my mother. I'm not sure about my father. I used to be very fond of my youngest sister." He paused, evidently trying honestly to add to a catalogue whose exiguity seemed to chill the warm room. "I quite admire cats," he said. "There is something about them," he added, "which . . ." He could not find the words. "Which is quite admirable," he ended lamely.

"Poor Robert," said Crabbe, coming over to him and pressing his very thin shoulder. "Poor, poor Robert."

Robert Loo looked up at Crabbe, genuine bewilderment in his small lashless eyes.

"But I don't understand, Mr. Crabbe. I just don't understand. I have everything I want. You must not feel sorry for me."

Maniam had missed the plane. Deliberately. He could have walked on to it without help, he could have survived the journey without undue nausea—despite the kick in the belly—but he was ashamed and angry about the spreading purple under his left eye and the big blubber upper lip. Now he lay on the spare bed in Dr. Sundralingam's house, saying: "What would they say if I walked into the office like this? They might laugh. And the C.P.O. might be angry about it. He might think that I had been fighting."

"So you have been," said Sundralingam, "in a way."

"I swear to God I never touched him. But he took unfair advantage. He got me against the wall under the Greenwich Mean Time. And there were all the instruments and radios and meters there. Supposing I had been responsible for breaking one of those things. And the aircraft was coming in too. He took very unfair advantage." The words came out half-chewed, what with the swollen lips and the stiff jaw.

"We fought for you," squeaked Arumugam. "The first duty is to a friend." He still had growling in his ears the noise of the Australian pilot asking for wind velocity and saying: "What the hell goes on there?" The fight had been broadcast, must have been heard in half the aircraft and airports of the peninsula.

"I can't remember the best treatment for a black eye," said Sundralingam. "I have been on this yaws campaign for so long now that I've forgotten my general medicine. Some people recommend a beef-steak, but I don't think that is quite right for a Hindu. Perhaps a pork chop?"

"Not enough blood," squealed Arumugam. "You've got to have blood." He sounded like young Master Pavy playing Hieronimo.

"Cold water compresses," prescribed Dr. Sundralingam. "And stay in bed. I'll send an official note to Pahang."

"Will I be safe here?" chewed Maniam fearfully. "Will I be safe alone here during the day?"

"My servant's here all the time," soothed Sundralingam. "He's a Malay, but he's all right." The Malay stood by the sick-room door, hunched, heavy-jawed, simian, the end-product of God knew what mingling of Achinese pirates, aboriginal bushmen, Bugis bandits, long-hut head-hunters. He took in Maniam's broken face with relish, crooning to himself.

"If he definitely loses his job," quavered Maniam thickly, "if that happens, he may try to get me again. He may send axe-men. Perhaps I should have got the plane after all." But he saw in vision the laughing office and heard the questioning C.P.O. "No, I couldn't. I see that. I'll have to stay here. But do spread it round that I've gone back. Say I've gone back by train."

"Yes, yes, yes."

"Vythilingham let us down," shrilled Arumugam. "He

was cruiser-weight champion at Calcutta University, you know. He would have made very short work of our Malay friend."

"Where was Vythilingam?" asked Maniam.

Parameswaran, the schoolmaster, who had been sitting still and pipe-puffing at the foot of the bed, now removed his pipe. "I can guess where he was," he said. "I will bet he was at the house of my colleague, Miss Rosemary Michael."

"But he took his black bag with him."

"That is a blind," said Mr. Parameswaran. "He is ashamed of it being known that he goes there." He put back his pipe and nodded several times. Middle-aged, grizzled, with a comfortable paunch, a golf-tee sticking like a nipple through his shirt-pocket, he was the photographic negative of any suburban Englishman. He was a Jaffna Tamil, but also a Rotarian. He knew lines from the *Golden Treasury*, apt for after-dinner speeches, and even a few Latin tags. He was not quite trustworthy, he trembled on the brink of a bigger world than Jaffna. Not that he had travelled very far. "A home-keeping youth," he was fond of saying. Also he had a wife and family (the wife, disappointingly, above suspicion—pure red-blooded Jaffna) and he never came to the agapes. But he seemed to know about them and he seemed not to approve.

"Are you sure of this?" asked Sundralingam. "It sounds quite unlike Vythilingam."

"No. It is only a guess. But she has mentioned his name in the staff-room to other ladies as being one of the innumerable men who have been seduced by her charms."

"Seduced?" echoed Arumugam in a squeal of horror.

"Seduced by her charms. That is what she alleges. She alleges it about many men, however."

34

"I don't know the lady," munched Maniam. "I've never met her."

"Oh, she is, I suppose, not unattractive," said Parameswaran. "She is not to my taste, however. She is also Christian and immodest."

"She's of very low caste," said Sundralingam. "I knew her parents in Kuala Hantu. She knows I knew them, but still she once told me that she was a Balinese princess. On another occasion she said she was partly English and partly Spanish. It was her Spanish blood, she said, that made her get brown so easily. In England, she said, she was quite pale. She despises her own race, you see."

"Of course," admitted Maniam, "she must be ashamed of her caste."

"There is too much of all this," said Sundralingham. "Too much despising of one's own race and too much despising of other people's races. That is going to be the big trouble of Malaya. You take this man Syed Omar. He has a mad hatred of Tamils. He imagines big Tamil conspiracies against him. Now he will nurse an even bigger hatred than before because of the thrashing he got to-day. But I personally did not want to thrash him, nor, I think, did Arumugam. You will believe me, perhaps, when I say that I felt sorry for him when he lay at the foot of the stairs. It was pathetic to see him with his poor cheap shirt on, all decorated with film stars, lying there in his blood."

Maniam protested through his sore mouth. "Look what he did to me. He deserved all he got."

"Yes, yes. But he should never conceive these hatreds. The trouble starts in his poor misguided brain." There were glistening pin-points in Sundralingam's large brown eyes.

"There is no occasion to get sentimental," said Parames-

35

waran. "I know the family and the family is rotten. I've taught seven of Syed Omar's children. The eldest, Hassan, is the lowest of the low. Lazy, truculent, dishonest, with his long hair and his American clothes, slouching round the town with companions equally low. There's a core of shiftlessness about the Malays. They know they're no good, but they try to bluster their way out of things. Look what they're trying to do here. They're trying to close the bars and the dance-halls and the Chinese pork-market, in the sacred name of Islam. But they've no real belief in Islam. They're hypocrites, using Islam to assert themselves and lord it over people. They pretend to be the master-race, but the real work is done by others, as we know, and if Malaya were left to the Malays it wouldn't survive for five minutes."

"True," said Arumugam's piccolo. "Without the Malays it would be a good country perhaps."

"The name Malaya is unfortunate," said Sundralingam. "But it may yet get back its original Indian name of Langkasuka. That has already been proposed. Still," he added, "if only people would get on with their work—the Malays in the kampongs and in the paddy-fields and the Indians in the professions and the Chinese in trade—I think all people could be quite happy together. It is the ambition of the Malays which is going to prove so tragic. For them," he smiled, not without compassion.

"Trouble is coming, certainly," cried Arumugam. "But if we all stick together there will be no difficulty."

"That," said Sundralingam, "is why we mustn't have Vythilingam doing anything he should not do. I do hope there is nothing in this rumour of yours," turning to Parameswaran.

Parameswaran, intent on puffing, raised one eyebrow and grimaced non-committally.

Maniam suddenly cried in terror. "I have just thought," he said. The Malay servant lounged by the door, not yet sated of the innocent entertainment Maniam's ruined face provided. "I have just thought," he repeated. "This servant of yours will talk in the market about my being here. And perhaps Syed Omar will find out." He tried to get out of bed, but Parameswaran immediately sat on his left foot, at the same time pushing him back to the pillow and saying: "Don't be a coward, man."

"I think." said Maniam, "I had better get back to Pahang after all. I can get the evening mail train. I can steal quietly to my house. Nobody will see."

"Don't be a coward," repeated Parameswaran. "Aren't you ashamed? Fancy being frightened of a Malay."

"I am no coward," declared Maniam from his ventriloquist's mouth. "I just don't want any more of his dirty tricks."

"There is no need to worry," said Sundralingham. "If Syed Omar tries it again we will set Vythilingam on to him. If you worry you will make a slow recovery. Try to relax."

Arumugam called over the Malay servant. *"Mari sini,"* he piped. The Malay servant shambled over, mouth open. "Do not say this *tuan* is still here," ordered Arumugam in bad Malay. The servant nodded, his eyes all animal wonder. "Keep quiet about it and you will get ten dollars."

"You see," said Sundralingham. "Nobody will know."

"Your old man knocked that Tamil about so much that he can't go back to Pahang." Thus Idris bin Sudin, friend of Syed Hassan. "He's staying at that doctor's place." Hassan guffawed.

The four friends sat in a hot drinking-stall, drinking warm orange crush, beguiling the tedium of the long Sabbath afternoon. The stall was one of many in the Park of Happiness, a palisaded Venusberg set in mud. There was an open-air stage for ronggeng dancing, a fœtid cabaret with a beer-bar, two houses of ill-fame disguised as coffee-shops, and a tattered cinema-screen whereon was shown the endless epic of the Javanese shadow-play. The Sabbath would not end till sunset; till then these vessels of pleasure must lie becalmed. Only the wooden and attap huts were sleepily open for the thirsty, each Chinese towkay dozing over his abacus, the Malay waitress sulking over an old copy of *Film*.

Of the four, only Azman wore full uniform. It was his turn to wear it. The drainpipe trousers, the serge jacket with the velvet collar, the string tie—they had bought these cheap from a hard-up private of the Special Air Service. Hamzah, Hassan and Idris were cooler, but far less smart, in jeans and shirt-sleeves rolled up to the arm-pits. This, however, was the authentic tropical dress. But a greater solidarity with their brothers of the West was the desire of all of them, and each was only too eager to sweat and stifle in these romantic garments, the armour of a new chivalry. But they were fair with each other : nobody ever tried to jump the roster. Soon each would have a suit of his own; in the meantime the common hair-style identified them as one tight cell of an international movement : it flowed down the neck, a congealed glossy stream, trickled over on to the cheeks in side-burns, and tousled lustrously on to the low brown forehead. Each had a pocket-knife, for whittling wood or carving cryptic signs on café tables, not yet used for any direr purpose, though the flash of the blade—shooting up from the handle at the touch of the spring—made a brave and intimidating show. They were boys who wished nobody any real harm, romantics who were distrustful of order, preferring colour to form. They liked to muddy the lake, the enemies of complacency, their music the siren of the police-car and their own hearts pounding up the dark alley.

"He got him," said Hassan. "He's tried to get my dad thrown out of his job, see, and that's why my dad bashed him. Beat him up, knocked his teeth out, kicked him in the guts, made him spew his liver up, smashed his nose." He gleefully performed a pantomime of violence and his friends chortled.

They spoke a vivid back-street Malay, unlike the new cold instrument of the Government, with odd splashes of film American to raise their fantasies to a more heroic level. So now Idris interjected cries of "Yer yeller! Yer chicken!" while two-fisting the edge of the table. Azman said: "He roughed your dad, though. Your dad was kicked down the stairs."

"He didn't do it," said Hassan. "It was the other two. That doctor and him with the girl's voice." He fluted a parody of Arumugam and then suddenly felt depressed. His dad shouldn't have done it. It was old-fashioned, that business of punching and kicking, it was Wild West. And his dad was an old man, too. It was a bit undignified. Fish-hooks, knives, razors, bicycle-chains—that was different, that was modern. He felt ashamed of his dad and wanted to change the subject.

"Move on," he suggested. "Let's move on. There's nothing happening here."

"*Ai, mek!*" called Hamzah. The sulky girl came to their table. She was pretty and her low-cut *baju* showed a delicious expanse of warm milky-brown neck. The boys teased her, guffawing rawly. Hamzah said: "I gave you five dollars. I want some change."

"Not paid yet."

"Have paid. Gave five dollars."

39

"Correct, correct!" cried the others. The girl went over to the dozing towkay.

"Eh, towkay, have paid five dollars. Want change!"

"She say not paid. You pay one dollar."

"Have paid. Change!"

The cameras whirred. Azman, teeth bared, frowning in menace, moved to the counter. Very slow, perfectly timed, only the pad of his feet on the sound-track. No music until, the knife slowly drawn, raised, pointed, the click and hiss of the shot-out blade down-beated furious chords. "All right, bub. We won't argue. We don't argue, see?" Menacing, caressing tones. "Keep your money. Chicken feed. But we don't come here again, see?" On the last hissed word the knife-point flashed at the towkay's throat. Cut. Put that in the can. Out they all went, jovial, happy laughing boys, waving a cheerful good-bye. Man, that was acting.

Hands in pockets, they kicked odd stones along Ibrahim Avenue, singing in authentic American. Trishaw-drivers coasted up and down the long glaring road, looking for custom, but the Friday siesta still held. "Only you," sang the boys, "can make my darkness bright." Hassan saw, suspended before him from the hot blue sky, retreating from him as he walked, a microphone. With kissing lips he let the words trickle into it.

"There he is," said Azman, stopping in mid-song. "One crab leaving the house of another." The Malays of this State called all Chinese 'pincered crabs', an allusion to their chopsticks.

"The wonder boy," said Hamzah. They stood, waiting for Robert Loo to approach. His father's shop was near the Park of Happiness. He walked somewhat mincingly, thin, in soiled whites, his brief-case under his arm. They had been in the same English school together, all of them, but

Robert Loo had left a year ago, complete with certificate. The Malay boys plodded on, moustached in the Third Form, the gap to the Fourth just too wide for them to leap. They resented this, a slur on their adulthood. They resented the treachery of the examiners, obviously in the pay of the Chinese. They resented the Chinese, too rich and too bloody clever. They resented Robert Loo's brief-case. They resented Robert Loo.

"I know what you got in there," said Idris. "You been robbing a bank. That's the loot." His Malay was too rapid and too colloquial for Robert Loo to follow. Robert Loo smiled urbanely.

"It's the documents," said Hamzah. "He's selling them to the enemy."

"Open up," said Azman in American. "It's de F.B.I."

"It's only music," said Robert Loo, smiling. "You wouldn't be interested."

"I can't hear anything," said Hamzah. "I must be going deaf." He put his hand-cupped ear to the case, dropping his jaw like a stage zany. Laughter.

"Music on paper," said Robert Loo. "Music has to be written, you know." He spoke in Malay, and, having spoken, realised the absurdity of what he had been saying. The Malay word for 'music' was *bunyi-bunyian*, which just meant 'sounds'. And of course, you couldn't write sounds. "I must be getting along," he said.

"Let's see," said Hassan. He whisked the brief-case from under Robert Loo's arm and, the straps not being fastened, plunged in his hand and pulled out the bulky score of the symphony.

"Music," he said. "So this is music." Holding the score away from mock-long-sighted eyes, pushing out his belly, he began to sing:

41

"Only yew-ew-ew-ew-ew
Can make the darkness bright."

"All right," said Crabbe's voice. "Cut it out." Robert
Loo just stood there, showing neither anxiety nor relief,
not even contempt. "Give it back," said Crabbe. He was
breathing angrily, his hands on his spreading hips. "Go
on, give it back." Sullen and puzzled, Hassan obeyed. All
the boys were sullen and puzzled. What was all the fuss
about anyway? After all, it was only a joke. And this was
Friday anyway, and everybody was off duty, and Crabbe
had no right to play the schoolmaster. A trishaw-driver
hovered, interested. Crabbe called him. "Go on," he said
to Robert Loo. "Get up. He'll take you home." He gave
the driver a fifty-cent piece, still seeming to suppress anger.
Robert Loo climbed aboard, his restored brief-case under
his arm, silent. "Go now," said Crabbe to the driver.
"Pergi, pergi." The Malays watched, puzzled, as Robert
Loo, without a backward glance, was borne jerkily away.
Crabbe waited till the trishaw was a hundred yards down
the road. He turned to the Malays, saying:

"What sort of a country are you trying to make? You've
got it in for everybody. For the Chinese and the Indians
and the Eurasians and the white men. You can't see a
Chinese without wanting to persecute him. You want to
knock the stuffing out of the Tamils. I suppose you'd
like to have a go at me, wouldn't you? For God's
sake, grow up. You've all got to live together here,
you've got to . . . Oh, never mind." He went back to his
house.

"Apa ada?" said Hamzah. "What's the matter with
him?" The others shook their abundant locks in puzzle-
ment. Slowly enlightenment blossomed in Hassan's head.
"I think I know," he said. He was ignorant, but he had

seen something of the world. "But perhaps I'm wrong," he added.

"What is it, then?"

"I don't know."

"What did you say you knew for, then?"

"Ah, never mind."

They threw a few harmless pebbles at Crabbe's car, parked in the porch, and then went on their way, singing. Hamzah suggested going to the Chinese gramophone shop, to pretend to want to buy some records. A good idea, they all agreed. That would pass the time nicely. Then sunset would be presented formally by the muezzin, the whores and hostesses appear, and adventure tremble in the shadows.

Lim Cheng Po came to tea. He took it in the English manner, enjoyed the tomato sandwiches and the fruit cake, said, in his Balliol voice: "A pity one can't get crumpets here." He was a solicitor from Penang. He came over for two days every two months to see how his assistant, who handled the cases this side of the peninsula, was faring, occasionally to take a case himself. He also visited his friends, of whom Crabbe was one. To Crabbe he was a breath of home, an unalloyed essence of Englishry. He was Henley and Ascot, vicarage garden parties, tepid bitter, Gothic railway stations, London fog, the melancholy of a Sunday summer evening. He was plump and not unhandsome, his Chinese blood hardly apparent. Only the eyes were lashless and small and the nose slightly squat. But the English voice and the English gestures swallowed up these details, as a pan of gravy soup might swallow up a shred of shark's fin. He talked now about the troubles in Penang that had just ended—terrorism and a curfew on that one-time peaceful island—and the troubles that, so he had heard, were soon to start in Perak. He had been warned to cancel his trip to Ipoh.

"Who starts it all?" asked Crabbe.

"My dear chap, that's rather a naïve question, isn't it? It just starts. Some blame the Malays, others the Chinese. Perhaps a Malay shakes his fist at a Chettiar money-lender and, for some obscure reason, that sets off a brawl in a Chinese cabaret. Or a British tommy gets tight in K.L. and the Tamils start spitting at a Sikh policeman. The fact is that the component races of this exquisite and impossible country just don't get on. There was, it's true, a sort of illusion of getting on when the British were in full control. But self-determination's a ridiculous idea in a mixed-up place like this. There's no nation. There's no common culture, language, literature, religion. I know the Malays want to impose all these things on the others, but that obviously won't work. Damn it all, their language isn't civilised, they've got about two or three books, dull and ill-written, their version of Islam is unrealistic and hypocritical." He drank his tea and, like any Englishman in the tropics, began to sweat after it. "When we British finally leave there's going to be hell. And we're leaving pretty fast."

"I didn't know you thought of leaving."

"Yes. Back to London, I think. I have my contacts there, and my friends."

"The Malays are to blame, in a way," said Crabbe. "I'm disappointed in them."

"Blame the middle-class Malays, if you like, the political men, but don't blame the kampong blokes. For them the world hardly changes. But there should never have been a Malay middle-class, they're just not the middle-class type at all. They're supposed to be poor and picturesque, sons of the soil."

"And yet," said Crabbe, "I don't like to think that it's impossible to do something about it, even at this late hour. There are lots of things we neglected in the past, but you can't really blame anybody. Perpetual Malayan summer, perpetual British rule. No seasons, no change. It was all very satisfactory, it worked. And, remember, there was no imposition of British rule. People just came because the British were there. Even the Malays. They flocked in from Sumatra, Java . . ."

"Just what do you think can be done?"

"Oh, I don't know . . . A bit of adult education, I suppose. Of course, religion's a problem, a nasty problem."

"What a thing to say," grinned Lim Cheng Po. "What do you want? Nineteenth-century rationalism, Voltairian deism? We're living in a religious age, you know. I suppose Anglicanism might be a solution. An Anglican Malay is an interesting conception, I admit."

"One could inculcate a little scepticism underneath the outward conformity," said Crabbe.

"That's pure Anglicanism, isn't it? And what would you do about your food taboos? It's always those that seem to spark off your massacres. It's just a hundred years since that nasty business in India. The Hindus and Muslims don't seem to have developed a more rational attitude towards beef dripping and swine fat, despite a century of the civilising British."

"One could spread the light a bit. One could discuss inter-racial marriage, for instance . . ."

"Discussion won't get you far."

"It's a beginning," said Crabbe. "Discussion is a beginning. Even just getting all the races in one room is something."

"They're talking in Singapore about an Inter-racial Liaison Committee. It won't do any good."

45

"Oh, Cheng Po, you're such a wet blanket. You're so damned Chinese."

"Chinese?" Lim Cheng Po looked offended. "What do you mean by that remark?"

"You've got this sort of divine disdain. You don't really believe that all the other Eastern races are anything more than a sort of comic turn. That absolves you from the task of doing anything for them. You've no sense of responsibility, that's your trouble."

"Oh, I don't know," said Cheng Po slowly. "I've got a wife and children. I've got a father living in Hounslow. I give tithes of all I possess. I work so damned hard precisely because I've got a sense of responsibility. I worry about my family."

"But you've no nation, no allegiance to a bigger group than the family. You're not quite so bad as Robert Loo, admittedly. He's completely heartless. His only allegiance is to the few quires of manuscript paper I bought him. And yet, strangely enough, it's he who's convinced me that something can be done in Malaya. It may be pure illusion, of course, but the image is there, in his music. It's a national image. He's made a genuine synthesis of Malayan elements in his string quartet, and I think he's made an even better job of it in his symphony. Not that I've heard that yet. I must get it performed."

Cheng Po yawned. "Music bores me," he said. "And your liberal idealism bores me quite as much. Let Malaya sort out its own problems. As for me, I've got enough to think about without getting mixed up in other people's politics. My youngest daughter has measles. My wife wants a car of her own. The curtains of the flat need replacing."

"Pale tea under the mulberries. A single flower in an exquisite bowl. Ideograms, painted with superb calli-

46

graphy, hanging on the walls," mocked Crabbe.

"If you like. Cricket on Sunday. A few martinis between church and luncheon. Gladioli by the open window. That's your world as much as mine."

"You'll never understand us," said Crabbe. "Never, never, never. Our mandarin world's dead and gone, and that's all you're looking for in England. You think the old China will stay alive in England, but you're wrong. It died forty years ago. I'm a typical Englishman of my class —a crank idealist. What do you think I'm doing here in early middle age?"

"Deriving an exquisite masochistic pleasure out of being misunderstood. Doing as much as you can for the natives" (he minced the word like a stage memsahib), "so that you can rub your hands over a mounting hoard of no appreciation."

"As you please. But I've got a year left before I have to go home, and I'm going to try something useful. Though what exactly I don't know . . ."

The western sky put on a Bayreuth montage of Valhalla. Towards it the Muslims would now be turning, bowing like Zoroastrians to the flames. It was genuinely the magic hour, the only one of the day. Both men, in whites and wicker chairs on the veranda, facing the bougainvillea and the papaya tree, felt themselves begin to enter a novel about the East. It would soon be time for gin and bitters. A soft-footed servant would bring the silver tray, and then blue would begin to soak everything, the frogs would croak and the coppersmith bird make a noise like a plumber. Oriental night. *As I sit here now, with the London fog swirling about my diggings, the gas fire popping and my landlady preparing the evening rissoles, those incredible nights come back to me, in all their mystery and perfume . . .*

47

Rosemary Michael entered without knocking, bearing her ridiculous beauty on clacking high heels across the sitting-room. "Victor!" she called and then said: "Oh, you've got a visitor."

"This," said Crabbe, "is my friend Mr. Lim, the last Englishman."

"How do you do?"

"How do you do?"

Rosemary listened to the Balliol intonation with hope and wonder. She could see, with her woman's miss-nothing eyes, that Mr. Lim was not an Englishman, but she was fluttered and confused by his voice. She was also a little tight. Clumsily she gave Mr. Lim her choicest, most exclusive Sloane Square vowels and, sitting down, a ravishing glimpse of her round brown knees.

"Have you come to live here, Mr. Lim?"

"No, no, just a visit. My home's in Penang, actually."

"Do you know London, Mr. Lim? I love London, I positively adore it."

"Yes, I know London."

"Do you know Shaftesbury Avenue and Piccadilly Circus and Tottenham Court Road?"

"Oh, yes."

"And Green Park and Hyde Park Corner and Knightsbridge and South Kensington?"

"Yes, yes, the whole Piccadilly Line."

"Oh, that's marvellous, isn't it marvellous, Victor, just marvellous!"

Lim Cheng Po was an Anglican and a cricketer, but he allowed a small Chinese man to enter his brain and, with a tiny smile, hint that Crabbe's mistress had arrived and it was time to be going. He said:

"It's time I was going. Thank you for your hospitality, Victor. Good-bye, Miss . . ."

"Rosemary. My friends call me Rosemary."

"An exquisite name and highly appropriate in its exquisiteness."

"Oh, Mr. Lim." She became all girl. As Lim Cheng Po drove off she stood by the window to wave to him, and then came running back to the veranda.

"Oh, Victor, what a very nice man. And what a lovely voice. Do you think he was attracted to me?"

"Who could fail?"

"Oh, Victor," she simpered. Then she pouted, kicking her shoes off as she lay back in the chair, saying: "I've been getting tight with Jalil."

"What will Joe say about that? Somebody's bound to write and tell him."

"I don't care. To hell with Joe. He let me down very very badly. I expected a ring and all I got was that horrible Blackpool Tower. I'll never forgive him."

"But he didn't send the Blackpool Tower."

"No, he didn't send me anything. Oh, Victor, Victor, I'm so unhappy."

"Have a drink."

"But I'm hungwy." A pathetic little-girl's rhotacismus.

"Have some dinner then. I dine at seven-thirty on Fridays. Have a drink first." Crabbe shouted to his servant: "*Dua orang!*"

Rosemary had several gins and then became reminiscent. "Oh, Victor, it was so marvellous. They had me on television wearing my *sari* and gave me a whole ten minutes' interview, and then next day you should have seen the letters I received. Fifty, no, a hundred offers of marriage. But I said I'd wait for Mr. Right even if I had to wait all my life and . . ."

"And now you've found Mr. Right."

"No, no, Victor, I hate him for treating me like that,

49

me, who could have married a managing director and an M.P. and a bishop and, oh, yes, a duke. Lord Possett his name was."

"This duke?"

"Yes. But I kept myself to myself, I sent back their flowers and their mink coats, and I never slept with anyone, Victor, not with anyone, and I could have slept with anyone I wanted to. I was a virgin till Joe came along, Victor, and I gave him everything. Everything." She screwed back the tears and looked inhuman. "He's had everything from me."

"And now you hate him."

"I love him, Victor, I love him. He's the only man in the world."

"You mean you enjoy sleeping with him?"

"Yes, Victor, I love him. It was love at first sight."

Rosemary made a hearty dinner. There was roast chicken and bread sauce and Rosemary vigorously swamped everything first with ketchup and then with Lea and Perrin's, refreshing her plate with these condiments frequently through the meal. With her coffee she had a Cointreau and then a Drambuie. Then she lay back in her arm-chair.

"Victor," she said, "is it true what Jalil says?"

"About Joe?"

"No, about you. He says you don't like women any more."

"I like some women."

"He says you prefer little boys."

"Does he, by God?"

"Everybody's talking about you and this Loo boy. That's what Jalil says."

"Really?"

"Is it true, Victor?"

"No, Rosemary, it's not true. He writes music and I'm trying to help him."

Rosemary giggled. "I don't believe that."

"Please yourself, my dear."

Rosemary fell into a posture of deeper languor, limbs spread, voice sleepy.

"Victor."

"Yes?"

"Are Chinese the same as Englishmen?"

"Yes."

"How do you know?"

"It's just something one takes for granted."

"Oh." The coppersmith bird hammered slow minutes.

"Victor."

"Yes?"

"You can if you want to."

"Can what?"

"Oh, Victor, Victor." She sat up and cried vigorously. "I'm so lonely, so lonely, and nobody in the world loves me."

"Oh, yes, a lot of people love you."

"It's true what Jalil says about you, it's true, it's true. I've never been so insulted in all my life."

"Perhaps I'm not as susceptible as His Grace."

"I'm going home, going home."

"I'll run you." With great eagerness Crabbe went to the porch where his car was parked.

"I'll walk home, thank you. I don't want a lift in your car. I hate you. You're as bad as the rest of them, and I thought you were different." She put on her shoes angrily and clomped out with her ridiculous beauty, leaving the room no emptier than before. Crabbe settled down to an evening's reading.

51

3

The job of Victor Crabbe was, appropriately, a somewhat crepuscular one. He, as acting Chief Education Officer of the State, was slowly handing his post over to a Malay. Sometimes this Malay, a youngish man with a most charming smile, would be deferential to Crabbe, showing great anxiety to learn; at other times he would enter the office as though, in sleep, an angel had visited him, teaching him all in painless hypnopædia. Then the Malay, still with great charm, would tell Crabbe what to do—settle a strike of pupils in a local school; write a letter in courtly English to the Director, apologising for the loss of a receipt voucher; sign the letter; send out for coffee and curry-puffs; generally make himself useful. The Malay himself would sit at the desk and smoke cigarettes through a Ronson holder, telephone Chinese contractors and give them hell—first announcing his official title loudly— and occasionally brood dramatically over thick files. So Crabbe demoted himself to the rank of the Duke in *Measure for Measure*, a god whom all men might touch, and wandered round the schools of the town to give funny lessons to the children ("the white man always make us laugh, make very happy"). Sometimes he would try to do more spectacular good, and this morning he visited the State Information Officer with schemes in his mind.

Nik Hassan liked to be called 'Nicky'. It was *chic* to have an English name in his circle. His friends Izuddin and Farid were called 'Izzy' and 'Fred' and Lokman bin Daud usually signed himself "Lockman B. Dowd". Very big-executive, very American, and a quite legitimate trans-literation of the Islamic name. Nik Hassan had tried to mould his personality round the connotations of his nick-name, and he sat like the boss of a gambling-joint behind his harmless official desk, moustached and smart in the busy hum of the air-conditioner. Crabbe greeted him and smiled dutifully at the counter-greeting. Nicky and Vicky. Education and Information. The comedy-team of the new Malaya.

First Crabbe told Nik Hassan about Robert Loo and his symphony.

"You see," said Crabbe, "apart from its æsthetic value—and I'm not really capable of judging that—it's just come at the right time from the political point of view."

"Music? Politics?"

"Yes. You know, of course, they they made Paderewski Prime Minister of Poland. Paderewski was a great pianist."

"A bit before my time."

"This symphony could be played as a big gesture of independence. 'We in Malaya have thrown off the shackles of an alien culture. We have got past the nose-flute and the two-stringed fiddle. We are adult. We have a national music of our own.' Imagine a full orchestra playing this symphony in the capital, imagine it on the radio—'the first real music out of Malaya', imagine the pride of the average Malayan. You *must* do something about it."

"Look here, Vicky, the average Malayan won't care a damn. You know that as well as I do."

"Yes, but that's not the point. It's culture, and you've got to have culture in a civilised country, whether the people want it or not. That's one of the stock clichés—'our national culture'. Well, here's the first bit of national

53

culture you've ever had: not Indian, not Chinese, not Malay—Malayan, just that."

"What sort of a thing is it?" asked Nik Hassan suspiciously. "Is it modern—you know, Gershwin stuff? Has it got a good tune? Do you really think it's any good?"

"I'm pretty sure it's good. I've not heard it, but I've read it. Whether it's good or not is not really the point, anyway. It's a work of art, it's extremely competent, it's probably highly original. But don't expect sound-track slush. It's not got a good tune anywhere in it, but it's terrifically organised, tremendously concentrated. That boy's a genius."

"Chinese, isn't he? Pity about that." Nik Hassan made a sour gangster's face. "Pity he's not a Malay. Though, of course, he could use a what-you-call . . ."

"Pseudonym?"

"That's right, a Malay pseudonym. It might carry a bit more weight. After all, everybody knows the Chinese are clever. We're a bit sick of hearing it. We're just dying for a Malay genius to turn up."

"Well, here's a Malayan genius for you. I'm pretty sure about that."

"If," said Nik Hassan, "if it's any good, they might think about playing it as part of the Independence celebrations. There's no harm in trying. It shows that we're alive in this State, anyway. Do you think he'd object to having a Malay what-you-call? You know, something like Abdullah bin Abdullah? It would make quite a bit of difference up in Kuala Lumpur."

"He," said Crabbe, "wouldn't mind in the slightest. He's quite devoid of ambition. But, frankly, I should mind very much. Why should he hide his real name, when he's got as much right to the country as you people have? Damn

54

it all, the Chinese have done as much as anybody, if not more, to, to . . ."

"All right, all right," said Nik Hassan. "I know. My dear fellow, I know. But it's a question of the line, you see. It's a line we've got to try and follow. I mean, to be honest, the line of the Chinese is supposed to be trade, isn't it? Money in the bank and a fleet of Cadillacs. The Malays have got nothing. The time's come to give them something. And, now I come to think of it, a little thing like this . . ."

"Not so little."

"It could be a boost. A boost. Is there any singing in it? You know, patriotic Malay words. That would help a good deal."

"There's no singing. But," said Crabbe, "yes. Yes. It's an idea. A choral finale. Beethoven did it; why not Loo? It might sell the work to the public."

"And if you could get the orchestra to stand up at intervals and shout 'Merdeka!'. Now that really would sell it. That really would make it political. That would get it performed."

"But," said Crabbe, "it's a kind of desecration. You can't do that to a serious piece of music."

"You're keen on getting it performed, aren't you? You said it was a political thing. Well, make it really political and it might bring the house down. But," said Nik Hassan, "is it good? Really good? I don't want to look a bloody fool, sending off a lot of tripe to K.L. I mean, we've only got your word for it."

"You can take my word."

"Well . . ." Nik Hassan handed Crabbe a small Dutch cigar and lit it for him. "We're friends, aren't we?"

"Oh, yes, Nicky, of course we're friends."

"If I were you, Vicky, I'd stop seeing that boy."

"So people are talking, are they?"

"What did you expect? It was a godsend to the gossips. What with your wife going back to U.K. and you not knocking about with women these days and then your always having this lad around at your place."

"Not so often."

"Often enough. Anyway, they're talking. And, you see, it puts me in a funny position when I do this job for you . . ."

"I'll send the damned thing off myself."

"And then, if it's any good, they'll want to know how I came to miss it. All I want is for you to tell me, quite honestly . . ."

"You can go to hell, Nicky. Why should I have to go round denying rumours? If people want to think what they presumably are thinking, I can't stop them. I'd be a fool to try and stop them. And you think it, too, don't you?"

"No, not really. I mean, it's a bit queer you're not bothering with women—that Rosemary girl's after you all the time; I've seen it—and, damn it all, I'm broad-minded enough, there's a lot of it goes on, but, I mean, it's your own affair, isn't it? You don't want to start bringing anybody else into it. It makes it awkward for other people, you see."

"My dear, dear Nik . . ."

"Nicky. They're talking about giving me the big Australian job. Have you heard that?"

"No. Congratulations."

Nik Hassan did not seem really pleased. "They're watching me, that's the trouble. Watching me all the time, seeing if I'm up to it. And you're never sure whether you're doing the right thing. If you drink, you're going against Islam, and if you don't drink you've got no social

56

talents. If you've got more than one wife, they say that won't go down well in a Christian country. But, damn it." He turned, face wrinkled and arms wide in perplexity. "Look at my wife, just look at her. A woman like her was all right in the old days. You know, no drink in the house and chewing *sireh* after meals and belching in public. And not a word of English. And not a damn word of decent Malay conversation for that matter. How am I going to get on, running a big department in Canberra? How are we all going to get on?"

"You'll get on all right, Nicky. You worry too much."

"Perhaps I do. But supposing somebody here starts telling K.L. that I'm helping—— Sorry, I won't say that. And supposing somebody says that I'm not helping to cultivate local talent. Where am I? Oh, Vicky, won't you tell me the truth?"

"There's nothing in it, Nicky. Nothing at all. You can trust me."

"I used to. Now I don't think I can trust anybody. We're starting our independence in an atmosphere of mistrust."

"But I've no stake in the country, not any more. It's only people like me who can really help. And it's that very mistrust I want to do something about. I want to try and cultivate better inter-racial understanding, for one thing. I had an idea last night, in bed. Why can't we have meetings, say, once a week, to try and mix up the races a bit more? We could discuss things, we could have dances, we could encourage young people of different races to go about together. We need a headquarters of some kind, of course. You know, a sort of club-house."

"Where's the money coming from?"

"Well, how about the Residency? The British Adviser's finished here. That place isn't doing anything any more.

We could have a subscription, we could make money on dances and shows. A caretaker and a couple of gardeners wouldn't cost much. Of course, there's the electric light bill . . ."

Nik Hassan shook his head. "Nothing doing. The Sultan's taking that place over."

"But, damn it, he's got three palaces already."

"Now he's got four. That's out. There's one thing though. I just thought of it. You remember Wigmore, the planter?"

"Yes, poor old Wigmore." Wigmore had been shot by Communist terrorists on his own estate. A fat harmless man, thirty years in the country.

"His will has been proved. He left twenty thousand dollars to that Tamil girl he'd been living with. He also left twenty thousand dollars to the state."

"What for?"

"God knows he'd got enough out of the state in his life-time. It's a vague sort of bequest. It just says: 'for the improvement of the lot of the people'. He was a vague sort of chap. Drank too much, of course. If only he'd left it to a dogs' home or the hospital, or something. Now there's got to be a committee to decide how the money's to be used."

"Who's on the committee?"

"Oh, we'll all be on it. We'll argue about it for a year, I suppose. And then the Sultan will claim the money for a new car. Of course, it's not a lot."

It wasn't a lot, but it was enough. Enough to send Robert Loo to Europe. Enough to buy a building of some sort. Enough for both?

"Vague, as you say," said Crabbe.

"Very vague. The Sultan could interpret a new car as improving the lot of the people, I suppose. The people are happy seeing their Sultan happy. I wonder if I could do the same thing about getting an honourable divorce? Buy my wife off, marry a new one—*soignée*, educated, a drinker, somebody who'd go down well in Australia."

"There's always Rosemary."

"Oh God, man, she's too bloody dark. Black as the ace of spades. I can't stand the touch of a black skin."

Robert Loo was wishing he had more practical knowledge of the violin. The muse had told him peremptorily to start writing a violin concerto; that is to say, she had hurled themes at him, fully orchestrated, with a solo violin soaring and plunging in the foreground, and this solo part insisted on being rich in harmonics and intricate multiple stoppings. Behind these sharp images was a bigger, duller image which would only be fully realised when the work was complete, for it was the image of the work itself. Robert Loo sat in his father's shop, neatly sketching first and second subjects for the first movement, the music-paper next to the abacus, occasionally laying down his pen to move his fingers—with the grace of one playing an instrument—over the wire-threaded wooden balls with which the amounts of bills were calculated.

His father's shop had started by selling provisions; then it had seem a natural transition to install tables and chairs and turn the place into an unambitious restaurant; later a first-class licence brought in a scant drinking clientèle allowed by law to sit over their spirits till midnight. It meant a long day for everybody in the family, but nobody really minded: a Chinese towkay's children will, with the thriftiness of the race, find fulfilment and diversion where they can. Life does not go on in some place remote from the coffee-urn and the cash-till; life is where you live.

Robert Loo sat, quite content, behind the counter,

against a cyclorama of tins of milk and corned beef. The shop was bright with sunlight, trade calendars, drink posters, the yapping of two younger brothers who made up orders for delivery. A solitary Malay blew into a saucer of black coffee. Outside were all the colours of the East and all the languages. But Robert Loo gazed on a world more real and shot with sounds and colours more intense than any the shop or the street could show. Two flutes in counterpoint, the sudden citrous tang of the oboe—the auditory images were so vivid, the thrill of creating them so deliriously pungent, that the outside world was burned up. Only when he heard a faint snatch of whistled song outside, or when a younger brother shouted in Cantonese —making a tone-pattern that was on the edge of music— did Robert Loo frown. It annoyed him that the sounds that impinged on the outer ear could get so much in the way. He was not yet perfect; only when he was like Beethoven, deaf, would he have final control. But he could feel satisfied with the conquest and the grinding into the dirt of the last four or five years. The small library of musical text-books in his bedroom, the help from Crabbe, the original spark when that other Englishman, Ennis, had shown him music for the first time and saturated him in the sound of his records and his piano—he could look back tolerantly on all this. He was free now, or nearly free. He was on his own.

But something about this violin concerto disturbed him. It was a visual image of the soloist that kept obtruding. He could *see* the concerto being performed, and, though the orchestra was shadowy, the soloist's fingers, the soloist's arm were terrifyingly vivid, as in a dream of fever. The fingers were strong and long, the arm was bare, and a kind of technicolor blue quivered behind. The bowing arm, the fingers on the strings, and then the violin itself, polished

60

brown, and the soloist's chin pillowed on it. Startled, he saw it was a woman. Who? Was this some memory of a film, of a photograph in a book on musical celebrities? Open-mouthed, he stared at the big luminous mirror opposite. It was set too high to reflect him, it carried only a shelf of looking-glass beer and the moving blades of the ceiling-fan. But this letting-in of the three-dimensional world exorcised the vision. He returned to his manuscript paper, sketched a passage of solo treble-stopping, and then suddenly the long fingers were on his, showing him that this was impracticable, that you could not, see, stretch the little finger so far when, see, the first finger had to be down here . . .

His father, Loo Kam Fatt, walked in from the street. "It comes now," he said. He spoke no English, he had no Christian name. He did not object to his eldest son's speaking English—that helped trade—nor did he mind that some of his children had become Christian—that could do trade no harm. Trade and gambling and a woman occasionally—that was a man's life. He had just won forty dollars on a bet that the fever-bird in the tree opposite Ng's shop would, this time, sing a passage of four notes, not three. There were thus, in him, the rudiments of a concern with music. This morning's win was a good omen for a new enterprise of his, an enterprise he had kept secret, for, coming as a surprise, it might give his eldest son all the more pleasure, because this too was to do with music, and he knew that his eldest son liked music, or certainly had used to like it. Loo Kam Fatt beamed, rubbed his towkay's paunch, and said again: "It comes now."

Robert Loo's three younger brothers were at the doorway, quacking with interest. The railway van had drawn up. Four men in the back of the van—Malays in shorts and torn vests—began easing out the crate, shouting instructions, counter-instructions and warnings in glottal monosyllables.

"Is what?" asked Robert Loo. But he knew what it was and felt slightly sick. One just doesn't think, doesn't expect. He should have known this would happen. He watched the crate dumped beside the counter.

"Will see now," smiled his father. "Will like."

Half the street seemed anxious to help. Hashim, the idiot boy from the barber-shop next door, was pulling out nails with a crowbar. Grindingly, laths of wood yielded to brown and yellow hands, a wrenching and screaming of twisted nails fanfared the discovery of the treasure beneath. This coyly revealed itself in a growing flank of red metal as the wood came away, the shavings and masses of packing paper. Soon it stood naked and shining in sunlight, stripped of its crude cerements, a portent and a god. "Ah," breathed the crowd.

"Lift to corner," said Loo Kam Fatt. To corner was pushed with happy groans and sighs, with padding of splay feet. Scavengers appeard, shining eyes darting swiftly and slyly about, to take off the wood that strewed the floor. The workers stood back to survey with awe the glass and metal music-god, whose name indeed, sprawled on its belly in flowing chrome, was APOLLO. A hundred black plates behind heavy glass, as if draining into the mysterious hidden viscera below, stood firmly on their edges. Loo Kam Fatt uncoiled the omphalic flex, saying, in tiny frustration: "This plug not right size. Must change." Out of air appeared a smaller plug and a screwdriver. "Man come from Singapore," said Loo Kam Fatt, "after six month. Change all records. This very good."

"Ah!" The god had begun to breathe, to glower with a glowing blue eye. This was the moment. Loo Kam Fatt, like a priest with a host, reverently put into the creature's tiny mouth a ten-cent piece. "Now must choose." He turned benignly to his eldest son. "You choose. Number one son must choose. Son who like music must choose." With gentle smiles, with the sense of an occasion, the crowd made way for the number one son. This was cere-mony. This was religion. Robert Loo, his heart like a heavy breakfast, came forward to greet the god, to com-mand it, to be sacrificed to it. Blindly he pressed a button. Inside, a turntable in a staff-car, moving slowly up the rank of records, searched, failed to find, moved down again. Silently it ordered a record to come forward. The record obeyed as silently. Then it fell flat on the turntable, trans-fixed, and the tone-arm came down. What had been a military formation became a harem. And now . . .

Joy lit all the Asiatic voices as noise filled shop and street. Drums and red-hot brass, a wedge of saxophones burst from the god. The god gave greeting. "Will bring trade here," shouted Loo Kam Fatt in his deafened happi-ness. "Park now closed down. No Muslim girls allowed dance now. No beer to be sold there. People here all the time. Come to hear music. Music very good thing."

Ten-cent pieces shone everywhere in eager waiting fingers. What was rice, what was coffee compared to the solace of art? The solo violinist waited, her bow at the ready, smiling patiently but clearly puzzled at the delay.

This music crept by Syed Omar in Police Headquarters, sitting puzzled while others were going out to lunch. He had just typed out orders to the police, instructing them that, on high religious authority, they must arrest any Muslim found drinking intoxicants, any Muslim woman plying the trade of dance-hostess, café-waitress or lady-of-the-town, any Muslim—man or woman—found in the act of committing or being about to commit or having committed adultery. They must also report any Malayan of any race or religion whatsoever found assisting or encouraging any Muslim to commit these crimes. A good morning's work, and he felt he deserved a small beer in Loo's *kedai* round the corner. But he was puzzled by a letter, a copy of which had just been given to him by the C.P.O. This letter was addressed from Police Headquarters, Kuala Beruang, Pahang; it was a glowing eulogy of Syed Omar, and it was clearly signed by Maniam. What puzzled Syed Omar was not the eulogy but the address. Why should a letter from Maniam be addressed from Pahang when Maniam was still living, convalescent, in the house of Dr. Sundralingam? He pondered for a while and then concluded that Maniam must be afraid of further vengeance from Syed Omar and thus pretended to be many miles away. The insincerity of the eulogy, of course, was to be taken for granted. It had done Syed Omar no good, for the C.P.O. had rightly divined that it was insincere and that Syed Omar must have behaved to Maniam very badly for Maniam to have written of Syed Omar in such a way. But Maniam's attempt at convincing Syed Omar that he was already back in Pahang must signify that Maniam feared that to write such a letter would cut no ice (that was the expression) with Syed Omar, and that Syed Omar was still expected to nurse hatred for Maniam and even to express that hatred in the usual manner. Probably this woman Neelambigai was now waggling her bottom in some better job than the one Syed Omar still held. So Maniam was making no sacrifice, not even humiliating himself—for it was well known that Tamils would sell their mothers, their honour, their souls to save their skins or to advance themselves. They did not know the meaning of the word humiliation, except when it applied to others, such as humble and deserving Malays like Syed Omar. Syed Omar read the letter through again:

. . . and so I wish to correct any false impression that may have arisen concerning my attitude to Tuan Syed Omar's character and work, owing to a quite superficial misunderstanding that arose between us shortly before my departure. I consider that Tuan Syed Omar is efficient, honourable and loyal, anxious always to give of his best, courteous to his superiors and considerate to his inferiors. I came to have the highest regard for his excellent qualities during the few months in which I worked in your Headquarters. With the coming of Malayan Independence Tuan Syed Omar should go far, as it is men like him that the country needs. . . .

Still, thought Syed Omar, still, this would come in useful. It was a good testimonial, even if it was insincere. But, then, all good testimonials were insincere. That stood to reason. But now Syed Omar felt a greater anger rising to think that he had to rely on the specially insincere praises of a cowardly Tamil. He felt murderous towards Maniam. He folded the copy of the letter with great care and put it into his thin wallet. It was a good testimonial. He would get Maniam.

Rosemary Michael heard loud music coming from Loo's shop as she tripped along Jalan Post Office. Men gaped at her, whistled after her, made unequivocal gestures at her. Teeth gleamed from Indian shops in frank concupiscence. A fat Sikh constable tried to pinch her bottom. So it was always; the whole male town did homage to her beauty. Complacently she accepted the homage. The music from Loo's shop blared for her, the very sun, which she far outdid in radiance, showered its hot gold on her alone.

Oh, but she had cause for radiance. It had come, it had come at last. Well, in a sense it had come. Joe had sent her a cheque for twenty guineas. The guineas made it seem rather like a fee, but of course perhaps Joe was really being considerate and ensuring that she had a nice even number of dollars—one hundred and eighty exactly. Joe wanted her to buy an engagement ring with the money. He couldn't send one, he said, because he wasn't quite sure what size to get. And she would know better than he what kind of stones and what kind of a setting to choose.

The money, of course, was not really enough for an even moderately good ring. But perhaps Joe was not really being mean; perhaps the poor boy didn't really know how much a really good ring should cost. Perhaps he was just saving money for their little home. Still, it meant that Rosemary would now have to·dig into her small reserve in the bank (she had called there on the way home to find out exactly how much it was). She must buy something really good, something commensurate with the gifts she had showered on Joe: the record-player, the golf-clubs, the Leica and the car radio. Joe must not appear less generous than she.

Joe had said in his letter that it was very likely he would be coming back to Malaya. With this import firm or export firm or whatever it was. Then, he said, she could transfer to a school in the town where he would be working, for it would quite definitely not be this town. Rosemary did not feel too happy about this. She had thought of herself living in a nice house in Hampstead or Chiswick, the beautiful mysterious Oriental princess who had married a commoner, who was not above preparing special dishes—exotic and spicy—for her guests,

66

but who otherwise queened it over a household of stolid British servants. Or, if not that, at least in Malaya she would be a mem, yawning all day over books from the Club library under the two fans of the sitting-room. She had not thought of herself as *working* after her marriage. But, said Joe, marriage itself would have to wait, because this firm did not believe in its employees marrying coloured women. He would only stay with this firm for a time and then he would, perhaps, get a good government job. After the initial mess-up of Independence they would be crying out again for expatriates like Joe.

Coloured women, indeed! *She* a coloured woman! She walked, head up, with an indignant hip-swing past Crabbe's house, round the corner, down the lane to her own quarters. Across the road she saw a car parked, broiling in the sun. Jalil's car. Coloured woman! She was a European, at home in Paris and London, fond of European clothes and European food with plenty of Lea and Perrin's. She loved the snow, tea and crumpets by the cosy fire, fog and primroses. She was also, of course, a Javanese princess, or Balinese, or Hawaiian. But she was not a coloured woman. Hadn't her rich tan always been admired in England? Weren't Europeans always trying to get sunburnt? What did they mean by calling her a coloured woman?

She sailed on her exquisite legs down the narrow drive to her house. Inside sat Jalil, wheezing, stopping this to hum a chesty chromatic scale when he saw her. He did not, of course, stand up. The room was full of cats, flowers—bougainvillaea, canna lilies, hibiscus, orchids—and the music of bees. Rosemary said:

"I've told you not to come here. Jalil, I've told you again and again. What are people going to think, you coming here all the time, what are they going to think?" But this was mere ritual, performed without conviction. Jalil said:

"Come eat, come drink, come make jolly time." This was the now traditional liturgical response. Two cats came to greet Rosemary.

"Oh, don't be silly, you know I can't, oh, you're ridiculous. Oh," she said, "what lovely orchids."

"Orchids I not bring. Orchids Crabbe send round."

"Crabbe? Victor Crabbe?" Rosemary picked up the card and read: "To an exquisite lady these somewhat less exquisite blooms." "Oh," cooed Rosemary, "oh, how sweet. Oh, the darling." She read the signature: "Lim Cheng Po".

"Crabbe send round. Come from Penang, from Chinese man." Jalil chuckled and wheezed.

Rosemary sat down in the other armchair. "I'm engaged, Jalil," she said. She had always thought her announcement of this would be rather different—leaping in the air, loud song, Jalil discomfited. Then, of course, she remembered the Blackpool Tower. It was Jalil who had spoiled everything last time.

"He not send ring. I know he not send ring. I watch every day."

"He's sent the money for the ring."

"How much he send?"

"Ooooh, two hundred pounds."

"Not believe."

"All right," said Rosemary, "if you don't believe me you can come with me when I go to buy it. You can take me to Penang. There." She pouted at him, triumphant.

"We go Penang make jolly time."

"I'm engaged, you see, Jalil, engaged. And you said he never would."

"He never marry. He tell me he never marry."

"Well, now I can prove you're a liar. We're engaged to

be married, and that means we're going to be married. So there."

"He not marry."

"Oh, what lovely orchids," said Rosemary again. She frowned, hearing Lim Cheng Po's voice, so English, so refined, so very English upper-class. And often she had had to tell Joe about his aitches. Well, perhaps not often, but on one or two occasions. What was the matter with her? Absently she stroked the cat with the Disraeli face. (It was on the table, sniffing the orchids.) "I wonder why," said Rosemary. "I wonder why he sent them. He's only seen me once," she smirked.

"He want sleep. Cheaper than hotel when he come from Penang."

"Jalil, what a filthy, filthy thing to say. I hate you. Get out, go on, get out." But Jalil chuckled and pushed down a cat from his lap. He said:

"He not marry you. He got wife in Penang. Only me marry you."

"I'd never marry you, never, never. I'd rather marry Vy than I'd marry you. You're horrible." Jalil rolled with pleasure at this tribute. He said:

"You want marry European. I European. I got three wives only. Is room for one more. If you not marry me I find other wife easy. Plenty Malay women want husband. I not care."

"Oh, Jalil, you'll never understand. Never. What would I do at Christmas? I don't want Hari Raya. I don't want Deepavali. I don't want Muslim feasts or Indian feasts. I want Christmas. I want turkey and Christmas pudding and mince pies and mistletoe and snow and carol-singers. I want a Christmas tree. I want my presents!"

On the last word she broke down and her face became inhuman. Crying, indeed, on what should be the second happiest day of her life. She wept, forgetting that it was lunch-time. Jalil chuckled gently.

Vythilingam worked quietly and efficiently through the long hot afternoon. He inoculated six dogs against rabies, diagnosed feline enteritis in a cat, inspected the sheep in the experimental sheep farm, confirmed that a pet monkey was suffering from pneumonia, went out in the Veterinary Department van to a kampong to treat buffalo for a new strange skin cancer that was spreading ferociously, came back to the surgery and there wrote a letter to Rosemary Michael.

His speech impediment prevented him from making a dignified oral proposal. On paper he could be fluent, even eloquent, and the stilted phrases of his letter pleased him. ". . . If you consent to become my wife I promise to fulfil honourably all the duties of a husband. Though not wealthy I have an adequate income, and I pledge myself to endeavour to support you in the manner to which you have been accustomed." The dead hand of eighteenth-century Indian administration, which in no wise could be tempered by the reading of translations of Marx and Chou En Lai, this lay on his prose style. "I remain, your sincere admirer, A. Vythilingam." He sealed up the letter, would take it round to her house, would stand there blinking nervously while she read it.

It was necessary that he should marry soon. That morning a letter had come from his mother in Ceylon, enclosing yet another photograph of an eligible Jaffna Tamil girl. Vythilingam sneered in hatred. How well he understood the agony of that bourgeois creation of that bourgeois dramatist, pride of that detestable country. "Frailty, thy name is woman." He had seen quite recently a Tamil film version of *Hamlet*, over-long by about two hours, but crisp enough in its way, despite Ophelia's eight songs and the dance of the grave-diggers. That scene in the bedchamber with its rumble and gurgle of bitter Tamil vilification, the black Queen scared on the bed, that was art, that was words. But there was the question of conditioned response. If his mother should come to Malaya for a holiday, as she had once or twice threatened to, if she brought with her some girl such as this black pudding with teeth on the photograph, it would not be easy to sustain an attitude of intransigence. He knew all too well what would happen. Before he knew where he was he would be sitting for his wedding photograph in his best suit with a marriage garland round his neck, tied for life to his mother's choice. His mother must not win; that was certain. Free will was, of course, an illusion, but one must at least seem to exercise it.

When it was time to go, Vythilingam packed his black bag with medicaments for Rosemary's cats. He wondered whether the time had yet come to make her a present of another animal. A sheep? Too large. A monkey? Destructive. A parrot? Psittacosis. A cockatoo? He went out to his car and found two men already in it, Arumugam and Sundralingam. They greeted him jovially.

"Hallo there! You've been a long time!"

"Hail!" squeaked Arumugam, witch-like.

"We're having a party," said Sundralingam. "In my house. Maniam's a great deal better."

"I must go . . ." began Vythilingam. "I have to go to . . ."

"My car's in the garage," said Sundralingam, "being serviced. You can drive us home."

"But first I must . . ." Vythilingam shrugged a nervous chin towards his black bag. "I have to . . ."

"No," said Sundralingam firmly. "We know these little

71

games, ha ha. You're coming with us. We'll look after you."

"We'll look after you," said Arumugam, in canon at the double octave. And then, as if a Shakespearean mood were on him, as, indeed, it had been on Vythilingam, he began to sing:

"Where the bee sucks, there suck I . . ."

"But . . ." attempted Vythilingam.

"Get in," said Sundralingam, firmly but not unkindly.

The music-god sang loudly to the shop and the street. Children stared with awe into its hypnotic eye, and many beer-drinkers, more than ever before, sat tranced and wrapped in a warm overcoat of tropical night and thumping great music. Old Loo, standing by the refrigerator, looked pleased.

"Look at him there," said Idris, sweating gently into the suit, "cotton-wool in his ears."

"Who?" asked Azman, to-night in tropical dress.

"Him. The wonder-boy."

The four guffawed. Robert Loo indeed sat as though trying to weave silence round himself, two tufts of cotton-wool ineffectual valves, for the noise dwindled from a lion to ants as it met the soft obstacles, but, marching tinily rather than leaping with spread claws, still entered. The maddening image of the violinist, her dress changed, for some reason, from blue to green, was more maddening than before: she would stand there forever, her bow ready, her cheek caressing the polished wood of the fiddle, waiting, smiling, waiting. Robert Loo opened the woollen doors and the raging golden ocean entered. It was no good trying to fight.

"Here's your dad," said Azman to Hassan. Syed Omar

72

had entered, gay in his newspaper shirt, black slacks, sandals. He greeted his son, saying: "So this is how you waste your time."

Syed Hassan grinned, embarrassed by his father's loudness of voice and dress, and mumbled: "Not doing any harm." Syed Omar loudly ordered a brandy and ginger ale. Loo Kam Fatt said: "Cannot do. You Malay. Police say no." Syed Omar said: "I am the police. You can serve me. You must serve me. I am the police."

Syed Omar sat with the four boys and sipped his brandy and ginger ale. "And what kind of a get-up is that?" he said, sneering at Idris's suit. "What are you supposed to be?"

"Nothing," said Idris.

"That's right, nothing. That's all you do, nothing. Trying to look like gangsters. You too," he said to his son. "I've seen you round the town wearing that same get-up. What's happening to the Malay youth of to-day?" he said. "Where are the good old Muslim principles your elders tried to teach you?"

"We're not drinking brandy, anyway," said Azman boldly.

"Couldn't if you tried," said Syed Omar with contempt. "You'd spew it up." He made a vomiting face, showing the white blade of his tongue. "You're not the men your fathers were, nor never will be. All this Coca-Cola and jazzing about. Where are the principles your fathers fought for?"

Nobody liked to ask where or against whom they fought. They remained silent. Syed Omar said: "What will happen to Islam when it's left to milksops like you to defend it? Tell me that." Nobody could tell him. Suddenly the music burst like a boil and Syed Omar jumped in his seat. "In the name of God," he shouted, in

English, "turn down that noise." Nobody moved. Suddenly a quiet passage started. "That's better," he said, as though the god itself had hastened to obedience. "You're soft," he resumed to the boys. "It's all these films from America. Soft living and soft thinking. Look at that muscle," he said to his son. "Rolling up your sleeves as though you've got something to show." He felt the hard roll on Hassan's upper arm, saying: "Soft, boy, really soft."

The boys looked at him in good-humoured contempt, at his round belly and his general flabbiness. "I could stand up to you in the ring," said Hamzah. "Five rounds. I reckon I could knock you out."

Syed Omar laughed. "That's right," he said. "Pick on me. The enemies of Islam and the enemies of the Malays are all around you, and you talk about knocking me out. Me, the same age as your father, me, a member of your own race. You sit there drinking horrible sweet drinks, and all around are enemies." He took in, in a dramatic slant-eyed gaze, the harmless drinkers. "And all the four of you can think of is hitting a poor old man whose day is nearly over, who's given the best years of his life to making the world safe for milksops like you." He called for more brandy and said: "Put it on my account."

The first show at the near-by cinema had just ended. Crabbe came in with Rosemary. Relenting of his boorishness of the other night, his crass rejection of those freely offered sensual treasures, he had taken her to see the town's first English-speaking film for months. A poor film, it had moved Rosemary deeply, its blonde heroine stirring new fantasies in her. As they sat at a table now, Rosemary said above the music: "Just like her, Victor, fair hair and blue eyes, both my father and my mother and my brother and sister too, all of them, and just because I happened to be born dark like this they didn't want anything to do with me. They threw me out, Victor, out on to the streets, just because my skin was the wrong colour. They did, Victor. And that's why I hate them, that's why I hate my own race, that's why I'd like to cut their throats and see them lying in pools of blood at my feet." Crabbe gazed at her in admiration. At the moment she was being the blonde film-star. Factitious passion did not make her face crumble: it merely enlarged her black eyes, dilated the Mediterranean nostrils, suggested, with its false image of a temperament that could be controlled, that she was really desirable.

"And you'd like to do that to Joe?" asked Crabbe. "Joe lying in pools of blood at your feet?"

Rosemary looked at him as though he were mad. "But that's the whole point, Victor," she said. "Joe isn't Scottish. Joe's English. I thought you knew that."

Crabbe gave it up. He greeted old Loo with a wave, called for gin, and gestured to Robert Loo that he come over to the table. Robert Loo hesitated, his father spoke swift urgent Chinese to him and pushed him towards Crabbe.

"What was that all about?" asked Crabbe, as the boy stood shyly by. "Come on, sit down. I want to talk to you."

"He's really quite handsome," drawled Rosemary, as though Robert Loo were one of the 'natives', and she but newly arrived from Sloane Square. "A bit like that nice man from Penang."

"I must see you," said Robert Loo, "I have to talk to you. It's very difficult."

"Well, sit down. Talk to me now."

"He speaks quite good English," said Rosemary, "for a Chinese."

"I can't go on like this," said Robert Loo. "I can't get my work done. Day after day this noise. And I can't get out."

"Sit down," said Crabbe. "Tell me all about it. Calmly."

Robert Loo sat down on the edge of a chair, hands clasped, as in a vicarage drawing-room. "I've written only five bars in two days. It's this noise all the time. And I try to write up in my bedroom, after midnight, but my father puts out the lights."

"What are you writing?"

"A violin concerto."

"Ah."

"Can you play the violin?" asked Rosemary loftily, out of a chumbling refined mouth.

"No, I can't. I mean, I know how . . ."

"I was taught the violin," said Rosemary. "I played it at school, and at the university. On television, too," she added. "Oh, all sorts of things. Symphonies by Bach, and fugues, and, oh, all sorts of things. *Ave Maria,*" she added, like a pious ejaculation. "And *In a Persian Market.*"

"I must speak to your father again," said Crabbe. "It's not altogether his fault, I can see that. He wants more trade, and so forth."

"He won't listen to you," said Robert Loo. "He says . . ."

"What does he say?"

"He says that people are talking."

"You see, Victor," said Rosemary briskly. "I told you people were talking, didn't I? But you wouldn't listen."

"I don't know what he means," said Robert Loo. "But he said you were up to no good. Please, please," he added in panic, "don't say that to him. He says you're a good customer and you mustn't be told anything to make you annoyed. But I still don't know what he means."

"I'll tell you what he means," began Rosemary with vigour and relish. "He means . . ."

"Do be quiet, Rosemary," said Crabbe. "Never mind what he means. That's not the point. The point is that you must be able to go on composing. Do you get no evening off? You can always come to my place and work there."

"He wouldn't let me go there," said Robert Loo. "And he says there's too much work to do here. I don't think he'll let me have any more time off."

"I'll speak to him," said Crabbe, not without grimness.

"Don't, don't. He sees we're talking about him now. I must get back." And he rose from the chair.

"Sit down," ordered Crabbe. "So," he said, with a certain malice, "the real world's impinging at last."

"Impinging?"

"You're becoming aware of other people. The artist, you see, can't function in a vacuum. If I were you," said Crabbe, "I'd start acting. Doing something. I'd even leave home and get a job somewhere, a job as a clerk, say. I'd assert myself."

"I couldn't do that." All the shock of intense Chinese conservatism confronting the heterodox, even the blasphemous. "I couldn't. He's my father."

"My father threw me out on the streets," said Rosemary, "to fend for myself. Alone in the streets of London at the age of ten. Then I was adopted by an Indian prince," she added. "I wasn't afraid of leaving home."

"There's only one way, perhaps," said Crabbe. "Your father must be made to see. There's a fair chance that your symphony will be played for the Independence celebrations. If he hears that broadcast, or, better, if he actually *sees* it being played, a large audience, the applause . . . He has to take your music seriously. He must be *shown*."

"You can come and work at my house," said Rosemary generously. "Any night."

77

"I can't get out," said Robert Loo. "I said that before. And I asked him again about becoming an accountant, but he said that he needs me here now. They're closing down so many other places, and he says we're going to get all the trade."

"Your symphony," said Crabbe patiently, "is, I think, going to be played. All you have to do is to add a short finale for chorus, a patriotic ending in Malay. Your symphony must have a more popular appeal. A political appeal. You can get that done, can't you? Somehow?"

Robert Loo sneered. "I won't change it. It's good as it is. It's what I wanted to write. They've no right to ask me to change it. Even if I could, I wouldn't."

"Oh, Robert, Robert." Crabbe sighed deeply, just, thought Rosemary, like Jalil. "You'll never learn. The real world's impinging, and you can't see it. What am I going to do with you?"

But Robert Loo was looking, fascinated, at Rosemary's right hand which held, in film-star elegance, a long cigarette-holder holding a long cigarette. "Do give me a light, darling," she said to Crabbe. Robert Loo saw himself looking, for the first time, at a woman's hand. It was a well-shaped hand—the beauty of any one isolated part of Rosemary's body was a divine wonder: it was only the totality, the lack of the animating soul, that failed to impress: she was a valuable lesson in æsthetics, proclaiming the kinship of the sublime and absurd. Robert Loo's eyes were led, as in an artfully composed picture, up from the long delightful fingers to the cunning of the wrist, up to the smooth round brown arm to the bare shoulder. This was the real world impinging. "I must go back," he mumbled. Crabbe nodded bleakly, dumbly.

When Crabbe and Rosemary left, the four Malay boys, free at last of Syed Hassan's father, made tiny whistling

78

noises at Rosemary's haunches. Then they sat a while in gloom. In a sense, all that had been said was true. They did nothing to justify their vaunted knightly trappings: the casque of hair, the one suit of sweating armour, the brave oaths and the slick knives. They had been visited, they knew, by Hamlet's father's ghost. O, what rogues and peasant slaves were they. They must start acting. Doing something.

"If my dad lost his job," said Hassan, "it would be his fault. A dirty Tamil."

"We could beat him up," suggested Azman.

"Knife him." Thus Hamzah.

"Hit him with a bicycle chain."

"Smash a bottle in his face."

"Knock his teeth out."

"Punch him in the *bodek*."

"Here," called Hassan angrily to Robert Loo. "We want to pay."

"Eighty cents."

"Too much. Fifty."

"Eighty cents."

"Fifty, or we'll smash up your juke-box."

Robert Loo smiled, said fervently: "If only you would."

That was not the correct response. How all occasions did inform against them. Sullenly they paid what was asked, sullenly left, Hamzah feigning a kick at the glass show-case filled with loaves and Chinese cakes.

Action. At two-thirty-five in the morning, Robert Loo, barefooted, his sleeping-sarong knotted tightly at the sternum, crept past his father's snores, past his brothers and sisters who breathed heavily in the heavy labour of sleep, and went softly downstairs. His electric torch caught rain-stains on the wall, scurrying cockroaches big as mice,

79

forlorn empty mineral-water cases. Entering the shop, he found moonlight sitting at the tables, the great music-god asleep in the corner. This he sought. He was not going to murder, for he had no murdering weapon; he was merely going to maim. He put out his torch and, by moonlight, made from the tray of an empty Player's packet a wedge of card, trimming it with fingers and teeth to the right size. This wedge he jammed into the coin-slit of the machine, jamming it hard in, closing the passage to noise-buying ten-cent pieces. He hoped to gain from this a day of silence, time enough to sketch out a good deal of the first movement of the concerto. He heard it now, violin soaring above the muted horns and the harps, and saw the soloist, smiling in green. Then, with a shock, he saw Rosemary, and heard no music. This would not do. His breath came faster. Seeing the long elegant brown arm again, he groaned, remembering Crabbe's curious word 'impinge'. Why couldn't they leave him alone? All he wanted to do was compose his music.

4

Rosemary returned from her week-end in Penang looking curiously over-dressed. It was the effect of the engagement-ring, whose tiny stone danced and flashed hugely in the sharp Malayan light, helio-signalling many contradictory messages: 'You'd like me, wouldn't you, but you can't now, see, because I belong to another; how beautiful I am, aren't I, someone was bound to snap me up; come and get me, brave the barrier of fire; the auction's on, this is only the first bid; I am, as you can see, essentially a respectable girl.' The ring seemed ubiquitous: the glow of its spectrum filled, like a perfume, any room she had been in: its song was as loud in the town as Loo's juke-box, now repaired. But, somehow, the ring sat on her as obscenely as a nun's coif would have done.

It put into Crabbe's head the notion of a party, a party not just for her, but also for the launching of his inter-racial sodality scheme. Of that, a ring that promised marriage was an apt symbol.

"You can help, you can be hostess."

"Oooooh, Victor, how marvellous, what a good idea, Victor, oooooh."

"We'll have Nicky, of course, and some of the Chinese Rotarians, and the Tamils."

"Oh, no, Victor, no, I can't bear the touch of a dark skin."

"It's not going to be that sort of party."

"How about those nice English boys in Boustead's, and the manager up at Durian Estate, and Jerry Framwell from Sungai Puteh, and . . ."

"No. It's not that sort of party. In some ways, it's going to be rather a serious party."

"How can you have a serious party?" she asked in wonder, flashing her ring.

"You'll see what I mean."

"Oooooh, Victor, in Penang the men just wouldn't leave me alone, I hardly dared leave my bedroom, and there was one very distinguished-looking man, you know, with greying hair and pots and pots of money, and he wanted to marry me, but I told him he was too late, and then Jalil was jealous and got tight and tried to get into my room at three in the morning. Oh, Victor, it was awful, awful . . ."

"Did you see Lim Cheng Po while you were there?"

She pouted. "Yes. He was in the bar one night. Oh, I hate him, Victor, hate him. He was very polite and stiff, and, oh, Victor, he has such a lovely voice, and he just offered me a drink and then he left."

"Well, you don't really like Asians, do you?" said Crabbe. "You can't bear the touch of a . . ."

"Oh, I don't know, I don't know, Victor. He's not really an Asian, is he? He has such a lovely voice. Oh, Victor, Victor, why is life so difficult?"

"It's not difficult any more, Rosemary. You're engaged."

"Yes, I'm engaged. To Joe."

"You're engaged to Joe."

The name hung in the air an instant like a faint common smell. It was as if, engagement having been definitely, sacramentally, achieved, Joe, its instrument, might well be discarded. Rosemary and Crabbe discussed arrangements for the party.

"Cheng Po will be over here on Wednesday. We might as well have the party then."

"Oh, yes, Victor, what a good idea, really, that *is* a good idea."

"I thought you hated him."

"Oooooh, Victor, I never said that. I never said anything of the sort. How could you imagine I'd say such a thing?"

It was carefully enough planned. Many canapés—no beef to annoy the Hindus, no pig-meat to enrage the Muslims —and various beverages, including harmless hideous coloured liquids lying, a clinking reef, in a tub of ice-water. Rosemary, brown bosom, flaming dress, flashing ring, high-heeled vigorously over Crabbe's large drawing-room as the sun set, setting out nuts and pretzels, perking up nodding flowers. This was, after all, on one level, her party.

When Nik Hassan came he was accompanied, to Crabbe's surprise, by his wife, 'Che Asma. She was a bulky woman in a tartan sarong and a green cardigan, who, in Malay fashion, kicked off her sandals at the door and padded on large horny feet to a hard chair in the corner. She took a wad of *sireh* from her bag and began chewing juicily, ignoring her host, dismissing her bare-shouldered hostess as a light woman, waiting for the other Malay wives to arrive. But no Malay wives had been invited. 'Che Asma had a shrewd, ugly face, obviously happiest when mobile. She curtly refused orange crush, lime juice, lemonade, and gave Rosemary an order for coffee. So coffee had to be made.

"I'm just as surprised as you are, Vicky," said Nik Hassan, smart in a grey palm-beach suit, his fine brown eyes gloomy. "But she would insist on coming, said I never take her anywhere. I hope to God she behaves herself."

83

"Never mind, have a drink, Nicky."

"I think," said Nik Hassan, "I'd better pretend to be drinking ginger ale. She watches me like a bloody hawk, man. Here." He summoned Crabbe's boy, a shifty Chinese who loved parties, and spoke quick Malay to him. "That's all right," he said. "He knows that ginger ale is a code for brandy-ginger ale." Loudly he said: "Ginger ale, please."

Mrs. Pereira arrived, a somewhat unappetising Eurasian lady of fifty, headmistress of a local girls' school. Her husband had run away from her, but he still sent her enough money to pay the rent. Gushing, she examined Rosemary's ring with catty claws, saying: "None of us ever thought he'd do it, Rosemary dear, but he's done it, hasn't he? I wonder why, now. Men, men, you can't trust any of them, can you?"

"I trust my Joe."

"I trusted Pereira. Never mind, dear, life is what it is. You can't change human nature."

Lim Cheng Po arrived, urbane, elegant, the soul of courtesy, with a silver bracelet for Rosemary.

"Ooooooh, that's so sweet, isn't it sweet, Victor, ooooh, it's lovely, oh, I can't wait to put it on."

"Not half exquisite enough for so exquisite a lady," said Cheng Po. "May I congratulate you, Victor?"

"Congratulate?"

"And may I say how pleased I am that Victor has made so exquisite a choice, and how happy I shall be to see him settled down again, and how I hope, my dear, dear lady, that you'll make each other very, very happy."

"Oh, Victor," Rosemary smirked, all vermilion lipstick, "do you hear what he says?"

Crabbe's head reeled seeing a new world form, in which the act of engagement came first and the choice of a betrothed followed. "No," he said, "that's not it. You see, it's not me, that is to say, Rosemary is engaged to . . ." Had he, he wondered, possibly proposed to Rosemary at some time or other, and everybody remembered except himself, and Joe was a kind of code-word like ginger ale? No, no. He came to, said to Cheng Po: "What will you drink?"

"Ah, pink gin, please, Victor."

Pink gin, Scotch and soda, brandy and water. The guests were arriving, the room was filling, talk and smoke rode the air. But Crabbe felt that things had got off to a bad start. 'Che Asma spat out vigorously a sliver of toast with a shive of luncheon-meat on it. *"Babi!"* she cried.

"Is isn't pork," said Crabbe. "We were very careful about that." She shrugged, unconvinced, not willing to talk to a man anyway, waiting for the Malay wives to come. But the only other wife present was Mrs. Foo, wife of Mr. Foo, the dentist, smiling, slim, delicious, in a *cheongsam* that showed thighs thinner, but not less delightful, than Rosemary's. 'Che Asma spoke to the air her detestation of such exhibitionism.

And here were the Tamil brethren. For Arumugam and Sundralingam there was much to worry about: Maniam alone in the house at night; Vythilingam inclined to be naughty; Rosemary at large. But they had not been able to think of a valid excuse for not coming, especially as Vythilingam had expressed his determination to get drunk on Crabbe's liquor. Arumugam and Sundralingam knew why: another letter from Ceylon that morning, another photograph of a shining Tamil girl, with the dowry pencilled baldly on the back: $75,000; the complex machinery of Vythilingam's soul churning and grinding; even at one point in the early evening, a show of pugnacity. And now Vythilingam was jerking out mouthfuls of air at Rosemary.

"Oh, Vy, don't be silly. It's hopeless, can't you see that? Look, my ring." The tiny diamond winked and signalled.

"I . . . I . . . don't think. . . ."

"We're still friends, aren't we? I mean, you'll still look after the cats."

"I . . ."

"Come along," sang Arumugam, in hearty falsetto, "come and join the boys."

"I . . . don't . . ."

"And," said Nik Hassan to Crabbe, "they think it's a good idea. That's just what they'd like, they say, to open up the celebrations. A good stirring Malay song all about our glorious mountains and jungles and tigers, and all that guff. Not too long, of course. They think they can get their orchestra from Singapore. And, of course, there's always the Federation Police Band."

"But that would just be the end of a rather long symphonic piece," said Crabbe. "The whole point is really the symphony itself."

"Couldn't all that be cut out? Couldn't he just send in the singing bit?" said Nik Hassan. He grabbed Crabbe's boy—who already smelt of Beehive brandy—and handed back his glass, saying: "I asked for ginger ale. This is just ginger ale."

"No," said Crabbe, "no. That's just it. They've got to have the whole lot."

"They haven't *got* to." Perhaps it was merely the presence of his wife that made him irritable. "I'm doing you a favour, after all, Vicky."

"*Me* a favour?"

"Well, him a favour. That boy a favour."

"But, damn it all, man, I thought we'd been into all that. Can't you honestly see that getting this thing performed is important to Malaya?"

Rosemary's bosom and perfume and ring were upon them. "Victor, Victor, I think that Vy's trying to get tight. Look at him." Vythilingam had been wedged into the corner by the drink-table, a solid wall of Arumugam and Sundralingam shielding him from temptation. Vythilingam had drunk off two neat whiskies and was pouring another. Sundralingam spoke loudly and pedantically to Mrs. Foo about the local yaws campaign.

"There is a most nauseating fluid exuding from the yaws sore, and the causative organism is found abundantly in that."

Mrs. Foo smiled winningly and nibbled at a sardine on a toothpick.

"As much as twenty years between the primary sore and the tertiary stage."

Crabbe cleared his throat and called: "Ladies and gentlemen." The words "spirochæte" and "ginger ale" lagged into the near-silence. With drink Vythilingam found the gift of speech returning. He too said, goldfish-twittering to the ceiling: "Ladies and gentlemen."

"I don't want to talk a great deal," said Crabbe. "First, let me say how glad I am to see you all here, and, more particularly, express my pleasure at the sight of representatives of all the races of South-East Asia mixing freely and in obvious harmony in the house of a wicked Englishman." There was dutiful laughter; only Arumugam nodded gravely; Vythilingam, as on a dummy flute, tried out mouth-twisting phrases. "We hear a great deal these days," said Crabbe, "about the prospect of racial discord in the new, independent Malaya. These ideas have been disseminated by unscrupulous elements who see in racial dissension an admirable instrument for the furthering of their own nauseating ends. I refer, of course, to the Communists."

There were pious noises of agreement. Rosemary stood puzzled, wondering at so strange an exordium to a speech about her and her engagement. Suddenly, surprisingly, Vythilingam said, quite clearly: "The Communists," and drank off more whisky.

"But," said Crabbe, "apart from the Communists, I don't think we can doubt that the component races of Malaya have never made much effort to understand each other. Odd superstitions and prejudices, complacency, ultra-conservatism—these have perpetually got in the way of better understanding. Moreover, the idea of a community —a single community, as opposed to many distinct com-munities—never seemed very important during the period of British management. There was a cold, purely legal unification provided by the State—a British importation— and a sort of superficial culture represented by American films, jazz, chocolate-bars, and refrigerators; for the rest, each race was content to keep alive fragments of culture imported from its country of origin. There never seemed any necessity to mix. But now the time has come." He banged his fist forensically on the top of a dinner-wagon. "There must not merely be mixing, there must be fusion."

"Confusion," said Vythilingam, nodding agreement. He was shushed.

"There must be inter-marriage, there must be a more liberal conception of religion, there must be art and litera-ture and music capable of expressing the aspiration of a single unified people." Nik Hassan grinned cynically. "I suggest that we attempt, here in this town . . ." Here Crabbe stopped. His heart sank at the vision on the veranda: Syed Omar, in newspaper shirt, making a spec-tacular entrance, crooning throatily.

"Big words," said Syed Omar, "big words. But they will not help us to get jobs." He came into the drawing-room,

88

blinking with drunken photophobia, and then stood swaying under the fan, his untidy hair stirred by its breeze. "Look at them," he said, "wearing their suits. Black bastards."

"Come on, now, Omar," soothed Nik Hassan. "Come to the kitchen, have some black coffee."

"Don't want any black coffee. Don't like anything black."

"For God's sake," whispered Crabbe, "pull yourself together, Omar. We don't want any trouble."

"I never wanted any trouble," cried Syed Omar. "I did my work, didn't I? I did my work better than the next man. And now I get my reward. I am out of a job." He sat down in the nearest arm-chair and began to sob quietly. Everybody looked embarrassed, everybody except Vythilingam. Vythilingam sang very quietly the song the Japanese had sung in celebration of the fall of Singapore.

"I think," said Mr. Foo, all fat smiles, "my wife and I had better be going."

"Not so soon," said Crabbe.

"Oh," cried Syed Omar, "I see. You do not want to be in the same house as a man without a job. You think I am only a dirty jobless Malay."

Vythilingam picked this up very clearly. "Dirty jobless Malay," he smiled to the whisky bottle.

Syed Omar was on his feet. "And if you are a clean Tamil I would rather be a dirty Malay," he cried. "It is your fault, it is the fault of your race that I am now without a job. Your Mister bloody Maniam and the whole damned lot of you."

"You'd better go home," said Crabbe. "Come on, I'll take you." The party, he felt, might as well be abandoned. But Syed Omar shook himself free of Crabbe's arm, saying: "I will say what I have to say to these black bastards."

89

"Such filthy language," protested Mrs. Pereira. Rosemary tried to cling, in a show of apprehension, to Lim Cheng Po. Vythilingam broke through his cordon, smiling, saying very distinctly to Syed Omar: "I know you."

"I know you too, you bastard."

In the scuffle that followed, nobody actually got hurt. Some of Nik Hassan's ginger ale was spilled on to Rosemary's dress, and the dress began to reek of brandy. 'Che Asma, disgusted, swept her hand across a row of spirit bottles, and two of these rolled over the floor, and Syed Omar tripped and fell over a bottle of rum, grasping, as he fell, at the nearest stable object, which was Mrs. Foo's right leg. The whole business was quite deplorable.

"Well," said Idris, panting a little, "what do we do now?"

"Quiet," whispered Syed Hassan. "He'll hear you." The house of Dr. Sundralingam was in darkness, but there was no doubt that Maniam was within.

"But what are we going to *do*?" asked Hamzah.

Nobody answered, for nobody really knew. Each carried in his mind a confused image of violence, and this was further confused in the mind of Hassan by a sense of filial obligation, of guilt and also, since his father had come home and said that there would be no more wages coming in and hence no more school-fees could be paid, by relief and even a curious gratitude to Maniam. Hassan envisaged for himself a fine idle adult future, feeling, at the thought, as they stood breathing quietly and quickly in the palmy darkness, a kind of promise of ecstasy in his loins, which whetted his desire to do some harmless harm or other to Maniam.

Inspired, he said: "Handkerchiefs round our faces."

"Have no handkerchief," said Azman. His whisper got

out of control on the last syllable, and a sudden voice-breaking bass rasped the darkness.

"Sssssshhhh! Fool!"

"I've got two," breathed Idris. Tonight he was wearing the suit, and had a handkerchief in top as well as trouser pocket.

They tied these yashmaks round their faces, and, as a car went by on the road parallel to the avenue where they stood, they saw each other's big brown eyes above them, and Azman started to giggle.

"Sssssshhh!"

"Front door locked," said Hassan. "Must be. We'll try kitchen door. Take off that jacket," he said to Idris. "Take off that tie. May see. May recognise. Leave under that tree there." Idris obeyed. Softly on sandals they trod grass; now and again a dried twig cracked underfoot, Hamzah stubbed his toe on a coconut shell, Idris squelched into an over-ripe papaya lying under its tree. Starshine above, faint rustle of palm-leaves, black, quiet, moonless. The kitchen door was locked.

"His boy sleeps here?" asked Azman voicelessly.

"Sssssshhh! Boy always go to town. Look, window there. Open."

"Listen! Maniam's breathing in sleep?"

"Help me up," whispered Hassan. "Will look. Knives ready."

Elbows on window-ledge, legs held by comrades, he looked in, darkness, saw nothing. "In," he whispered urgently, "help in. Knives ready." Hassan kneed himself up, over, in, soundlessly, feet on floor, knife out, eyes like blunter knife trying to cut darkness. No sound. "Azman," he whispered. "Azman next. Then Idris. Hamzah stay out there. Watch. In here nobody."

Idris, Azman, now in also, Azman pulled out pocket-torch, shone through room dimly with dying battery. Nobody. Sundralingam's room, perhaps. Bed empty, mosquito-net down, wardrobe, dressing-table, Chinese nude calendar on wall. Cautiously the three soft-footed out of the room, opening door creaked a little. In new room Hassan felt for light-switch.

A blaze of glory shone on Maniam sitting up startled in bed. Like 'Che Asma who, just at that moment, was knocking bottles off Crabbe's drink-table. Maniam wore a tartan sarong. His eyes wide with surprise and fear, he clutched tightly the bolster—sweat-absorbing bedfellow of sleepers in the East—known as a Dutch wife.

"What? What? Who?"

It was always as well to leave things to impulse. Hassan found the right thing to say.

"*Jangan takut,*" he said, then remembered that the language of sophisticated crime was English. "Don't be afraid," he amended.

"What? What? What do you want?"

"We come to protect you," said Hassan. "Are enemies wanting to kill you. We will stop enemies wanting to kill you."

"What do you mean? Who are you?" Maniam's great eyes, his black skin oiled with sweat, Maniam's hands pudgily clutching his Dutch wife.

"You pay little money only. We stop enemies from killing you," said Hassan.

"Where do you keep your cash, bub?" asked Idris hoarsely. His American was better than Hassan's English. "You gotta hand over, see."

Maniam eyed the knives. "How much do you want?"

"Twenty bucks," said Azman.

"A hundred bucks," bid Hassan, giving Azman a rough elbow-jab. "Pay up and you be all right."

"I've got no money," said Maniam.

"I bet there's money there in your trousers," said Hassan. A pair of crumpled green slacks lay over the bedside chair. "Pay up."

"Or else," added Idris. He juggled his knife in menace, dropped it on the floor, picked it up, repeated, "Or else."

"My wallet's in the next room," said Maniam. "I don't know how much is in it. I'll get and fetch it."

"That's right, you go and fetch it," said Hassan. "We'll wait here."

"Yes," said Maniam, out of bed with eager agility. "You wait here."

"Idiot," cried Idris in Malay. "There's a telephone in there. Stop him." Azman, nearest to Maniam, grasped his sarong, which immediately unwound down to Maniam's ankles: black round buttocks were disclosed, short hairless legs, Maniam's shame. "Let me go," he said in anger. He tried to get into the living-room, his dropped folds of sarong hobbled him; eluding Azman's grasp too vigorously, he was tripped by his own wide stride and the folds at his ankles; he went over, striking his nose hard on the door-knob. He lay cursing an instant, aware of a maimed face just healed, now maimed again. "Damn you!" he cried.

"You get the money, bub," menaced Idris. "And no more tricks, see?"

"A car! A car coming!" cried Hamzah from without. "Allah!"

"Out the same way," ordered Hassan. "Through the window, quick."

"We get the money first," said Idris. "Here in trousers."

"Out, out, I order," ordered Hassan. "Out now, quick, quick."

"I bring trousers," said Idris. He grabbed them from

the chair. The naked Maniam tried to rise, called: "Help! Murder!" as he heard the car engine come closer. The boys dashed. Azman had already scrambled out into moonless garden, clumsily landing on Hamzah the helper. Idris, trousers under arm, followed, Hassan tumbling after. The big eyes of the car, turning into the drive, caught their yashmaks, their legs doubtful whither to run. "Help! Help!" from Maniam at the front door. "Get them, quick! There!"

In the back of the car, Vythilingam was loudly singing: ". . . And the rising sun shall rise yet higher, destroying with its flaming fire the evil will of the wicked West, but smiling warmly on the rest," in demotic Japanese. Arumugam was out, ready with fists, voice girling high: "Where, where?"

The boys ran, scattered. Idris and Hamzah met the big arms of Sundralingam, realised it was not a question of catching but of recognising, realised too late that this sort of adventure was not for small towns, but part of the culture of cities. Hamzah knifed Sundralingam gently in the forearm. Sundralingam wailed, Hamzah and Idris got away. Arumugam was down, kicked by Azman. "Run, run!" They ran. Running, Hassan remembered the jacket, with the string-tie in the pocket, lying under the tree. To-morrow it was his turn to wear full uniform. He ran that way, ready to scoop it up from the tree's shadow. Even in this panic and flurry he saw clearly that he was rightfully the leader, having the brains to remember to remove a clue from the vicinity of the crime. (Crime? Had there been a crime?) Thus Arumugam, athletic and virile under the feminine dress of his voice, caught him, being quickly on his feet again, off his mark. Hassan struggled in muscular arms, his turn now to call for help, but the six fugitive feet were padding down the road, abandoning him. Caught in an unarmed combat grip, raised in agony to his toes, Hassan was marched, the voice squealing in his ear, towards the house and the waiting Maniam and Sundralingam. Vythilingam snored.

The yashmak jerked off, in the third-degree light of the house, Hassan's scared face was scanned. "Syed Omar's son," said Sundralingam.

"Yes, yes," squeaked Arumugam. "Like father, like son. This is Syed Hassan."

"They got away with my trousers," said Maniam.

"What is this he has?"

"That is a jacket."

"Was there money in the pocket?" asked Sundralingam. Then he sucked the tiny wound on his arm.

"There was my wallet. Some money, yes, not much."

"Your face," said Arumugam. "They hit you on the face."

"Yes, yes, they did that, too."

"*Pembohong*," gnashed Hassan, "liar." Arumugam tightened the screw of the hold. "Ow!" cried Hassan.

"Well," said Sundralingam, "I shall ring for the police. This is very, very bad. Will Syed Omar never be out of trouble?"

So comparatively early in the evening still, and the party broken up, though the drawing-room had a morning-after look and Syed Omar groaned over his black coffee.

"But damn it," said Crabbe, "it sounds to me as if losing your job was nobody's fault but your own."

"Other people," said Syed Omar, eyes shut against the light, slumped in an arm-chair, "other people have done what I have done and have kept their jobs. I lost one file only, though I do not think I really lost it, but somebody stole it deliberately. I never claimed to be much good at typing. I have taken a few days off. I once had a bottle of whisky in the desk drawer, but that was only because I had fever. Other people have done worse and have not been given the sack. I have been framed. Maniam is at the back of it all."

Lim Cheng Po yawned delicately and continued to keep his distance from Rosemary, who sat temptingly by him on the couch. Rosemary pouted, feeling also a twinge of superstitious foreboding because her engagement party had fizzled, or exploded, out. She looked with distaste at Syed Omar, blaming him, blaming Crabbe too, then deciding also to blame Lim Cheng Po for the failure of the evening; and it would be their fault, too, if Joe now wrote breaking off the engagement.

"And who's going to get your job?" asked Crabbe.

"I don't know, I don't know," groaned Syed Omar. "Some Tamil woman, I suppose, some other relation of all those black bastards."

"Really," protested Rosemary, from her best refined mouth.

"I suppose I'll have to find something for you," sighed Crabbe. "There may be a vacancy in my office. Though," he added, "it's not really my office now."

Then there was the sound of transport, too heavy a sound for a private car, and headlights showed up the withered pot-plants in Crabbe's porch. "Whoever it is," said Crabbe, "they've come too late for the party." Slammed metal doors and boots. Inspector Ismail stood on the veranda, saluted, showed many teeth, and said, "Ah, I thought he would still be here. Forgive this intrusion, Mr. Crabbe. There is trouble with Syed Omar's son. Syed Omar had better come to the station."

"Trouble? What trouble?"

"Trouble?" Syed Omar's mouth was fixed for the

dentist's chair, his eyes huge now, despite the light.

"Your son and his friends tried to kill Mr. Maniam with knives. They stripped off his clothes, hit him on the face, kicked him while he was down, stole his trousers and his money, assaulted Mr. Arumugam too and tried to stab Dr. Sundralingam to death."

"No!"

"Oh yes," smiled Inspector Ismail. "We have everybody down at the station now." He sounded happy, as though everything were set for a party, the more pleasant because unexpected. "I think Syed Omar must come too."

"Oh, God God God," said Crabbe. "Why, oh why do they do these things?"

"Unfortunately," smiled Inspector Ismail, "they only caught Syed Hassan. The others got away. But the gentlemen think that Syed Hassan will be enough. For the moment, anyway."

"Look, I can't believe all that about killing and whatnot," said Crabbe. "Let me have a word with Maniam and the others. It was probably only a stupid childish joke, anyway. They must drop the charge."

"But," smiled Inspector Ismail, "it is really a police matter. They had weapons, you see. And housebreaking in very serious."

"I'll drive Omar down," said Crabbe.

"Keep out of these things, Victor," said Lim Cheng Po. "Keep out of these Asian matters. You will find yourself in terribly deep water."

"I'll drive him down," said Crabbe. "Stay here with Rosemary. Have a drink. Have something to eat. I shan't be long."

"My son," said Syed Omar, "my son, my son. They are ruining us all, the whole family." He wept.

"Come on now, pull yourself together."

"I am impotent, impotent."

"Oh, come on. Stay here with Rosemary, Cheng Po. I'll be back soon."

Lim Cheng Po and Rosemary were left together, under the wind of the fan, among the dirty glasses; the faint brandy-song of the cook-boy wafted in from the kitchen. Lim Cheng Po went over to the table to get a drink, saying: "Victor's a fool. He shouldn't do these things." Rosemary stood up, knowing she looked her best tall and straight, like a smooth brown tree, and sobbed: "Oh, I'm so unhappy, so unhappy."

Lim Cheng Po turned, startled, a glass in his hand. "Oh, my dear, dear lady, you mustn't be unhappy. What does all this business matter to you?"

"Oh," wailed Rosemary (men are so stupid), "oh, it isn't that. I'm so unhappy. I want to die." She waited for consoling arms. Lim Cheng Po said: "There, now, come and sit down. Have a drink. Tell me all about it."

"I don't want to sit down. Oh, life is terrible, terrible."

"There, there, there." And here they were, comforting arms beneath a so English, a so refined voice, a smell of hair-cream, after-shaving lotion, invisible talc, Imperial Leather soap, good cloth, man. Rosemary sobbed into Lim Cheng Po's chest, sobbed dryly because tears would ruin her mascara.

"There, there, there."

"So unhappy, so unhappy."

"Better now?"

"So unhappy."

Lim Cheng Po, Anglican, Royalist, cricketer, respectable husband and father, allowed his animal reflexes out for an avenue walk on the lead. Rosemary had a pleasant smell, her flesh was agreeable to palpate, to kiss her left temple lightly was less of a bore than having to say "There, there,

98

there" all the time. Eyes closed, she raised half-open vermilion lips to him. He was debating whether to touch them with his own when Vythilingam walked in, swaying but slightly, not very drunk.

Vythilingam had been left, apparently sleeping, in the back of his own car, while his friends, disgusted that he had once more failed them in the moment of need, had gone to the station in a police-van. But, in fact, Vythilingam had been drunkenly aware of violence proceeding outside, and he had not greatly wished to be involved. If his friends were being assaulted, that was perhaps a good thing: he was growing tired of their brother's keeper clucking over him. If his friends were assaulting others, that, too, was a good thing: the Jaffna Tamils had suffered enough from the rest of the world. He erected an impregnable tower of drunkard's snores in the back of the car, and only when silence returned to the house and its garden did he strike the stage set. Then he drove with drunken care to Rosemary's house, smiled nervously to find her not yet in, and walked, tracing wave-patterns on the road, to the house of Crabbe. There he found her being embraced by a Chinese from Penang.

The whisky ventriloquised through him, the dummy. "Stop that," he called, with great strength and clarity. Lim Cheng Po was only too ready to stop it. Rosemary turned, startled and thwarted.

"Vy!"

"Stop that," he repeated, though it had already stopped.

"My dear fellow," said Lim Cheng Po, in civilised reproof.

"You think," said Vythilingam, "you can do anything with me. "But" (he had some slight difficulty with the labial), "but I am a man." He paused, to let them take this in, to think of what to say next. "Like other men."

"Go home, Vy," said Rosemary, keeping her temper. "Go home and sleep. You've been drinking too much."

"I wait." He paused and swayed. "I wait for an answer."

"Do go home." She stamped her delicate foot. "Please, please go home."

"So that. He can. He can."

"I can what?" snapped Lim Cheng Po. He had not enjoyed any of the evening.

"Any man who comes along," said Vythilingam. "Any man can do it. With her."

"Vy, what a filthy and disgusting thing to say." Rosemary's face disintegrated. "Get out, get out this minute, do you hear?"

"Except me."

"Look here, old man," said Lim Cheng Po, "pull yourself together." That seemed to be the leitmotif of the whole evening. "Go home now, have a good night's sleep, you'll feel better in the morning. You're upsetting this lady, you know."

"I only want," said Vythilingam. "I only want," he repeated. "To marry her. To . . ." (he stumbled over another labial plosive) ". . . protect her." He nodded and swayed. "From herself."

"I don't want your protection," cried Rosemary. "Get out, get out, or Mr. Lim will throw you out."

"My dear lady . . ."

"He's always after me," cried Rosemary. "Always annoying me. He wants me to marry him. And I won't, ever, ever."

"Your dear Joe," said Vythilingam, "won't marry you." He smiled round the room, as at a circle of invisible friends. "Ever."

"What do you know?" cried Rosemary in anger. "What do you know about it? Shut up, do you hear?"

"He won't marry you. Joe only wanted one thing. And he got it." Vythilingam nodded several times, smiling.

Rosemary peeled off Sloane Square, Hartnell, decorations-will-be-worn, fog, primroses, crumpets by the fire, and let fly vulgarly at Vythilingam. Lim Cheng Po was distressed. "Bitch," said Vythilingam, with some difficulty, and, with more difficulty, "bloody bitch." Then he added, with courtly formality, "I ask for your hand. In marriage."

"Never, never, never, do you hear? Never!" Rosemary's eyes flashed danger, lights on a crumbling tower. "Now get out!"

"I think," said Lim Cheng Po, "I'd better take you home." He took her wrist.

"No," said Rosemary, "let him go home. How dare he say such things? Filthy, filthy things! Send him away or I'll hit him!"

"I suggest you go home," said Lim Cheng Po to Vythilingam. "We don't want any trouble, you know. Especially in Mr. Crabbe's house."

"I ask for her hand. I wait for an answer."

"You've got your answer. Never, never, never! I don't want to see you again, after the filthy, filthy lying things you've said! I don't want to see you again, ever!"

"Come on, dear lady," said Lim Cheng Po, leading her to the door. Rosemary sobbed. Vythilingam swayed slightly, smiling still. A madhouse, thought Lim Cheng Po, what a madhouse Asia was. He would be glad to be out of it. The church bells on Sunday, bitter and darts in the pub, civilisation. Crabbe could keep Malaya.

5

Crabbe sat at home in the early evening, gloomily drinking gin and water, waiting for the alcohol, like some great romantic symphony, to poison his nerves to a mood of quiet and resignation. It had been a hard day. The pupils of the local Anglo-Chinese School had decided to go on strike, and had maintained a day-long picket of the school yard, bearing revolutionary ideograms on cards and banners. Crabbe had been sent to investigate, but had found out nothing. The Communist cell lay hidden, somewhere in the multi-stream fourth form. He had appealed to them in English, and a Chinese Inspector of Schools had addressed them in Kuo-Yü—a language as remote as the tongue of Caedmon to the impassive hearers. The pupils had agreed to go back next day and had been much praised for their public spirit.

And this tiny revolt, by some kind of chain reaction, was connected with Syed Hassan's foolish escapade. Undistributed middles had led to a number of incredible conclusions in shop and bazaar, over sucked coffee and fingered rolls of silk. The Malays, it was said, had started to rise: parang and kris were being sharpened. They had begun to make a breakfast of the Tamils, they licked their lips at the prospect of a great Chinese dinner. It had never been young Hassan's desire to meddle in politics—he had merely wanted disinterested violence or intimidation of the most token sort—but his single night in the lock-up had made him, to other Malay youth at least, a kind of Horst Wessel. Now he was out on bail of five hundred dollars, which Crabbe, of course, had had to find. And now there were some who were saying that Crabbe was behind the coming rising of the Malays: he had, they said, secretly married his amah and had entered Islam.

Syed Hassan had betrayed his three friends very readily, arguing that, as the four shared responsibility for the crime, so they must equally share the quantum of the punishment. The English had taught him arithmetic but no ethics. The keen sight of Maniam, Arumugam and Sundralingam had apparently pierced through yashmak and darkness without difficulty, for Idris, Hamzah and Azman were immediately identified as the other criminals. For these three no bail could be found, so they had to languish behind bars. This caused further murmuring against Crabbe: why this favouritism? Why could the white man not dip deeper into his deep coffers? After all, Hamzah's father was a dredger in a tin-mine and Azman's uncle had, for three weeks at least, tapped rubber, and it was well known that the English had made themselves rich through tin and rubber, natural riches which belonged rightly to the Malayans, meaning the Malays.

So it was with relief that Crabbe read the message that the peon brought:

"Headmaster of Durian Estate School murdered. Please investigate. I would go if I could, but someone must stay in the office. Please take train tonight."

True enough, expatriates were now expendable: it was right and proper that the new masters should stick to their offices. Crabbe looked at his watch, saw that he had an hour before the slow train left for Mawas, packed shirts and razor, and sat down comfortably to finish the bottle of gin. If he didn't, his cook would in his absence. The great

Brahmsian slow movement of the sixth glass was broken rudely by the telephone's percussion.

"Is that you, Vicky? Nicky here."

"Vicky here, Nicky."

"It's about the money that Wigmore left. You know, the twenty thousand bucks to the State. There's going to be a meeting next week."

"Good. I shall be there."

"All right, if you want to, Vicky, but it won't do any good."

"What do you mean?"

"It's already been decided. Just as I said. The Sultan wants a Cadillac."

"But damn it, he can't do that. The terms of the will are quite clear, aren't they? It says something about the good of the State, doesn't it?"

'It's just as I said. They're prepared to argue it out. They say the highest good is the Sultan's good."

"Who say that?"

"The Sultan and the Raja Perempuan and the Tungku Makhota and the Mentri Besar."

"And you?"

"Well, damn it, what can I do? I've got my job to think about, and, besides, I suppose they're right really. I should leave well alone if I were you, Vicky. You don't want to get into trouble."

"I don't mind in the slightest getting into trouble. Who's the executor of Wigmore's will?"

"Protheroe. He's the trustee as well, if you want to know. And he's not objecting."

"For the usual reason, eh? He doesn't want to be thrown out of the State."

"It's just not worth it, Vicky. He says the terms of the will cover a Cadillac."

"I'm going to get Lim on the job. I'll contest this. It's a bloody disgrace."

"Don't do anything stupid, Vicky."

Crabbe slammed the receiver down. Then he called his cook and told him he would be away for a couple of days. "And," said Crabbe, "I know exactly how much brandy's in that cupboard. And whisky." The Chinese smiled ineffably.

Jalil wheezed at the two cats that lay on the only other arm-chair and somewhat roughly removed them. Then he sat down, breathing heavily at Rosemary's back as she, feigning to ignore him, steadily filled an air mail letter form at the table. "Who you write?" asked Jalil.

". . . I am longing for you to hold me in your arms again," wrote Rosemary, "and tickle my ear with your moustache. Oh, darling, it sends such funny shivers through me."

"You write him. I know," chuckled Jalil. "But no good. He not marry you."

". . . And am dying for the day when you and I can be together again and say these things to each other properly," wrote Rosemary. "All my love, dearest one." There was enough space after her signature to implant a kiss. Rosemary raised the thin blue letter to her richly rouged lips, pressing it to them as though covering a lady-like belch with a dinner napkin. Then vigorously she folded the letter, sealing it with a little condensed milk which she allowed to trickle from the tin on to her finger-tip. Ritually she replied to Jalil:

"Oooooh, go away, Jalil, you shouldn't be here, you know you shouldn't, I told the amah not to let you in."

"Come eat, come drink, come make jolly time." Jalil yawned. A cat yawned.

"No," said Rosemary. "I'm going to bed early."

"I come too," said Jalil.

"Jalil, what a filthy, what a horrible, what a downright nasty thing to say." Rosemary began to file her nails. There was silence. The brief ceremony was over.

"How long since you hear from him?" resumed Jalil.

"That's none of your business."

"How long?"

"If you must know, we write to each other every day. We never miss. That's because we're in love, but you wouldn't know what love is."

"I know what is love. Love is man and woman in bed."

Rosemary smiled, superior. "That's what you think. That's because you're an Asian. You Asians don't know anything about real love."

"How long since you hear from him?"

"I've told you." Rosemary's voice grew schoolmistressly sharp. "He writes every day."

"You get letter from him today?"

"Of course I did."

"Yes. You get letter today. But not yet."

"What do you mean?"

"He not write two weeks, more. Today letter come. But not yet you get."

"Jalil," threatened Rosemary, "if you're up to your nasty tricks again I'll hit you, I'll throw you out, I'll call for the police. I haven't forgotten that other business with the Blackpool Tower."

"Every day I ask Sikh in Post Office about letter for you. Today he give me. Letters more safe with me. Here is letter." In quiet asthmatic triumph Jalil drew a blue air mail letter from his breast pocket. "He write at last. He send bad news. I know. I not read, but I know. Now you read."

In rage Rosemary hurled herself at Jalil. A cat fled to the kitchen, another hid under the table. The force of her onslaught toppled Jalil's chair over, and he lay, legs in the air, as she scratched at his face. He panted for a while and then began his deep chuckle as he grappled, finally seizing her wrists. They were on the floor now, and frightened cats looked on as they rolled, Rosemary spitting, trying to bite. "This time," wheezed Jalil, "you get. You really get this time."

"Pig. Swine. Rotter." Rosemary's off-the-shoulder dress was now off more than her shoulders. Jalil's asthma roared in her right ear. Her skirt was in disarray. Cats climbed and leapt, watched with huge eyes, tails were high with fright, fur staring like quills. "Now," panted Jalil as though dying. Rosemary screamed for her amah, but nobody came. And still, crumpled in her left hand, she gripped the letter she had wrested. "Only I love," sweated Jalil. "Now. You see. Now." He dredged his lungs deeply and desperately for a spoonful of air. Rosemary tore at his right ear, turned it like a radio knob. Jalil hardly noticed, concentrating on breathing and his tearing hands. Then Rosemary upped with her knee.

Over in the corner she watched him crawling towards her, her own eyes big black lakes, herself panting. Panting filled the room, fan and refrigerator were silent. As Jalil got to his feet, his black Eskimo hair over his right eye, gasping towards her, Rosemary fumbled at the kitchen door, tottered through to the door of the servants' quarters, opened the door and tripped through the untidy cell (the floor paved with cigarette tins saved up for a ceremony of lights, a bulky sewing machine, cardboard boxes filled with trinkets, the amah out without permission) to reach the outer door which, thank God, was open. Crying, clutching the letter, she ran through the oven-like evening of the empty avenue, shoeless, whimpering towards Crabbe's house.

Crabbe's house looked empty: not because of shut doors or darkness—it was not quite lamp-lighting time—but because there was no car in the porch. How naked a porch then seems: caddis-cases, dried shed lizard-tails, corpses of cicadas, frogs hopping freely, cigarette-ends, dust, a great smear of oil, normally hidden by the bulky metallic body, now appear as symbols of desolation. Rosemary tried the glass-and-metal front door, but it was locked; round by the servants' quarters she called: "Boy! Boy!" but nobody came. (In fact, Crabbe's boy was there, but so was Rosemary's amah.) Rosemary went round to the veranda: there the folding doors were in place, but she rattled at panel after panel. She weakened at the knees with relief when one panel meekly swung inwards, the key panel with the tiny handle, its bolts unfastened, almost a true door. Inside the living-room that smelt of enclosed heat, she stood undecided and then called: "Victor! Victor!" Darkness gently began to lower itself into the chairs, to settle on the surfaces of tables and cupboards. Perhaps he was in the bedroom? Rosemary padded down the long corridor, passing the second bedroom which Crabbe used as a study, to the big chamber which held his solitary single bed. "Victor!" In the room the mosquito net was down, ghost-grey in the falling light. Crabbe was nowhere: the lavatory door stood wide, there was no sound of bath or shower. Rosemary sobbed gently, gorgeous in her disarray, the crumpled letter still in her fist. Disturbed by the noises, a toad hopped towards the bathroom, a chichak ran up the wall. Wearily she parted the mosquito-net's folds and half lay on the bed. Then she smoothed out the letter and tried to read it. The crumpled words swam, blurred, got mixed with diamonds, great splotches of tears dissolved some.

But, of course, she had known all the time, had always known.

. . . And if you met Sheila I am sure you would be great friends. She is not a bit like you, of course, she is very English and has blue eyes. Anyway, she says she will go on working till I find something, she has a good job, she is a confidential secretary, and it is perhaps just as well that I didn't get the job with that export or import company, whatever it is. Anyway, I want you to still wear the ring, and to think of me whenever you look at it, it will perhaps bring back happy memories of you and I together. I do not regret buying it for you at all, darling, for they were good times, weren't they, and it's nice to think we each have things to remember each other by. But, as the saying goes, East is East and West is West, and it would have been very difficult for both of us, darling, if we had got married. And if we had had kids it would have been very awkward for them, wouldn't it, so perhaps everything has worked out for the best. You're bound to find a good husband soon, for you are marvellous looking, and any man who is an Asian would be proud to have such a smasher for a wife. When Sheila and I are married, which should be next month, I know when we are in bed together I shall often think of you and the things we did. Good-bye, now, dear, and God bless you, and don't think too badly of your loving Joe.

Rosemary now pumped out floods of grief on to Crabbe's pillow. Her face cracked, split, liquefied, its horrid disintegration burrowed into the worn cotton; howls and bayings and ghastly sobs and chokings racked her body and made the bed shake and tremble. (Indifferent on the wall, a male chichak hunted a female with loud chuckles.) Only the lovely patina of Rosemary's flesh, the wonder of curve and line which was not her but the whole species, only these did not join in the personal dissolution, though her limbs writhed and her breasts laboured in that transport of misery. Occasionally she gasped out "Joe!"—a flat animal cry that her slack vocal cords made unfemininely deep, that her nasopharynx, choked with mucus, robbed of all resonance. The earth did not swallow her up, but gently the dark did.

Robert Loo, hesitant in full dark, with a moon rising, heard these strange sounds clearly from the veranda. Surely that could not be Mr. Crabbe? He clutched more tightly the brief-case under his arm, wondering whether to enter. Listening carefully, he decided that the voice was the voice of a woman: Mr. Crabbe evidently was in bed with a woman, and he was making her cry aloud either with pain or with pleasure. The cries were like nothing he had ever heard before, but they did not frighten him, they did not even arouse much curiosity: the only significant sounds in Robert Loo's life were musical sounds, preferably imagined ones, and these sounds were too grossly external and certainly not musical. Still, Crabbe was in and, when he was sated of whatever he was doing, there was much for him to hear and certain actions for him to take. Robert Loo now entered the dark living-room with confidence. He moved over to the table where, he knew, there was an electric lamp, and he fumbled for the switch of this lamp. Light sprang on to the darkness, a great rose-coloured circle of it. Robert Loo sat in an arm-chair, took scoring paper from his brief-case, and then placidly began to orchestrate the bar which had waited so long to become palpable dots and lines and curves: the first bar of his violin concerto—the opening cry of the orchestra set out fully from piccolo to basses. Meanwhile the woman's sobs continued. Flutes, oboes, clarinets, the downward-leaping theme on the bassoons, the wedge of harmony on the horns. He calmly and neatly wrote out the notes with a thin-nibbed fountain-pen.

The sobs began to slow down, like somebody dying, like the end of Honegger's *Pacific 231*. The noises of pleasure or despair became articulate sounds, a name called miserably, with a modicum of hope.

"Victor!"

Robert Loo raised his head, his pen halted in the middle of a group of quavers.

"Is that you, Victor?" Then sighs, deep sniffs, a jolting of the bed. Robert wondered, a tiny crease of frown over his eyes. Crabbe apparently was not in. He must have gone out for a moment, leaving her there. Then why those strange cries?

"Victor, come down here, Victor."

Robert Loo sat undecided. Then he put down his wad of scoring paper, his pen, and went half-way down the dark corridor leading to the dark bedroom. "Mr. Crabbe isn't here," he said gently.

"What's that? Who is it?" A further jolt of the bed, as of someone sitting up. A touch of fear in the voice.

"It's me. It's Robert Loo. Who are you?"

"What are you doing here?" A note of greater confidence, even of curiosity.

"I came to see . . ." But this was ridiculous, this colloquy at a distance and in the dark. Walking to the bedroom, Robert Loo found the corridor light-switch. Yellow clinical light disclosed the long bare wall of the corridor, the glass louvers all along one side, busy insect life, a young black scorpion high up near the low ceiling.

"Don't put the light on," warned Rosemary. "Don't. I'm a sight. You mustn't see me."

"I only wanted to ask," said Robert Loo, standing on the threshold of the room. "Has he gone out? When is he coming back?"

Suddenly the whole orchestra burst out again. "Never! Never!" A huge lost howl. "He'll never come back! I've lost him, lost him!" Another jangling of the bed as she turned to pour more tears into the already soaked pillow. Robert Loo stood and wondered further, finding himself now somehow involved in these terrible cries of suffering woman. He could hardly retreat from them: having advanced so far, having spoken, he had to say something. He was mildly surprised that Crabbe should have been carrying on some large film-like or operatic affair with a woman whose identity was becoming clear. He had read many operatic scores, only for the music, but the libretti had occasionally made a, mainly subliminal, impact. And at school they had read *Antony and Cleopatra*. "He ploughed her, and she cropp'd." He entered the bedroom, meeting the force of a lung-emptying sob, then the oceanic ingurgitation of air. He switched on the light.

Like some strange beast in a gauzy cage, Rosemary lay, her black hair abundant over the bed, her brown limbs sprawled in her abandon, her dress crumpled and in disarray. Stabbed by the light, she turned her swimming face in protest, her mouth square with crying.

"Turn it off, turn it off!" Her bowing arm moved—down-stroke, up-stroke—as she cleaned tears from her eyes with her fist. Robert Loo looked at that brown bare arm in mild fascination. Then he spoke.

"I'm sorry," he said.

"You don't know what it's like, you just don't know!"

"And where has he gone to?"

"To another woman! He's left me for ever!"

"Please," said Robert Loo. "I think this is important."

He sat on a chair by the bed, a chair cushioned by Crabbe's striped pyjamas. "I need to see Mr. Crabbe very badly."

Rosemary stopped crying. She looked through films of water at Robert Loo and said: "You wouldn't know anything about it. Nothing about real love. Like Joe and me." The name started her off again.

"Oh, I see," said Robert Loo.

"And I've nobody to turn to, nobody!"

"Can I do anything?"

"No! No! No!" She sank again into the salty water, indulging herself before even so inadequate an audience, into the delicious warm brine-tasting depths of her grief. Robert Loo wondered what he should do. A dance hostess with whom, he knew, his father had once been friendly, had tried, in a similar transport of despair over a man (not his father) to take caustic soda. This was, he knew, the usual Chinese way. Even in his mother's cupboard there had once stood a bottle of that standard agonising Lethe water. The Chinese were resourceful and even kept a store of death ready bottled. He remembered the story of this dance hostess: how the caustic soda had been wrenched from her fingers and she had been brought to a reasonable philosophy by Beehive brandy. He would get this shaking mound of a wretched woman some of Crabbe's brandy. He thought he knew where it was kept.

Even then, as he poured a measure into a beer-glass, he almost forgot his mission. He examined the half-scored bar, not too sure whether the horn-harmonies were well disposed. But he returned, soft and leisurely, to the bed-room, opened the mosquito-curtains and said: "Drink this." Between residuary sobs she drank it like water, sitting up, Robert Loo on the bed's edge, his finger-tips on the base of the glass.

The heaving of her shoulders subsided. "Why did you come here?" she asked.

"To see Mr. Crabbe. I've left home, you see."

"Oh, so they found out, did they?"

"Found out? What?"

"About you and him."

"I don't understand. It was trouble with my father. He hit me."

"So he'd found out, had he?"

"No, my father saw it. He saw these Malays steal the cigarettes from the shelf and run away with them. Then he blamed me. He tore up some of my music and hit me. Before some customers."

"Oh."

"So now I want to go to England. To study. Mr. Crabbe will arrange everything."

"England!" Like some Hollywood Pitt she howled the word in agony. "Joe's in England. Joe, Joe, Joe!" She collapsed again, her limbs somehow tangled round Robert Loo. Even he felt he had to make some perfunctory gesture of comfort. He began to stroke her bare arm, tentatively but, as he was a musician, rhythmically. "Nobody to turn to," said the pillow in a choked pillowy voice. Robert Loo went on stroking, the rhythm engendering a sort of *alla marcia* slow movement. Quiet strings, a monotonous alternation of minor, or rather modal, chords. Dorian mode. At her shoulder entered a most pathetic theme on a solo trumpet. The sudden sforzando made him grip it, involuntarily, just for an instant. There was a certain creative excitement, expressed in glandular constrictions which he knew well. Rosemary moved slightly. He found that his hand had seemed to travel otherwhither. "No," said Rosemary, "nobody to turn to. Nobody to comfort me."

"I'm sorry." That trumpet-tone was curiously breathy, almost asthmatic.

"Turn out the light. I'm ashamed to be seen like this." There was a two-way switch dangling from its cord by the bed. With his left hand Robert Loo made near-darkness. The corridor light still shone, but Rosemary's face was all but hidden. The still stroking hand met more nakedness than it had expected: it was out of its depth now, out of the shallow end of hand or arm. Not being able to swim, one could not struggle back to shore: and, anyway, there was no breath to swim with. This asphyxiation was something new, and it seemed to make drowning an urgent necessity. Another man, someone read about, someone heard singing ridiculous passionate words in opera, began to endue Robert Loo like a limp outer garment. He had become that: the head soaring somewhere, a launched balloon, the arms dangling sockets to be filled by engines expert at stroking and then caressing. Music squeaked remotely from the ceiling; a toad bellowed from the waste-pipe. There was a crescendo which seemed to require a new form of notation. Surely no one before had ever written *ffffff*? Impossible. And then he saw that it was in fact impossible. The whole structure collapsed, but the memory of the act of creation, the intention of the whole vast composition mercifully hung around.

The comforters, relaxed in sarongs after the day's work, kicked off their sandals at the top of Syed Omar's steps and made their obeisances to the wives, to the elder children, and to the gloomy head of the house. Syed Hassan, withdrawn, presented only his shamed back to the household, playing the radio, fingering the knobs like a rosary of penitence.

"There he sits," said Syed Omar, "the bail-bird, await-

ing his day of trial, the bringer of disgrace to his father."
The radio burst out angrily like a rude unfilial word.
"Turn that off!" shouted Syed Omar.

Orange crush was brought for the three visitors. "Well,"
said 'Che Yusof, late colleague of Syed Omar, most clerkly
in horn-rims and neat receding hair, "have you found anything yet?"

"I wait," said Syed Omar. "Crabbe has promised me a
job in the Education Office. But the white man's promises,
as we know, are not always fulfilled."

"Still," said 'Che Ramli, fat master in the Malay School,
"he found the money for the bail, did he not, this man
Crabbe?"

"Yes," said Syed Omar, "he found it, and now I wonder
why."

"One should not be so suspicious," said 'Che Yusof. "It
may be sheer goodness of heart, generosity of nature, a
desire to help the Malays."

"I wonder," said Syed Omar. He turned to his son. "You
can turn that radio on again," he said. "Loud." A news
bulletin in bubbling Tamil gushed forth at once. "That
will do," shouted Syed Omar. Then he bent towards his
friends, and his friends bent towards him, and, fixing 'Che
Yassin, Land Office clerk, with slitted eyes and hissing
teeth, Syed Omar spoke his worst fears. "You know this
man Crabbe, you know that he does not go after women,
you know of his relationship with at least one Chinese boy
in the town."

"You mean," said 'Che Ramli, "he is a member of the
tribe of the prophet Lot."

"That is one way of putting it," said Syed Omar. "Now,
I am fairly sure that he has as yet made no advances to
my son, though this may be a beginning, this may be a
means of making us all obliged to him. But already, in

the coffee-shops, some people have hinted to me that the thing I fear is already actual; otherwise, they said, why should Crabbe have helped one more than another? Two men today I have struck with my fist," said Syed Omar. "One I merely grazed with a coffee-glass. And early this evening one man suggested to me that I myself was involved with Crabbe and his perversions." Syed Omar swelled his chest. "I told him in no uncertain terms that that was not so. He apologised and stood me a drink. And he then said that there were possibly some chances of employment for me in the North-Eastern Transport if I knew how to drive heavy vehicles. I told him," said Syed Omar, his chest not yet relaxed, "that there was no vehicle I could not drive. Thus," he said triumphantly, "you see that an ill wind blows some good to somebody, if not everybody."

His friends pondered this proverb for a time, sipping their orange crush. The bubbling radio Tamil then stopped, followed immediately by a fast screeched song of urgent amorousness—drums and twangs and a high woman's voice. "Turn off that row!" called Syed Omar. "We can't hear ourselves drink, let alone talk!"

"You told me to turn it on," replied Syed Hassan, "less than a minute ago."

"And now I tell you to turn it off!" cried Syed Omar. "Don't argue, boy!"

"I wish you'd make up your mind," said his son, sullenly.

"What's that?" said Syed Omar, half rising, "what's that you say? You hear," he said, turning to his friends, "you hear how he answers back. I have spoiled the brat with too much kindness. Too much kindness is the only fault I can chide myself with." He sat down, simulating the arthritic movements of a broken man. His friends tuttutted, saying: "Never mind, don't take on so, no cause to blame yourself, the younger generation is everywhere the same, no gratitude."

Syed Hassan spitefully turned the radio knob to its maximum, so that the high swollen voice, garnished soon with shrieks from the valves, filled the room and made the glasses and the few cheap ornaments tingle and rattle. There were shrill and deep shouts of protest from all present. With a sour face and a thrust-out jaw Syed Hassan obeyed his father's yell, and the painful music rushed in a diminuendo to silence and a click.

"Come here, boy!"

"I'm tired, I'm sick," cried Syed Hassan. "On to me all the time!"

"That's right. You have disgraced me before the whole town. You are now disgracing me before my guests and friends. How dare you. HOW DARE YOU." Syed Omar pulled up the right sleeve of his shirt, disclosing a fat un muscular arm. The friends showed embarrassment, saying: "No, no, please, no. We're going now, anyway."

"No," protested Syed Omar. "He thinks he is such a big man, defying his father, defying law and order, cringing behind the white man's help. The law will, God help me, God help his poor mothers and brothers and sisters, punish him in its own time, but I have my rights too. I will not be disgraced before my friends. Come here, boy."

The comforters were leaving, scrambling for their sandals at the head of the house steps, in their haste shuffling into the wrong ones, saying: "Sorry, yours, you seem to have taken mine, that's right, that's the one, thank you," and so on. Meanwhile, Syed Omar, with his right arm ready, called them to stay, to witness the act of just punition. But, bowing with sketchily joined hands, they smiled their way clumsily out, down to the darkness. Syed Omar, no whit deflated, turned to his son, saying: "Now."

"I wish," said Syed Hassan, his back to the wall by the radio, "I wish that I wasn't here. I wish I was in the lock-up with the others."

"Say that again! Say that again!" And from the women came shocked cooings.

"I'd be better off there. You wouldn't be on to me all the time. And I know what you're thinking, and I know what you said to those friends of yours."

"Have a care, boy." A big flat hand came up for slapping.

"All right, hit me. I don't mind."

"You will, boy, you will!" At this point, 'Che Maimunah, who was evidently Syed Omar's mother, sidled in between the contestants, preaching peace: "There will be enough tears soon, God knows. Be quiet now, both of you."

"Keep out of this, woman. This is my affair, I am his father."

"Sit down," ordered Maimunah. Zainab, the other wife, said: "Sit down, sit down, you are both waking the younger children." Sulkily the men obeyed, but Syed Omar, un-willing to see so many feet of good strong drama discarded on the cutting-room floor, burst out with a despairing "Ruined, ruined, ruined," as he slumped into his chair.

"Oh, shut up," muttered his son.

"You hear? You hear?" cried Syed Omar in gratitude. "You ask me, you stupid women, to sit down and be quiet, do you? You want your husband to be insulted, do you, in his own house, by his own son? By God, I will choke him with my own hands." On his feet, he made like an ape or a bear for his delinquent boy, but Syed Hassan was ready with fists.

"Strike your father, eh?" Syed Omar launched an un-handy cuff, then another. Syed Hassan side-stepped with skill, and his father's podgy left caught the wall, not hard, but enough to call forth religious cries of pain and rage.

"Keep off," warned Syed Hassan, "keep off, keep off." He was cornered between the radio and a flimsy dresser that held blue crockery. Almost above him was the poster of the Chief Minister and his loving silk-clad arms, the legend 'Peace.'

"Come here and take your punishment," said Syed Omar. "Come and be hit."

"No! No!" As the breathing bulk of his father advanced, Syed Hassan downed with his head and butted. No great harm was done: Syed Omar nearly lost balance, saved himself by clutching at the dresser; only one blue plate rolled on to the floor, and it did not break. But Syed Hassan stood now in the room's centre, crying out: "I'm going! I'm leaving! You'll never see me again!"

He was at once peppered with hot Malay and snaked about with women's arms. His father for some reason spoke violent English at him:

"Don't be a bloody fool! If you jump bail you'll be in big trouble!"

"I'm going," said Syed Hassan in Malay. "I go now," he said in English. He hacked away at the lianas of brown flesh that wreathed him about. A few strides took him to the door. Here he paused before his exit, waiting for some great exit-line to come, but nothing came. The dramatic instinct of both father and son was stronger than their dramatic talent. He said, in Malay: "You have ruined my life, all of you! May God forgive you!" Then he leapt the house steps into the night. He hurried down the soggy path, reached the road, and began walking at a great pace towards Crabbe's house. When he was satisfied that nobody was following him he slowed down, wiping the sweat from his neck and face and chest with a large soiled handkerchief.

In the town there was harsh light, and loud soothing music sang all about him. He was cooled by a new sense of freedom, heartened by the knowledge that Crabbe would help him to get away, willingly (for he was a rich man) forfeiting the bail-money, efficiently calling up cars and lorries, consulting rail time-tables, devising disguises. It was the job of the British to help the Malays. That was well known, that was in the history books. And if Crabbe was slow in helping, there was always blackmail. How would Crabbe like his pederastic activities reported to K.L., eh? He wouldn't like that, would he? But, essentially, it was as a friend that he would approach him, one glad to help, knowing it was the duty he had travelled eight thousand miles to fulfil.

Turning into the avenue where the school-teachers' houses lay, Syed Hassan was surprised to meet Robert Loo; surprised, anyway, to meet him at this hour. He should be in his dad's shop, cringing at the rich music of the juke-box and dealing with the cash sales. At the end of the avenue and round the corner was Crabbe's house. Robert Loo had undoubtedly been there. *Kaum nabi Lot:* the tribe of the prophet Lot. Syed Hassan smacked the phrase on his lips, thinking of Sodom and its destruction and the prophet's salty wife. "Hello," he said. "It's you, is it?"

"Yes, it's me."

"Where've you been?"

The Chinese boy hesitated. "To see Mr. Crabbe. But he wasn't in. So I'm going home."

Syed Hassan smiled with contempt. "I," he said, "have left home." Robert Loo looked at him with interest. The two youths, the brown and the yellow, faced each other at the cross-roads, under a dim street-lamp. "So Crabbe's not in," said Syed Hassan. "We'll see, we'll see."

"Why did you leave home?" asked Robert Loo.

"My father tried to hit me. But nobody hits me, nobody, not even my father."

"That's strange," said Robert Loo. "That happened to me too."

"Your dad tried to hit you?"

"He did hit me. Before the customers. And I walked out. It's my music, you see, I've got to go on with my music." Robert Loo spoke with sudden passion, and Syed Hassan smiled again, saying: "But you haven't left home. You Chinese are frightened of leaving home, you're frightened of your fathers."

"I did leave home," said Robert Loo, "but I'm going back again. Just perhaps for a night. Or two nights. I've got to think, you see, I've a lot to think about."

"And he'll hit you again. He'll beat you till you scream blue murder." Syed Hassan spoke the words with satisfaction. "But nobody's going to beat me."

"Over there," said Robert Loo, "there's a little stall. They sell coffee and orange crush. Perhaps we'd better go over there and talk."

"Talk," said Syed Hassan. "Talk's never enough. That's all my father does—talk, talk, talk. Yes," he said, "we'll drink some coffee. If you'll pay."

"I'll pay."

Syed Hassan felt somewhat ashamed of his brusqueness, his rudeness, his boasting. "All I meant," he said, "was that I've no money. That's all I meant."

"All right. I've two dollars."

"It's very kind of you," said Syed Hassan with stiff courtesy. "Thank you."

"You're very welcome." They almost bowed each other

over to the ramshackle stall, lit by a kerosene lamp, over whose cracked cups a thin Tamil presided.

"It's difficult to say these things in Malay," said Robert Loo. "And in Chinese, too." He sucked the lip of the brimming coffee-cup. "Some things the British brought with them. Along with their language." His brow let the kerosene lamp etch out the puzzle. *"Love,"* he said. "Do you know that word? *Love, love. I love you.* In Mandarin we say: *'Wo ai ni.'* But it's not the same."

"I know that," said Syed Hassan. *"I love you.* It's on the films. Then they *kiss."* He used the English word; the Malay word *chium* meant to plough the beloved's face with one's nose: it was not the same thing, despite the dictionaries.

"I'm in love," said Robert Loo in English. He burst out with it; he had to tell someone. "That's why I've got to go back home, you see. I'm in love. Everything . . ." He paused, juggling in his mind with Malay and English; the English words fell into his hand. "Everything *feels* different. If my father hits me again, even that will feel different. This coffee tastes different from any coffee I've had before."

"It's not very good coffee," said Syed Hassan.

"I don't mean that," said Robert Loo. "It's a different world. It's hard to explain . . ."

"In love," mused Syed Hassan. "Who are you in love with?"

"I can't say." Robert Loo blushed. "It's a secret."

"And you've . . ."

"Yes, yes. I never knew it would be like that. Everything becomes different. I feel older . . ."

He felt older. Syed Hassan felt envy. That was an experience he still had not had; he felt bitter because the whole thing seemed so typical: the Chinese cutting out the

Malays even in that particular business. But, in the act of formulating the words of resentment, he remembered his father. Race, race, race—his father's dinner-table theme. The Tamils had done this to him, and the Sikhs had done that, and the Chinese were pig-guzzling infidels, and as for the British. . . .

"Is she Chinese?" he asked.

"No," said Robert Loo. He said it almost fearfully, startled on the brink of confidences he must not make. "No, she's not. She's . . ." Yet he wanted Syed Hassan to know and envy. Only the beloved's name must not steal forth into air which, where she was not, was rank, polluted, slave's air. "Do not show your body to the moon, my darling, for fear that even her silver beams may smirch it." From where did that come, where had he heard that? Was it some old Chinese poem? He thought not; it had come, like his symphonic themes, from nowhere. "She's not Chinese," he said at length. "Nor Malay. She's . . ." Then he recollected that he did not really know what she was: the external world had meant so little that its great abstractions had never quite registered. Trying to assign her to the correct column of some bureaucratic form, he only became aware of her warmth and smoothness and the various scents of her—secondary attributes which nevertheless had power, in sheer memory, at this moment of savouring the enhanced taste of coffee and trying to finish the sentence he was uttering, to attack his knee-joints like monstrous rubber hammers.

"It doesn't matter," said Syed Hassan. "I don't really want to know." Then, with an eagerness that was new to him, he said: "I'd nothing against that Tamil really. What I mean is, it wasn't because he was a Tamil. My father's a fool. He doesn't know that he lost his job because one of his friends has been trying to get it for his daughter.

One of his friends that was at the house tonight. 'Che Yusof it was. At least, I'm pretty sure it was. You learn a lot going round the town. More than you learn at school."

"But," said Robert Loo, "they say that if you hadn't done that . . . What I mean is that those Malays wouldn't have come into our shop and tried to steal. And then my father wouldn't have hit me for not seeing them. And then . . . " And then, of course, he would have spent the evening as usual, a drudge thinking about the music he wanted to write, chafing under the blows of the juke-box. Tonight he seemed incapable of finishing any sentence. Curiously, now in the silence, the remembered noises of the juke-box did not seem so terrible. The mere sensuous impact of trumpet or saxophone, whatever it happened to be playing, was an echo, even though a faint echo, of that excitement and abandon. He wanted to taste, smell, hear: his senses were terribly alive.

"We ought to go to some dance-hall," he said. "We ought to go and drink beer and listen to music and watch the women dancing. After all, we are men."

"There's nowhere now," said Syed Hassan. "We could go to your shop, of course. But the Park's been closed down by the authorities. We can't go to the Park any more."

"And we haven't much money."

"I've no money."

"I suppose I'd better go home," said Robert Loo. "I'm not really frightened of my father. Not any more."

"Fathers," said Syed Hassan. "They don't know much really. They're stupid, like kids. Ignorant. You've just got to put up with them."

"You're going home too?"

Syed Hassan grimaced, shrugged. "I suppose so. We've

got to remember our *tanggongan*. *Tanggongan*. What's that word in English?"

"Responsibilities."

"Responsibilities. A good long word. We've got to remember our responsibilities."

6

'Was it,' wondered Crabbe, 'intended for him?' The poem was called *Lines for Early Middle Age*, and it was signed Fenella Crabbe, but it was impossible that Fenella—twenty-eight or twenty-nine—should think of herself as middle-aged, or even, being a woman and a good-looking woman although a poet, have a proleptic Eliotian image of an aged eagle with tired wings demanding to be released from the dressing-mirror. Besides, there was nothing of the nobility of the eagle here. It was himself, the hanging flesh on cheeks and chest dancing as he ran up the stairs: it was the kind of farewell he had not expected:

> "The afternoon hour has struck for you to
> Enter, become your body, pay
> The forced grin of affection due to
> What is now you. That is to say:
> You are this pate and mouth of missing teeth . . ."

"Pouring in, old boy," said the man opposite. "Just pouring in. Money in oil. As one door shuts, another door closes. Ha ha. But nowhere for anybody to live. Government servants sleeping in the monsoon drains. Wives going home after a month. Ha ha. Still, that's where you ought to go when you've left Malaya. Borneo. Borneo. I've just come back." He thrust his head into the aisle. "Boy!" A Chinese in a white coat responded listlessly. "What will you have? Beer?"

"Not Malayan beer," said Crabbe. "It doesn't agree with me any more. Gin and tonic, I think."

"You heard that," said the man to the boy. "And beer for me. A small Polar."

> "You are these sagging bulbs and bags beneath,
>   And the leering social face in that far mirror
>   Recognised with shock (but no, no error)—
> That is you, too."

"But you ought to drink beer," said the man reproachfully. "That's my line. I sell beer all over the East. Thirty years on the job. Three thousand a month and a car allowance and welcome wherever I go. Jones. You must know me. Everybody knows Tommy Jones. They may get rid of you, but they'll never get rid of old Tommy."

"No," said Crabbe. But the second stanza was more encouraging:

> "Youth was a knife and lakes and air,
>   Metal and glass; you could bestow
>   Your body as a gift of swords to spare.
>   It was different then. It was not you . . ."

"All the way along the line," said the man. "Last night I was given a dinner in Anjing. The towkays always do their best for old Tommy. Almost as though I was doing them a favour selling them the stuff. And the night before in Kuala Musang. And then Tikus tonight. And Ular tomorrow night. Drunk as a lord. Where do you get off?"

> "Be patient. It will learn to be concise
>   Again, the hot room shrink to austere ice.
>   The silver will evoke a salmon's leap,
>   And bone-rungs strong enough for a single step
>   Will make a one-way stair."

"Needn't answer if you don't want to," said the man huffily. "I was only trying to make conversation, pass the time a bit." He was thin, long-faced, domed and grey-moustached and carried a tidy paunch.

"Sorry," said Crabbe. "I get off at Mawas. Then I go to Durian Estate by launch. I'm sorry. I was reading this, you see. Something written by my wife. It was a bit of a shock finding it here."

"Your missus writes for the papers, does she? Well, well. I never did like brainy women myself. No offence. Everyone to his own taste."

"That's one brainy woman who didn't like me much. She went home," said Crabbe.

The man had taken the paper from Crabbe and he handled it as though it were a rag that had wiped vomit. "You buy this sort of thing? Never have much time for reading, myself."

"No," said Crabbe. "An army major got off at Pelandok and left it on the seat. I haven't seen a copy for a long time. It's a very progressive review."

"Eh?" The man looked at Crabbe with suspicion. Then he flicked over the pages gingerly. *"The New Presbyter*, it's called," he said. "And then, written very small, it says: 'Formerly *The Old Priest.*' That sounds a damn silly name for a paper."

"It's a kind of pulpit," said Crabbe. "It tells us what we've got to believe. And it has a sort of funny column. There, just next to my wife's poem. Called 'Dear, Dear Isle.' "

"I don't see anything funny in that."

Crabbe sipped his gin and tonic. The tonic, manufactured by a Singapore firm with a monopoly, had a curious musty taste which disturbingly evoked the smell of the old Manchester Free Trade Hall. Crabbe heard the heavy brass at the end of the *Tannhäuser* Overture. His first wife, in skirt and blue jumper, stood next to him with a score. Would they never let him alone? Even on Malayan Railways, chugging through jungle, they were there. Both of them.

"That's not funny," said the man. "A bloke here gets a prize for sending in a cutting about a woman who put flowers on her dog's grave. That seems a very reasonable thing to do. I'm fond of dogs myself. Are you sure this is meant to be funny?"

"I think so," said Crabbe. "But one gets so out of touch."

"That's it." With vigour and eagerness the man put down the periodical. The air-mail paper rustled like thin sheets of metal. "Out of touch, and a bloody good job too. They're all crackers back there. It stands to reason. Paying five bob for a packet of twenty. And four bob for a gin. You'd hardly believe that, would you? But it's true. I've got a sister back there. She writes to me now and again. You'd hardly believe the things they put up with back in England. I've not been back for thirty years. And I'm buggered if I'm going back. But," he said in triumph, "you've got to, haven't you? They're kicking you lot out. But not old Tommy. Beer's much too important."

"It binds the races together," said Crabbe.

"Eh? What's that?" The man listened narrowly, half incredulous. "Say that again. By God, that's clever. That'd make a damn good advert. I'll write that down." He searched in vain for a note-book. "Ah, never mind, I'll remember it." He looked at Crabbe with more favour. "That your line, eh? Slogans and so on? Information Department and what not?"

"Education," said Crabbe.

"You'll never educate them," said the man with finality. He looked at space, sneering, leaning back comfortably.

"You ought to get into oil. Money there, over the water. It's a good job your lot are going. You won't never do any good."

"You know," said Crabbe, "I don't think I am going. It's a funny thing, it's just suddenly come over me. There was a man, a Ceylonese, back in Kuala Hantu, and he said I'd never go. He said I'd end my days up-river. Funny. I just can't see myself getting on the boat. Or the plane. I just can't see any future beyond being here."

"You'll go home," said the man, "leaving your black bastards like the rest of them. Kids all over the place with no fathers, crying out for food."

"You ought to write for *The New Presbyter*."

"Women," said the man. "I've had my pick." He sucked his teeth. "But I've always provided. One of the kids is in the Free School, Kenching. You'd hardly believe that, would you?"

"No."

"Well, it's true." Dreamily he said: "There's always somebody waiting for me. Last night in Anjing. And in Tikus tonight. There's always somebody waiting for old Tommy. And you too, I expect. I've known some of you school-teacher bastards before. Think butter wouldn't melt in their mouths. But she'll be there in wherever-you're-going, Eh? That's true, isn't it?" He showed black teeth and tweaked Crabbe's right knee. "A woman waiting for the old bastard."

"Probably."

"A woman at the end of the line. Always a woman. Have another drink."

The train stopped at a village called Berang-berang. A Sikh went by swinging a lantern, rare lamps lit up the inevitable back-cloth of palms, bare feet padded along the platform. A Malayan family, laden with food in cardboard boxes, a callow English private in jungle green, a cheerful young Chinese in a soiled white Christian priest's habit—these got on.

"Next stop for me," said the beer salesman. "They'll be waiting at the station with the brass bands. It's a long time since they seen old Tommy. They won't half lay on a spread. Eh," he said suddenly, a poking finger making for Crabbe. "Eh, you. Don't know your name."

"Yes?" said Crabbe.

"You come too. Not in no hurry, are you?"

"I've got to get to Mawas."

"You can get to Mawas by road in the morning. I know. Trust old Tommy. Know this part like the back of my hand. What you got to do in Mawas?"

"A man's been killed. By the terrorists, I should imagine."

"Oh, well, that's nothing. Nothing you can do. Plenty of that goes on these days. You come and meet some of old Tommy's pals."

A sudden relief washed over Crabbe like shower-water. He realised that, for some reason, he wanted to put off going to Durian Estate. Why, he wondered. It wasn't the corpse, which would now be buried. It wasn't the need to dispense official comfort to the bereaved, to promise official financial help. It wasn't the prospect of meeting the manager and pretending not to be embarrassed by his whisky tremor. It wasn't the thought that he himself, crossing to the tappers' lines and the schoolhouse, might well be sniped at. It was something unseen, unknown, and far more solid. And the feeling of apprehension had, for some reason, come over him on reading Fenella's poem in *The New Presbyter*.

"Yes," he said. "Thanks very much. I'd like to come."

"No trouble about getting somewhere to sleep," said the

man. "If we do sleep, that is." He winked. "They'll fix you up all right. Do anything for a pal of Tommy's."

Tikus was a small town with an attap hut for a station. But that it would not be a small town for long (money in tin?) was evident from the girth and fleshy chuckles and clean white trousers of the two Chinese shopkeepers who had come to meet good old Tommy. "Told you," he said triumphantly to Crabbe, "didn't I? Brass bands and all, eh?" Indeed, a small Sikh boy with a top-knot, detailed by his station-master father to collect the tickets, sat on the platform blowing a mouth-organ. "This," said Tommy to the towkays, "is Mr. er—— Don't know your name," he said to Crabbe. The two Chinese slapped Crabbe on the back in welcome. Any friend of old Tommy's friend of theirs. They spoke no English. The ghastly debased Malay of the bazaars chirped out of prosperous bellies as the four got into a waiting Hillman, Tommy asking about old so-and-so and old so-and-so, not seen the bastards for years.

"Old bastard!" roared one of the towkays.

"Old bastard yourself. What you laid on for us, eh? Bring on the dancing girls!"

They drove down the main street, under sodium lighting, to a filthy shop-house crammed with shining refrigerators, tape-recorders, outboard motors ('Why?' wondered Crabbe; 'we're nowhere near the river') and brandy. A Chinese girl in pyjamas, bearing a soup-bowl, preceded them up the stairs. Good old Tommy, mounting straight after as honoured guest, whistled one sharp blast through his teeth, making the old Roman sign with snail's horn fingers that jabbed jocularly at her right buttock. The towkays roared, the girl turned at the stair-head, yapped a protest, and baptized Tommy briefly with a hot drop from the bowl. A few strips of shark's fin thatched his bald

133

dome. "Thinks the world of old Tommy," he cried. "Ha ha. That's my girl."

Two old men, shrunken relics of old China, greeted Tommy with shy laughter, and shook hands seriously with Crabbe. The six of them sat round a table, Crabbe's foot, as he took his chair, clanking loudly against a concealed spittoon. "Ha ha," cried Tommy. "Don't kick the pee-pot over." He took charge of everything, the life and soul, smacking his lips over the soup and calling for more chilli sauce, urging his hosts to down their own brandy with the fearsome Chinese salute: "*Yam seng!*"

"*Yam seng!*"

"*Yam seng!*"

Down went the brandy, neat half-tumblers of it, and more bottles were opened.

"You," said Tommy to Crabbe. "Don't know your name. Shouldn't be drinking this really, you know. All right for you, you've got no responsibility to the firm, but I'm never off duty, never off duty. Should be on beer. Still," he said, "there always tomorrow. *Yam seng!*"

"*Yam seng!*"

Over the fish-dish—something sole-like, exquisitely seethed in a strange sauce, garnished with roots and fruits of the country—Tommy became sentimental. "Bloody good firm," he said. "Always looked after old Tommy, know a good man when they see one. Given my life to that firm. And they know it. Never let them down. Never let me down. Here, gorgeous," he said to the pert painted serving wench, "come and sit on old Tommy's knee." But the time for dalliance was not yet. They had to eat their way through sweet-and-sour pork, a duck of miraculous tenderness, prawns and stuffed pumpkin, lychees in ice-water.

"*Yam seng!*"

134

"Yam seng!"

One of the two serving-girls, taking up chopsticks and used dishes from the table, sang to Crabbe. The towkays smiled, listening. Old Tommy tried to join in, but was shushed. "Wanted to make a jewess of it," he said. "Never mind." It was a pentatonic tune, austere and thin as the girl's body, evidently erotic, but its eroticism checked and chilled by the pure simple melodic line. 'They're civilised,' thought Crabbe. 'Despite the dirty ceiling and the cigarette butts swelling in the cuspidor, they're civilised.' And he felt, through the brandy, that this was perhaps the only country in the world for any man who cared about history. What an incredible, head-reeling collocation of cultures: Islamic texts sprawling on the Great Wall, a twelve-legged god looking down in exophthalmic frowning benevolence.

"Extraordinary collocation of cultures," he said to old Tommy.

"That's what I always say myself, old man." Tommy belched loudly. "And the very best of luck." The girl who had baptized him on the stairs now sat on his knee, chewing gum steadily. "That's right," he said. "You come to daddy." He stroked her thin leg. "Like going to bed with a bicycle."

And now Crabbe had his own feather-light chattering burden. Desire for a Chinese woman did not come easily: even at their lowest social level they were works of art, engendering a hardly kinetic emotion.

"Works of art," he said. "This lad's a fine musician. Marvellous, marvellous. And who'll do anything for him? You won't, will you, for all your big talk?"

"Beer, beer, glorious beer," sang Tommy. "Fill yourself right up to here." He was doing his duty now, doing his job. Six great bottles of one of the Hong Kong brews had been brought to wash down the brandy and the fragments of rice and *mee* and meat-fibres that clung to the back teeth. "Beer," cried Tommy. "What did you call it? International something-or-other you called it. Should have written it down." His girl, doing her job too, wiped his frothy mouth with a paper napkin.

"Binds the nations together," said Crabbe. "Like music. And you won't do a damn thing about it. Or about Rosemary. Or Vythilingam. Or old Syed Omar. Who'll do anything for them when I'm gone?" His girl hugged him, smoothing his back hair with a cool hand. The towkays were out of it. They sat there quietly, bemused, smiling faintly, glad that their guests were having a good time. They, too, were doing their duty, were now gently handing it over to their delegates of the long night.

"Beer's a bit warm," said Tommy. "Must have it cold. Remember." He beat time with a stained forefinger, reciting a slogan in a refined accent: "The Climate Is Torrid. Warm Beer Is Horrid." He drank down a full six inches and again had his mouth wiped. "But lovely stuff just the same. Knew a chap," he said, "big fellow, nearly seven feet tall, couldn't abide it cold. Held it in his big 'ot 'and. Made it 'ot as 'ell. He liked it that way. Nabby Adams, his name was. Police. You wouldn't know him."

All the towkays rose as one man, ready to go, knowing that their guests were in good hands.

"In the morning," said Tommy. "Talk business in the morning."

"*Terima kaseh,*" said Crabbe putting out disengaged fingers. "*Hsieh hsieh, towkay. Wan an.*"

"Knows a bit of the lingo, eh?" said Tommy. "Me, I'm not clever that way."

"Beer," said Crabbe, with finicking articulation, "is itself a language."

"By God, that's a good one. Must write that down." But his head drooped on to the thin shoulder of the patient girl on his lap. "Ready for bed. Take me home, love." The towkays waved benignly from the door.

Crabbe's girl's name was Chin Chin, a name frivolous in sound but meaning 'Truth.' Led by the hand of Truth,. he followed Tommy—in full song under the moon—down the empty street. Tommy's girl giggled, her arm in his, looking back to chirp Chinese words to her friend and colleague.

"Where?" asked Crabbe. "Where we go?"

"Sini, sini." It was a squalid-looking lodging-house, a vista of many stairs, a smell of turmeric and aniseed. In the distance, farther along the line, Tommy was singing, still doing his duty, advertising bottled euphoria to the sleeping town.

Chin Chin's room was small, fanless, with a bed, a cupboard, photographs of Chinese film stars with Caucasian features, the odour of hidden hung dresses. She had no underwear and was naked before Crabbe had taken off his tie. Crabbe stood, looked, wondered, tossed a coin in his head. It came down 'No.'

"No," said Crabbe. "Thank you, but no."

"Not like?"

"Oh yes, like. But not now. Other time. Sleep now."

She grimaced, wrapped a sheet round her body, lay face downward on the bed with her limbs spread, starfish-like. In two minutes she was asleep. Crabbe found a cushion and settled with the dust on the wooden floor. Before he fell asleep he had a dim notion that he ought to be keeping his body pure for this event hidden in the near future, and he felt a tired satisfaction that he had succeeded in postponing it, even if only for a few hours.

.   .   .   .   .

137

When Robert Loo left, Rosemary lay still for a time in the dark, no particular thought in her head, feeling no particular emotion, her body quite numb. The headlights of cars occasionally shot the room with moving brief silver, and then for an instant she was in a tower, high up, above everything, with searchlights playing upon her. The cars were going to Mr. Godsave's house, where there seemed to be a party, perhaps a farewell party for Mr. Godsave, the last white man in the Police Department. She heard distant drinking voices, and sometimes they seemed to be talking about her.

"Where's old Rosemary, eh?"

"Yahoooooo! Give her some stick!"

"The Trojan horse where fifty heroes slept."

"Rosemary, my darling," sang somebody, "Rosemary, my dear. Rosemary, da da-da-da da . . ."

One of the voices was the voice of Joe. "Then I put my hand there, and I did this, and I did that, and then I . . ." And then a great shout of drinkers' laughter. And then the grind-out of brakes and revving-up as more cars arrived.

"She was a grand girl in her way, you know."

"Always ready, I will say that."

"I mean, we were lucky to find her here, really."

"Oh, God, yes, when you think of the five-dollar doses in the Park, and those bloody Chinese keeps: gimme, gimme, gimme."

"But a bit too much for a whole tour. I mean, all right for a year or so. But not three, no, no, no."

"Say six months."

"Oh yes, six months would do nicely. And then, after a bit, come back for more."

"But as a permanency . . ."

"Oh, my God, a permanency . . ."

She got out of bed, and the voices merged into the word-less noise of happy drinking. She padded to Crabbe's bath-room, switched on the light, and saw herself in the wide mirror: Medusa hair, eyes puffed with crying, lipstick smeared where she had been inexpertly kissed by a Chinese boy, the polished brown glory of her upper body. She gasped under the cold spray of the shower, washing off and out with soap so much and so much. She scoured her teeth with Crabbe's tooth-brush, brushed her hair with Crabbe's brushes, and then put on a pair of Crabbe's silk pyjamas. And still no thought passed through her head. She sniffed and sniffed as though she had a cold, and, look-ing in the handkerchief drawer of Crabbe's dressing-table, found not only clean handkerchiefs but a bundle of letters. Most of them smelt old, musty, like half-eaten apples, and the dates, she noticed, belonged to another age. "Dearest Vic." "My own dear Victor." "Darling." Love, love, love. She read through six or seven, still sniffing. The story was that Crabbe was away, working in some college away from this woman, a place where there was no accommodation for married couples, and that, even though he was away, she thought of him all the time and missed him so much at night. Rosemary saw her mouth began to twist in the mirror, and got a swift image of stone masks she had seen above the proscenium of a Liverpool theatre. A howl came from somewhere outside, a pye-dog. She refused to cry, she had done crying. The drinking voices waxed very loud. Rosemary could not decipher the signature of the letters: Mal, May, Maya, something like that. She, too, had sent such loving letters, but Joe would not keep those in his handkerchief drawer, if he had a handkerchief drawer. He would show them to his English friends, and they would laugh at them, or they would make Zulu clicks of envious concupiscence.

"Smashing bit of stuff."

"Get up them stairs, eh?"

"Howwwwwwww!"

But that was the dog outside. Rosemary thought of her cats, how she had left them without food, how they relied on her, but tonight she was too weary for responsibility. Tomorrow she would not go to school, she would be ill. Tonight she would stay in Crabbe's house; her cats would not starve: they had shared three tins of pilchards at lunch-time. And the amah would be back to give them milk. For a moment she hungered sentimentally for her cats: they had promised nothing, given nothing, taken all, did not pretend affection. They were a symbol of home: the cat by the fire, the fog swirling outside, the television pro-gramme just starting.

"Oh, Joe, Joe, Joe," howled the pye-dog.

Rosemary swished silkenly down the corridor in bare feet. The sitting-room was but dimly illumined with a solitary wall-light. She switched everything on, including the dining-recess lamps, and then stood by the kitchen entrance and called: "Boy!" There was no reply: only a heave and rustle as of somebody turning on a bed. "Boy! Boy! Boy!" Nobody answered, nobody came. Rosemary turned back to the big bright room and poured herself brandy. She went to the refrigerator for water, and the click and swing of the heavy white door did what her call could not do. The cook-boy appeared in vest and under-pants, anxious for the safety of the pre-cooked meal he had placed in the humming cold: Crabbe's dinner or lunch, tomorrow or whenever he should return. "There you are," said Rosemary. "I want food."

"A?" A noise which God gave only to the Chinese lower classes—throaty, short, loud, interrogative, disapproving, incredulous, insolent.

"Makan, makan. Saya mahu makan," shouted Rosemary. "What's this?" She pulled from the refrigerator a
dish containing a chill curry. The cook-boy tried to grab
it too. They tussled for an instant, and, for some reason,
Rosemary did not feel that this was undignified. "Heat
that up," she said, letting it go, "and make some chapattis."

"A?"

"Chapattis, chapattis. Don't you know what chapattis
are? You-all Chinese cooks call yourselves cooks. . . . Here,
where's the flour?"

But the cook-boy had seen on the table by the refrigerator a glass of brandy waiting for water. He became loud
and agitated. He slip-slopped off to the sitting-room and
came back with a near-empty bottle. He wailed, he be-
seeched, he was near tears.

"All right," said Rosemary. "I'll tell tuan that I drank
it. But you'd better start making those chapattis."

"A?"

"If you don't start heating up that curry," said Rosemary loudly, "I'll say that you drank that brandy. I'll
finish off the bottle and say that you drank it all."

The cook-boy got busy. Rosemary sat in an arm-chair
and switched on the radio. A play was on, some silly
London play on the B.B.C. Overseas Service:

". . . Listen to that nightingale, like some very competent imitation of a nightingale."

"Like a gramophone record of a nightingale."

"It's all been used before, there's nothing new. That
moon over there, ridiculously bright . . ."

"Vulgarly full."

"The night-scented stocks, proud of a perfume that any
Piccadilly tart could buy." (At the mention of Piccadilly,
Rosemary's mouth began to square for tears.) "But you
know . . ."

"Yes? What do I know?"

"There are no new words either. Oh, God, I'm not afraid of being vulgar. I'm not ashamed of using the old, old clichés. You know, don't you, don't you, Rosemary? You know that I . . ."

"I think I know, Arnold, I think I've always known . . ."

"Darling . . ."

At the mention of her own name, Rosemary rose in shock and anger, ready to do injury to the mocking instrument. She blubbered instead, switching it off, hearing in the fading voice of 'Arnold' the refined stage-voice of Lim Cheng Po of Penang. "Oh, Victor, Victor," she sobbed. "Where are you? I could be a good wife to you, Victor." The loud sound of frying came from the kitchen: her tears dripped like hot fat. She sat down, sobbing—somewhat stagily now—through a litany of names of those who might comfort her, take her in their arms to say: "Don't cry any more, darling. The bad, bad days are over now." From the list certain names were absent: Joe, Robert Loo, Jalil. One name, surprisingly, was present:

"Vy, Vy, oh, Vy. Oh, why did I hurt you like that?"

Why should Robert Loo's name be present? His interest was purely historical: he was not to be read in any anthology. His poem had been jejune, over-brief, uncontrolled, inarticulate really, a poem not to take seriously, not even to read, merely a link in a long process of evolution: Bale divided the interlude into acts; Surrey first used blank verse; Wyatt introduced the sonnet—forgotten scullions to the great world, table-scrubbers, potato-peelers, onion-cleaners, meat-choppers for the master cook who will soon arrive from Stratford. But that cold, polite, refined Oxonian from Penang had made possible the entrance of Asia, and time and grief had handed the key to a dull and harmless Chinese boy, a boy who had at least stammered an overwhelmed gratitude, not merely yawned and said: "Let's have a cigarette."

The cook-boy came now and said obsequiously: *"Makan sudah siap."* Rosemary sat at the table, mistress of an empty house, and spooned out curry on to her plate. The chapattis were pale (at home they had always been golden) and heavy (at home they had always been so light). But she tore off great pieces and dipped them in the fiery sauce and munched with appetite, letting the viscous driblets stain Crabbe's pyjama jacket. She made parcels of mutton-pieces and potatoes and posted them express. She broke large chunks of fish with her chapatti glove. She called for water, no, not water, beer.

"Beer!" she cried. The cook-boy hesitated. "Brandy," warned Rosemary.

Rosemary ate four chapattis, half the fish, all the mutton, most of the sauce, most of the *sambals* of shredded coconut, hard-boiled egg, chutney, banana-slices and red cabbage. And as she drained her beer she remembered something she had long convinced herself had never happened. She sixteen, in her beauty's first heady phase, the meal with that man in Kuala Hantu. A curry with chapattis on Satu Road, and afterwards, with chillis in their blood, they had not gone after all to the cinema but to his flat near Bukit Chandan. And he?

"Black as the ace of spades," said Rosemary aloud in wonder. "No, I couldn't. It never happened."

But he had been handsome really. He had done an engineering course in Brighton. He had a white Jaguar which he drove at speed. He danced divinely. Where was he now? What was his name? Sundralingam? Mahalingam? *Sundra* meant beautiful, *maha* meant great. The names, now all too literally interpreted by her, were apt, apt enough. At the moment of climax their language had been Tamil, a rapid bubble of sincere sensuality.

"He was cold," said Rosemary aloud, "cold as that fish there." She was now thinking of somebody else, someone in West Kensington on a January morning. "Joe, too," she added, "really." She tried crying again, but she was too full to cry. She picked her teeth with a match from the box on a side-table. She called for coffee. After some argument, quelled by the mention of brandy, coffee was made and brought. While the table was being cleared, Rosemary lounged on the couch, sipping Cointreau, her eyes in far space. In far space the men of her life marched like stars. When the boy had gone back to his quarters, Rosemary said to a Corot reproduction, hanging over Crabbe's desk: "He's quite clever, really. And awfully kind. And I have been rotten to him. And he has got it bad. Poor, poor boy. I could do so much for him."

Soon she lay in bed, comfortable, a cigarette in her mouth, hands behind her head, the bedside fan whizzing. "I'm glad I gave up Joe," she said. "I told him that it would never work. But he insisted and insisted. And now he's leapt into somebody's arms, as they all do. Marrying on the rebound. And he'll think of me all the time when he's with her, knowing it's not the same, nowhere near as good. But I told him it wouldn't work. No qualifications, no ambitions, no money, no prospects. And me with all mine." She snuggled down in the bed, silk against her clean, smooth body. "And his speech was so bad. 'You was' he used to say sometimes. And think of the children. Eurasian children. I'd be ashamed to show my face."

As she turned on her right side, she saw, crumpled on the floor, almost out of sight under the bedside table, the blue air-letter that she had received that day. That was the letter saying that Joe had had to fly into the arms of another woman, that life was intolerable but he realised now that Rosemary would never change her mind. Farewell, O cruel. Rosemary got out of bed, picked up the letter, crumpled it still further, walked over to the lavatory with it and flushed it away. The words went crying away into the town drains, away to the river, to the sea. Poor Joe. Rosemary went back to bed and slept.

Robert Loo could not sleep. Excitement made his limbs dance under the thin sheet. He danced to the last movement of the Second Brandenburg Concerto, to the scherzo of Beethoven's Seventh Symphony, to the development of the *Meistersinger* Prelude, to the finale of *L'Oiseau de Feu*, to Holst's Fugal Overture. But the rhythms were not enough, and what sang above the rhythms was not really relevant to his highly-charged, almost febrile state. It was too universal, too general, too mature, too little concerned with this mad spring of love. Had music ever really been able to convey that? He listened in his mind to Wagner, leafing through the love-themes of *Die Meistersinger*, the great duet in *Die Walküre*; in Beethoven there was nothing; perhaps one of the songs of Hugo Wolf?

Fever, fever. His eyes must have been bright when he entered the shop, his head burning. Why else had his father been so considerate, his mother fussing round, sending him off to bed with Aspros and brandy? Or perhaps, thought Robert Loo, it had not been that at all. His father was hopeless with accounts, his brothers worse. He, the musician, had the musician's aptitude for playing with numbers: perhaps this one night had been enough to abash his father with a sense of his son's indispensability. But no, he had been away before, sent by Crabbe to Singapore to have his quartet recorded. His quartet? He tried to hear it in his mind, but it seemed to be played on miniature instruments by elves, incredibly high up and thin. All the music he had written before this night must, of course, be immature, must be re-written or, better still, destroyed.

Most probably his father and mother had been shocked by the possibility of the break-up of the family, and his own impiety, his pulling out of a brick, was discounted in the terror of the prospect of the whole vast structure collapsing in thunder and dust. Perhaps his mother had screamed at his father, accusing him, with blows, of tyranny and exploitation, and his father had been cowed and scared of the high-pitched storm.

Robert Loo felt that he could now dictate terms. He would ask for liberal time off—most afternoons and at least two evenings. Sometimes, after the closing of the shop at midnight, he would say:

"I'm just going out to see a friend. I'll be back in an hour or so."

"Very good, my son. God knows, you work hard enough. You deserve a little relaxation. Do you need any spending money?"

"Thank you, Father. I think I've got as much as I need." Then off, in the blue warm aromatic night, to see her, her waiting, arms open in perfume and desire, in some light gown that fell easily from her shoulders.

'But, look here, you need all this time to write your music.'

'My music? Oh, yes. Of course, my music. But I think I feel a new style developing, my second period, or perhaps my real first. That needs time to germinate.'

'And what's it going to be like, this new music?'

'I don't know yet, I just don't know. Warmer, gayer, speaking more to the heart, more rhythmical, tuneful, full of the spirit of the dance.'

'Something like this?'

Robert Loo's interlocuter, who was also Robert Loo,

sprang through the open window, flew over the street, switched on a light in a high room opposite and set a loud radiogram playing. Robert Loo, lying on his bed, came fully awake and listened.

It was the fat Indian clerk who lived in a solitary room above the chemist's shop opposite. He could be seen in silhouette, walking up and down, eating something, playing music, insomniac. The music was some standard American dance-tune, of the regulation thirty-two bars, with the regulation near-impressionist harmonies, its orchestral palette limited to brass and reeds and somewhat sedative percussion. No development, no variations, only a key-change from chorus to chorus. "No," said Robert Loo aloud. "Nothing like that." And then a voice sang, relaxed, without effort, against the pre-Raphaelitish chords of very early Debussy:

> "Oh, love, love, love——
> Love on a hilltop high,
> Love against a cloudless sky,
> Love where the scene is
> Painted by a million stars,
> Love with martinis
> In the cabarets and bars.
> Oh, love, love, love . . ."

Robert Loo listened entranced, hardly breathing, indescribably moved. Oh, love, love, love. His heart yearned, seeing himself in a white tuxedo, moving with grace round the small dance-floor, Rosemary in his arms, she ravishing in something backless and close-fitting. Words of love on a balcony, the band playing in the distance, under the moon, palms swaying. He felt the palms as something exotic, not the common dingy scenery of his town and state. Rosemary said:

"Let's go in and dance. That's a lovely tune the band is playing."

He smiled, draining his martini. "I'm glad you think so."

"Why? did you . . . ?"

"Yes, I wrote it. For you. I wrote it this afternoon when you were on the beach." (Ah, the romance of those large striped umbrellas!)

"So that was it! And you said you had a headache!"

"Yes. I wanted it to be a surprise."

"You darling."

And, yes, he would, he would! He would revert from this stage of hard-won mastery of counterpoint, of orchestration, of thematic development, to breathed clichés of wind and voice for her, for her. All the ore that waiting lay for the later working he would melt before its time to make her ornaments for a day.

'And so you've no longer any objection to composing something for people to listen to, even to sing? An anthem for the workers of Malaya, perhaps? A Strength Through Joy song?'

'No, no! Anything, anything for her!'

He slept fitfully, and in the morning his father brought him breakfast in bed: two boiled eggs and a pot of tea. He was too surprised to say thank you.

"You eat both those eggs, son. Eggs give stamina. You can't work on fresh air."

"No, Father."

7

In the morning Crabbe and Tommy Jones met, quite by chance, in a Chinese *kedai*. The loud radio somewhere down the street announced ten o'clock Malayan time, and then came the news in the cheerful sing-song of Mandarin. They drank treacly coffee and wondered what they could possibly eat. The shop was dingy and gay and full of half-nakedness—vests and underpants, pimply shoulders and hairless brown legs—and rang with ground-rows of Hokkien vowels and the clop of wooden clogs. Tommy Jones looked in gloom at the clouded glass display-case of cakes in primary colours. "Don't really fancy anything," he said. "You do anything last night?"

"Slept."

"Yes, I know. Don't know what's coming over me lately. Couldn't do a thing. I could eat a bit of fried fish if they've got it."

"With vinegar?"

"That's it." But he made no move to ask or order.

"I've got to get transport," said Crabbe, "to Mawas. Do they have taxis round here?"

"Eh," said Tommy Jones, plucking at the vest of a passing boy. "Polar beer. A big one, cold."

"A?" But beer was brought. Tommy Jones gulped it greedily, cutting the phlegm, and said: "That's a bit better." The morning film seemed to drop from his eyes, for he said to Crabbe: "You've had a shave."

"Yes. She brought some water in a flower-vase."

"Oh, I'll have one later. Got to see this new Malay shop here, try and get them to take a regular order. Bit difficult with some of the Muslims."

"You can tell them that they've just discovered a codicil to the Koran."

"Eh?"

"Making it all right to drink."

"You ought to be in this business," said Tommy Jones gravely. "You'd do all right. I'll put in a word for you when I get back to Hong Kong. Don't know your name, though."

"I've got to get to Mawas," said Crabbe. At that moment a Land-Rover pulled up outside the *kedai*: from its covered body came protesting squeals and loud comforting words. The man who jumped down from the driver's seat was known to Crabbe: Moneypenny, an Assistant Protector of Aborigines who was based at Mawas. He now entered the *kedai*, very big and boyish in khaki shorts, fair-haired, mad-eyed, almost as brown as a Malay, with a child's sulky mouth and native tattoo-marks on his fine throat.

"You've saved my life," called Crabbe. "I'm coming with you."

Moneypenny gazed at Crabbe with eyes focused at something far behind him, as though trying to pierce impenetrable jungle. He did not smile in greeting but merely said: "Oh, it's you, is it? You can help to hold down that blasted pig in the back."

"Pig?"

"Jungle-pig. There's a couple of Temiars with it. The bloody fools took it for a walk on a bit of string and they got lost. Spent half the morning looking for them." At this moment a large snout poked out from the back of the truck, small intelligent eyes looking bewildered at the street of trishaws and dustbins and idlers in sarongs. A small curly man in a yellow shirt and trousers much too big for him, evidently a cast-off gift from Moneypenny, jumped down, crooning at the pig encouragingly, showing all his teeth in a most affectionate smile. The great bristled body of the pig, pushed from behind, began to appear.

"Eh!" Moneypenny, still on his feet, shouted in a strange language. The Temiar looked hurt but began to push the pig back again. Moneypenny sat down.

"How long you been on this job?" asked Tommy Jones.

"Six years."

"Do they drink beer, this lot of yours?"

"They'll drink anything you give them. But they won't be able to for long. They've all got to be turned into Muslims, that's the new official policy. No more walks with pigs then." Crabbe desperately tried to make the blue far-focused eyes come home to himself, to the table. He asked about the murder on Durian Estate.

"Oh, that. The foreman said he'd been sleeping with his wife and got the Reds to do him in. And now the widow's sleeping with the foreman."

"How did you find that out?"

"It came through on the bamboo wireless. Everything comes through." Moneypenny refused a drink. "Got to go back and see how our American's friend's getting on. I only called in to get some condensed milk for the pig."

Crabbe and Moneypenny said good-bye to Tommy Jones. As they prepared to mount the dusty Land-Rover Tommy Jones came running out, calling to Crabbe:

"What was that about the what-you-call?"

"What what-you-call?"

"About the Prophet inventing beer?"

"No," said Crabbe, "not quite that." He suggested

various Jesuitical ways of persuading Muslims to reconcile their hard desert faith with the mild pleasures of the West. He realised he was still not quite sober. Moneypenny had borrowed a tin-opener from the shop, and already the jungle-pig was guzzling ecstatically, the Temiars encouraging it with gentle mooing noises and happy laughter.

"I'll tell them about you in Hong Kong," said Tommy Jones gratefully. Moneypenny impatiently engaged gear. "Eh!" shouted Tommy as they moved off. "Don't know your name!" Crabbe waved smiling at the thin paunched figure standing alone among the small Malay boys and the Chinese in their underwear, the prophet of harmless solace in a harsh world, not altogether ridiculous or ignoble. They never met again.

"Who," asked Crabbe, "is this American?" He sat next to Moneypenny; the pig no longer needed holding down: its snout ranged the sticky patches on the floor behind them. Moneypenny drove badly, almost bitterly lashing the vehicle to unnecessary speed, savagely jerking the gear-lever. Around his neck he wore a Temiar amulet: its charmed stones clinked as they bumped towards Mawas.

"Him? He's from some university or other. Under the auspices of some organisation or other. He's trying to give the Temiars an alphabet. He's part of the vanguard."

"Which vanguard?"

"The British are going. Nature abhors a vacuum. His name is Temple Haynes."

The river had appeared on their left, far below, eye-achingly silver. The jungle could be seen beyond. Crabbe laughed, a brief snort only. "You've got to hand it to them," he said.

These words seemed to have a violent effect on Moneypenny. "Christ," he said. He lurched to the side of the road and stopped the Land-Rover. His hands were shaking.

"What in the name of God did you want to do that for?"

"Do what?"

"You laughed. Didn't you see that butterfly?"

"What butterfly?"

"Went sailing in front of the windscreen. And you laughed at a butterfly."

"I didn't see any butterfly. In any case, where's the harm?"

"Oh, my God. You've broken one of the taboos. You couldn't know it, I suppose. But for God's sake be careful in future." He sat there, breathing heavily, Crabbe unable to say a word. The aerial factory of insects twittered away in the distance. "And," warned Moneypenny, "if we get any thunder today, for God's own sweet sake don't choose that time to run a comb through your hair. It's very serious." The pig was now snoring most gently, its Temiar guardians watching tenderly over its sleep. "I'm going to drive slowly," said Moneypenny. "I don't want anything bad to happen." They crawled along now.

Crabbe sat still and silent, as though for his photograph, thinking: 'Oh, would anybody believe it, would anybody believe it back home? They just don't know, they're all so, so innocent, sitting in their offices in Fleet Street and Holborn.'

Soon they came to the outskirts of Mawas. Moneypenny stopped, arbitrarily it seemed, at a tree-choked point indistinguishable from any other point in the long jungle continuum on both sides of the road. The river had long disappeared. But three little men in loin-cloths, armed with bamboo blow-pipes, came softly out of the mess of frond and liana and decaying palm-stumps, smiling and greeting. Moneypenny spoke briefly and made a cabalistic sign. The pig was aroused with considerable strokes and ear-tweaks, and pig and men climbed down amid a clank of empty cans, the men laughing and waving as they took their leave. In an instant the jungle had taken them.

"Well," said Moneypenny. He sighed. "What do you want to do? You've missed the estate launch. That went" —he looked narrowly at his wrist-watch—"an hour ago. You'd better stay the night with me. Although Haynes has got the only spare bed." He started the engine and wrenched the gear-lever with his teeth clenched, seemingly in hate. "You can toss for it. One of you will have to sleep on the floor."

"I slept on the floor last night."

"Oh, well, you won't mind doing it again, then. Our Temple's a bit more used to gracious living."

"Is he a nice chap?"

"Oh, yes. He talks a lot about phonemes and semantemes and bilabial fricatives. He has a van with recording apparatus in it. He's a good chap."

They came now into Mawas, a decent-sized town for this *hulu* region: a wide main street and a few shops; a clean police station with pot plants outside; even a cinema. Here the estates—two up-river, one down—could victual themselves with rice, fish and buffalo-meat; here the tappers could make sedately merry on a night off. Moneypenny drove to a wooden shack labelled 'Department of Aborigines'. This had been translated—in fresher paint—into official Malay: *'Pejabat Kaum Asli'* (literally, Office of Tribe of Originals) and, in paint hardly dry, into weird cuneiform symbols which were quite unfamiliar to Crabbe.

"That's his alphabet," said Moneypenny. "Temiar Alphabet Mark One. But Mark Three's already on its way." He spoke with a kind of gloomy vicarious pride.

In the cool office sat Temple Haynes. Before him stood three tiny aborigines. On the wall hung a large sheet of glazed rag-paper with pictures on it: men, women, children, horses, pigs, houses, trains, aeroplanes, buffaloes, trees. Temple Haynes pointed at pictures in turn with a stick, inviting the little men to name them. He seemed pleased to see Moneypenny. "I don't seem to be getting very far with this dialect," he said. "They keep saying the same thing. They seem to be giving everything the same name." He read off a weird word from his notebook. "That," he said.

"Yes," said Moneypenny. "That means 'picture'."

"Why do you have more than one picture of each thing?" asked Crabbe.

"That," said Temple Haynes, "is for plurals." He stood up. "I don't think I've had the pleasure." Moneypenny admitted that he had forgotten Crabbe's name.

"Crabbe," said Crabbe.

"Crabbe," said Temple Haynes. "I met a Crabbe in London. Fenella Crabbe, the poet. Are you any relation?"

"My very distant wife. Soon no longer to be a wife."

"I'm genuinely sorry to hear that," said Temple Haynes. "I think very highly of her work." The three aborigines looked up at Crabbe reproachfully.

Temple Haynes seemed pure Mayflower: unemphatic features, clear hazel eyes as sane as Moneypenny's were mad. He wore no crew-cut: ample light-brown waves were combed neatly from a middle parting. But his sharkskin trousers were American-tailored, delicately moulding his rump as he turned round to put out a non-cancer cigarette. He wore a drip-dry cream shirt and a polka-dot bow-tie. A moygashel jacket hung over a chair. "I guess that's the lot for this morning," he said to Moneypenny. "Could I have them again at two?" Moneypenny coughed sounds of dismissal. The three little men made vague obeisances and shambled out.

"Where's my clerk?" asked Moneypenny. "I've letters to write."

"He went away," said Haynes. "About an hour ago. He very kindly yielded the office to me."

"If you want lunch," said Moneypenny, "you can get it at Ang Siow Joo's. I never eat lunch." He gave them both a mad look and then sat down at his desk.

Haynes and Crabbe walked in the heat outside. "I'd read one of her things in a review back home," said Haynes. "A long poem about Malaya. Very impressive, I thought."

"Never read it," said Crabbe. "Didn't even know about it."

"Really?" Haynes gave Crabbe a swift sincere glance, mildly incredulous. "Then we had this short course at the Anglo-American South-East Asian Society in London. A very useful background course. She gave two lectures. She came with a rather distinguished Malay whose name I've forgotten."

"I haven't forgotten," said Crabbe, thinking: 'What the hell does she know about Malaya, anyway?' "That would be His Highness the Abang of Dahaga."

Hearing the rasp in Crabbe's voice, Haynes glanced at him again in mild inquiry. "Anyway," he said, "she's making a name. And she's a great help to all of us who are coming out here for the first time."

"All of you?" said Crabbe. "All of who?"

"Various organisations," said Haynes vaguely. "There's work to do in South-East Asia." It was the rather smug voice of the records of *Four Quartets*, though much younger. "I'm concerned, as you'll have guessed, with the linguistic angle. Then there's the angle of inter-racial relations. And there's method of teacher training, time-and-motion study in industry, behaviour-patterns, statistics, sociological surveys and, of course, demographic studies. A great deal to do. It'll cost a lot of money, of course, but it's the best possible investment. We can't afford to let the Communists get away with it."

"Where are we going?" asked Crabbe. "Are we going to have a drink?"

Temple Haynes smiled indulgently and looked at his wrist-watch—waterproof, self-winding, with the date and the current lunar phase. "What can one drink at this hour of the day?" he asked.

"Coca-Cola," growled Crabbe.

Haynes laughed gaily, but there were no butterflies about. "There's no need to feel bitter about anything," he said. "A lot of us contemn the drinking of that beverage as much as you Europeans seem to do. Although I must confess I found Europe full of Coca-Cola signs. No," he continued, "you mustn't identify us with the Hollywood or G.I. image. If you wish me to prove my adulthood, I'm quite willing to come and drink gin with you. Not that I really enjoy gin outside of a martini, and you can't get martinis here."

They strolled into Ang Siow Joo's. It was midday and Crabbe had had no breakfast. He ordered pork rissoles and boiled Chinese cabbage. Haynes's leather case contained more than notebooks: from it he took thin sheets of rye bread, peanut butter and silver-wrapped Swiss cheese. He ate sparely, lighted a non-cancer cigarette, and amiably watched Crabbe finish his crude meal.

"This afternoon," he said, "I must do a little more dialectology. The real job, as you know, is isolating the phonemes, or, rather, discovering what is phonemic and what is allophonic. That is fascinating and very important." He chattered on, and Crabbe felt lost and boorish and crude. The British, he decided, had been merely gifted

157

amateurs: Singapore had been raised on amateur architecture, amateur town-planning, amateur education, amateur law. Now was the time for the professionals. Thoughts struck him. He said:

"What are they going to do about music?"

"Music? That, of course, is not my department. But Lewis and Roget, both from Columbia, are getting permission to initiate a pretty exhaustive survey of South-East Asian music. It will take years, of course, but they hope to produce some kind of definitive treatise, complete with copious recorded examples."

"And if you find a promising South-East Asian composer?"

"I repeat," said Haynes, "that is not my province. My province is purely linguistic. But," he smiled, "if such a prodigy is found, I fancy that he'll be well taken care of with scholarships. I think there's already a foundation in existence to promote the encouragement of native artistic talent."

"Take this boy's name," said Crabbe, "now. And his address. Pass them on. Please."

"I think you're more in a position to do that than I," said Haynes. "After all, it's not my field. As I told you, I'm a . . ."

"I know," said Crabbe impatiently. "But I may never get the chance. Please take his name, please write to these people."

"If you wish." Haynes was most good-humoured and accommodating. He wrote in a pocket diary Robert Loo's name and address. "There," he smiled; "I've got that down."

"Thank you," said Crabbe. He felt relieved: perhaps, in time, all his burdens would be lifted.

"I think now," said Haynes, "I'll take a brief siesta. I

have work to do at two. Shall we stroll over to Money-penny's house?"

The house was round the corner, a little way up the hill. It was filthy and bare, stripped down, like its tenant, to sheer primary function, disdaining all secondary sensation. Thus the bathroom which Crabbe visited showed signs that Moneypenny now regarded even a lavatory as super-erogatory. The floors were covered with rugs of peanut-shells. Everything was pared to the human limit: tapioca and taboos. The spare room, which Haynes had taken, was a sweet cool oasis, aseptically clean, swept and scoured by Haynes himself, smelling of insect repellent, containing neat clusters of bottles on shelves: paludrine, quinine, penicillin ointment, vitamin tablets, toilet requisites of all kinds. But the rest of the house, including Money-penny's own room, where Crabbe sought his siesta, was a growling grim annexe to the jungle where Moneypenny spent most of his time, that green monster hotel with water running through.

Crabbe slept long, not hearing Haynes's neat, timely departure. He awoke after four, hot, wet and dry-mouthed. There was nothing to drink in the house, not even cold water, for Moneypenny had long sold his refrigerator. But Crabbe remembered that the American, being of a race with as little sense of guilt as history, would not be so self-deny-ing. Haynes's van was parked in the shack of a garage, and in it Crabbe found a deep-freeze—powered he knew not how—singing away, in its belly bottles of mineral water, clipped to its lid an opener. He sat and drank, thinking vaguely about Fenella. It was, he felt, not really remarkable that, travelling to the small world up-river, he should already have come into a finger-tip or finger-nail contact with her twice. She was making her name known at last, perhaps because free at last of him. But he could not get out of his head the feeling that this reading her last night, hearing about her today, was somehow ominous: it was as though the river and the jungle together were singling him out for attention, approaching him in terms of his own past. Death? Did this mean he was going to die? Absurd. He was fit, despite his small cushions of fat; his digestion was good; his heart, despite occasional palpitations attributable to the heat, to too much tobacco and midday drinking, was sound enough. The up-river journey was safe; he would keep out of the way of the snipers. Above all, he had no wish to die: there was plenty for him to do still, all over the dwindling Colonial Empire. He shrugged away last night's memory of Mr. Raj's words in Kuala Hantu, words about his never going home, his complete assimilation to the country. That, of course, could not be, and it would be stupid to give that prophecy an ironic interpretation—leaving his bones up-river, the Englishman's grave quickly becoming a native shrine to be loaded with supplicatory bananas and flowers. And yet he still felt a desire to postpone his trip to Durian Estate.

Though less now, he thought, envisaging another day with the sane Haynes and the mad Moneypenny, their clean and dirty worlds. Tomorrow he would take the launch, get the job over, return quickly to the State capital and the stress of his problems there. He drank one more bottle of Haynes's mineral-water—slightly scented, effervescent, saccharine, with an extravagant claim on the label ('it excites the pancreas to fresh efforts') and wondered what he should do now. Then Haynes himself appeared with a plan for his evening.

Haynes seemed mildly pleased that Crabbe should be crouched in the van among the tape-recorders and cold storage. "Welcome," he said, "to American territory." And then: "There's an event of some interest taking place tonight in one of the villages. A new stage for the native shadow-play has been erected, and there is to be an opening ceremony. I wish that Cunliffe could be here."

"Cunliffe?"

"A friend soon to come to this territory. He majored in anthropology and has already published a treatise on Mexican folk-ceremonies. Perhaps you would accompany me? My knowledge of Malay is slight, and I'd like to take a few notes. Perhaps photographs too." He beamed modestly at a fine delicate instrument lying on the shelf of the van—a camera with many knobs and calibrations. "I think even the observations of the amateur can be of some use. An amateur present is obviously better than a professional absent."

In Moneypenny's house no dinner was served. Guests had to feed themselves with what few raw materials they could find in their host's store-cupboard, cooking these laboriously on an oil-burner whose wicks were charred and slow to yield to the match. Crabbe heated a can of soup for himself, Haynes prepared eggs Benedict and had slices of spam with a tinned salad, Moneypenny ate cold boiled tapioca, grumbling in snapped sentences about civilisation.

"Another week," he said, "and Barlow should be back from K.L. I can't stand this sort of life," he said, sneering at Haynes's neat plateful, "it's artificial. I want to get back into the jungle. It's the only possible life for a man."

"How is Barlow?" asked Crabbe.

"The same as ever. The nice little professional anthropologist, the sort of bloke who likes office-work."

"But," suggested Haynes with scholarly courtesy, "you would surely be the first to admit that the professional anthropologist has his uses. I mean, the fact that he has a terminology, a classificatory system, the fact that he comes with a background of intensive comparative studies. . . ."

"Balls," bawled Moneypenny rudely. "You've got to get into the jungle. You've got to come face to face with the living reality. There was Barlow at the university reading books and dishing up the books in his essays; there was I actually doing the job. There's no substitute for actual experience."

"I'd venture to disagree," ventured Haynes. "Training . . ."

"You're just as bad," snapped Moneypenny. Clearly he had had a boring afternoon in the office. "Making alphabets without knowing a word of the languages."

"Really," protested Haynes with mildness, "I never laid claim to be a linguist. I'm a linguistician, which is rather different. I mean, what I'm after chiefly at the moment is the phonemes. I've no wish to be able to speak any of these languages with fluency: a working knowledge is all I aspire to."

"Yes," said Crabbe. "That's right. It's a question of what patterns you can make emerge out of your inchoate experiences. For instance . . ."

"You," said Moneypenny, "can shut up. What do you know about it, anyway? Coming up here slumming, laughing your bloody head off at butterflies. When you're a guest in my house, you'll behave. Understand?"

"But . . ."

"No buts," said Moneypenny. "You stick to your Chinese catamites and your black mistresses. Don't start telling me what to do."

"I never said a word . . "

"Well, don't." He began to get up from the table. "Just don't, that's all."

"And I don't quite like what you said just then," said Crabbe, with heat. "About black mistresses."

"We know what goes on," said Moneypenny, standing

162

with his plate by the kitchen door. "We may be far from *civilisation*," he sneered, "but we know all about you people. We don't want you, me and the Temiars. Leave us alone, that's all we ask." He stomped into the kitchen, rinsed his plate sketchily, returned. "I'm going to bed," he said. "You can please yourselves what you do." He entered his bedroom.

"We will," said Crabbe, and began to say more, but Haynes plucked his sleeve gently, shaking his head with a faint smile. "Bloody mad," said Crabbe.

Crabbe and Haynes drove gently to the village, four miles away, where the *wayang kulit* ceremony was to be held. "I can't stay the night there," said Crabbe. "I just can't. He's so obviously cracked. He may get violent."

"You can sleep in my room," said Haynes. "I've a li-lo. And the door has a lock."

"Yes. Thanks. After all, it's only for one night."

In the village they received a kind, an urbane, welcome. The headman even brought warm orange crush. And the shadow-play master invited them, with most courteous words, to sit on the stage itself, behind the drummers and pipers, the ox-hide shadow-puppets and the hanging lamp, the large taut cloth on which the silhouettes would be pro-jected, to witness the humble processes by which the age-old heroic drama was enacted.

"Hindu in origin," said Crabbe to Haynes. "Hardly a trace of Islam in the whole thing. Take your shoes off," he said, as they began to mount the steps. "That's the custom." In their socks they crouched in the corner of the attap hut, the enclosed heat most oppressive, listening to the oboist skirling away in improvisation, the drummers and gong-players trying out their sticks. The master sat cross-legged, immediately behind the screen, on each side of him the many figures—gods, demons, the comic inter-

163

mediaries between the supernatural and sublunary worlds
—the manipulation of which was his priest-like office.

"The heat," gasped Haynes. And from Crabbe's own
forehead sweat dripped or gathered into a kind of meniscus
to be scooped off. But the master, cool, brown, entranced,
now uttered the word "Om", identifying himself for the
instant with God Himself, calling on many gods and devils
to be kind and patient, not to take offence at the crude
representation of their acts soon to come, not to be
incensed at the ox-hide caricatures of their numinous
essences. He offered a delicacy—scorched rice; he abased
himself before their greatness. And he remembered the
one true religion, invoking the protection of the four arch-
angels of the Koran.

Soon he took in either hand a godly figure—a body and
head and extravagant head-dress, all carved in lacy com-
plexity, mounted on a hand-stick. These he waved at the
screen, as though delicately fanning it, and the raised
voices from the audience beyond it told that the spell of
the tale—so well known to all, so hard for Crabbe to interpret to Haynes—was already working. "The whole cycle,"
said Crabbe, over the oboe's sinuous cantilena, the gong
and the drums, "takes a week. It's Hindu epic, the age-
long struggle between gods and demons, the . . ."

"I don't feel well," said Haynes. He didn't look well. He
was ghost-white, and sweat oozed and shone on his face
and bare arms. "It's the heat." Crabbe caught the eye of
the oboist, an ancient man with dignified moustaches, and
mimed that they were going round to the front, to watch
the real thing, the shadows. The old man nodded that he
understood and then puffed his cheeks to his instrument.

"Better," said Haynes on the steps. He breathed the
dank night air deeply. "It was surely hot in there. I can't
take all that much heat."

Crabbe's own shirt was soaked, his trousers stuck to his rump. He reached down for his shoes, saying: "Perhaps you ought to have a drink of something. Something cold. Let's go back to the . . ." Then he yelled with pain. The drums and gongs were loud: only Haynes heard him. "In my shoe," said Crabbe, his face screwed up. "Something stung me. What . . . " He tipped the shoe, and from it fell the squashed body of something.

"A scorpion," said Haynes. "A black one, very young. You'd better get that seen to."

"Christ," said Crabbe. "My foot's on fire." He hobbled towards the van, Haynes helping him.

"Well," said Haynes, "we are a couple of fools. This is what happens when we come out for a pleasant instructive evening." He held his shoes in his hand still. They both padded in their socks over the short trampled grass, reaching at last the friendly civilised van. They drove towards the town. "Somewhere here," said Haynes, "there's a doctor. An Indian. I met him a couple of nights ago. He'll give you a shot of something."

The doctor was in—a lonely, talkative Tamil who gave Crabbe penicillin and told him not to worry. "Just rest it up for a couple of days," he said. "And I'll give you a sedative. Do you see anything of my friends?" he asked. "My friends of the Jaffna confraternity? Vythilingam should be coming up any day now, to examine the cattle. And how is Arumugam? That voice is a terrible handicap, terrible. A pity he can't get in touch with a speech therapist. But I don't think there are any in Malaya."

"There will be," said Haynes. "You can be quite sure of that."

"Yes," said the doctor, "poor Arumugam." Meanwhile Crabbe groaned.

. . . . .

"But I thought I was doing the right thing," squealed Arumugam.

"The whole thing is most unfortunate," said Sundralingam. "He will be quite right to be angry." They were sitting round the bed of Maniam in Sundralingam's house. Maniam's nose was a strange colour and painful: for the second time he had had to delay his return to Kuala Beruang. So now he fretted in his tartan sarong, clutching his Dutch wife, adding little to the worried talk of his two friends.

"But it was partly, no, mainly, your idea," shrilled Arumugam softly but urgently. "You said that he must not be lured away from the circle by this Rosemary woman."

"Yes, I know, but to steal his letters was surely going too far."

"I didn't steal them. I merely collected them from the Post Office. My idea was merely to see who they were from, and if one was from this Rosemary woman to steam that open and find out what was going on." Arumugam's voice rose yet higher with self-righteousness. "And then I was going to give him his letters, saying that I had collected them for him as a friendly gesture."

"And then you put the letters in your back trousers pocket and forgot all about them."

It was too true. Arumugan, the efficient, who whipped in with ringmaster's coolness the roaring delicate aircraft, the inheritor of Jaffna's immemorial tradition of reliability, Arumugam had slipped up badly. Then he said: "But it was an easy mistake to make. We had so much trouble with Maniam."

"That's right," said Maniam, through his clogged nose, "blabe be."

"And there was the question of my trousers," continued Arumugam. "They got torn slightly when we were fighting that day with Syed Omar. And then when his son came to beat up Maniam they got stained with blood. Your blood," he said to Sundralingam.

"It wasn't very much blood," said Sundralingam.

"And after that I spilled coffee on them," said Arumu-gam. "So I put them away in a cupboard. And I forgot all about them. And then Vythilingam said that this Rosemary woman had sworn at him when he saw this Penang Chinese making love to her in Crabbe's house, and then he said that he hated her and he never wanted to see her again. So after that I never thought about getting his letters and I forgot about the letters I'd put in my trousers pocket. So you see," he ended, "it is all easily under-standable."

He crumpled the letters absently with twitching hands as he talked. Sundralingam took them from him. "There is nothing very vital," he said. "A circular from Calcutta, two local bills. But this," he said, "is an air mail from Ceylon."

"I suppose," said Maniam from the bed, "I'b to blabe for everythig."

"No, no, not that," protested Arumugam. "It was just unfortunate, that's all."

"No great harm done," said Sundralingam. "The letters are a fortnight late. But the postmark on this letter from Kandy is not very clear. We can make it less clear by rub-bing some dirt on it and then blaming its condition on the Post Office."

"Or the peon in the Veterinary Department," suggested Arumugam.

"Yes. There's no great harm done. But never, never, never try anything like that again."

"No," piped Arumugam meekly. "And who is this Mrs. Smith?"

Sundralingam looked closely at the name and address on the back of the air mail letter. "I don't know," he said. "I never knew he had any English friends in Kandy."

"His bother," said Maniam. "His bother barried ad Eglishbad."

"His mother, of course," cried Arumugam. "How strange to think that Vythilingam's mother is called Smith." And then, with a naughty girl's giggle, he said: "Let us open it up and see what she has to say."

"Now really," reproved Sundralingam. "That, as you know, is not right at all."

"The letter is not stuck down. Tropical air mail letter forms don't have any glue on them. It's just got a couple of staples from a stapling machine."

"Mr. Smith's office stapling machine," said Sundralingam, turning the letter over and over. "Why ever did she marry an Englishman?"

"Bodey," said Maniam cynically. "She re-barried for bodey."

"Imagine," said Sundralingam, fascinated, "imagine those two bodies in bed together, the white and the black. Horrible."

"Horrible," squealed Arumugam. "Let us open the letter."

Sundralingam, with deft doctor's hands, eased out the staples. He smoothed the letter open and began to read. It was quite a short letter, written in convent-school English. Arumugam tried to read it over his shoulder, but Sundralingam said: "Do have some manners. I will read it first and then you can read it." Arumugam meekly sat down on the bed again.

"No," said Sundralingam in shock. "No, no."

"Whatever is the matter?"

"The date?" asked Sundralingam urgently. "What is today's date?"

"The twenty-third," said Arumugam. "But why?" His voice reached C in alt. "Why? What's it all about?"

"When does the next plane come from Singapore?"

"Tomorrow. Why? What is all this mystery?"

Sundralingam looked up at him in deepest reproach. "Now you'll see what you've done with your stupidity. Tomorrow she will be here."

"Here?"

"Yes, yes. It says here that she intends to fly to Singapore on the twenty-first. It's a one-day flight from Colombo, isn't it?" He didn't wait for Arumugam's professional confirmation. "And she's spending two days in Singapore while this girl buys new clothes. And then coming here on the next available plane."

"What girl? Who is this girl?"

"A girl for Vythilingam. An orphan. Both her parents were killed in a car smash."

"How much?" asked Arumugam automatically.

"Eighty thousand," said Sundralingam automatically. "And Vythilingam's stepfather is going to Penang on business. And she wants Vythilingam to call him 'father'."

"No!"

"And she wants to be met at the airport. A fine mess you've made of things," said Sundralingam. "You and your great inquisitive nose."

There was shocked silence from invalid and delinquent. At last Arumugam said: "What shall we do?" The intonation-pattern finished almost at the upper auditory limit. "We daren't give him the letter now. He'll kill me."

"The letter was lost in the post," decided Sundralingam. "Perhaps she sent another letter after. Or a cable confirming everything. Or perhaps she has rung him up from Singapore already."

"Do." Maniam shook his head. "He dever bedtioded adythig about that. He cabe id to see be this bordig."

"The letter got lost," repeated Sundralingam. "Letters sometimes do. It will be a nice surprise for Vythilingam. His mother will walk into the Veterinary Department while he is giving medicine to some small animal. With this girl. It will be such a surprise. There is no great harm done."

"But perhaps he doesn't want to see his mother," said Arumugam.

"Nonsense! What man does not want to see his mother? And this girl. Eighty thousand dollars," said Sundralingam. "Perhaps, after all, it is time we all married," he sighed.

"Never!" cried Arumugam jealously.

"Anyway, it will be your duty to meet her at the airport. You will see the plane come in. You will be able to send a loudspeaker message to her asking her to meet you in the waiting-room. Then you can take her to her son." There were tears in Sundralingam's eyes. "Mother and son meet after long years. With future wife."

"It will be a surprise."

"Oh yes, it will be a lovely surprise."

8

Rosemary sat at her Public Works Department escritoire, in a sea of fed cats, and tried to write a letter to Vythilingam. She had, as she had promised herself, taken a day off from school, having told Crabbe's boy to take a message to her amah to take a message to the school to say that she was ill. But never had she looked better. A large evening meal, deep sleep in a better bed than hers, a full evacuation, a hot bath (her own house had only a cold shower), a breakfast of bacon and eggs and sausages from Crabbe's boy—these had smoothed and restored her. She had come home, changed into a sunny model dress from Penang, tied her hair in a ribbon, fed her cats on corned beef and undiluted condensed milk, and now sat ready for a new life.

She sat wriggling on the standard-pattern Windsor chair, her pink tongue-point dancing about her lips, trying to write, wrestling with a profound stylistic problem. By her pad she had Vythilingam's stiff proposal, whose Augustan periods were intimidating and inhibited her normal chatty flow. The cats, digesting in broody attitudes, looked at her sleepily, taking in nothing of her delicious beauty.

As she shifted from ham to delectable ham, biting her tongue in concentration, the sun warmed her gently, muffled by the lettuce-green curtains but making brighter the mustard-coloured carpet, the pepper-and-salt cushions. She tried to continue her letter, but was half pleased to be interrupted by the opening of the door behind her. She said automatically:

"Ooooh, go away, Jalil, you're not supposed to come here. I told the amah not to let you in." Then she remembered Jalil's disgusting behaviour of the previous evening and turned to give him vinegary words. But it was not Jalil: it was a Chinese boy. Loo his name was. He stood there smiling very shyly, a clean shirt with a tie to show he was in love, pressed trousers. Rosemary could not remember his first name. "Hello," he said.

"Oh," said Rosemary, "it's you." Then she said guiltily: "Why aren't you at school?" His smile began to go slowly, and she remembered that he was no longer at school, but worked in a shop. So she said: "I was only joking. It's me who should be at school."

"I know. I've just been there and they said you were ill."

"Oh," said Rosemary. "Oh, yes, I am. I've such a terrible headache." She suddenly clapped her hand to her brow, screwing up her clear healthy eyes, whose whites were as white as peeled picnic eggs. The cats were aware of her feigning and did not look up at the sound of distress. But then some of them scattered like birds, for Robert Loo was awkwardly down on his knees, saying: "Poor dear. Poor darling." He blushed to say the words, as though he had stolen a theme from some other, inferior, composer.

"Oh, I'm all right, really," she said. "It comes and it goes." Robert Loo remained on his knees, wondering what he should do now. Some cats sat on window-ledges, one on the table, looking at him. This was the first amateur performance they had ever seen. Robert Loo turned his embarrassed eyes away from them and noticed the writing-pad and pen, the opening words: 'My dear.' "You're writing a letter," he said, some new equivocal feeling rising in him.

"Yes, I've been trying to. Do get off your knees, you'll make your trousers all dusty."

Robert Loo got up, as awkwardly as he'd got down. "Are you writing to him?" he asked; "to that man Joe?"

"Joe?" Rosemary smiled disdainfully. "Oh, not to him. I've finished with him. He begged me to marry him, but I won't. I was writing to somebody else."

Hope and despair and anxiety rose in Robert Loo. "Is it me that you're writing to?" He was already reading in his mind two letters, like two simultaneous staves of a score: 'After last night I realise that, young as you are, you are the only one who could make me happy . . .' 'After last night I want us never to meet again. It was beautiful, but it was all a mistake, let's forget it ever happened . . .'

Rosemary smiled again, almost with the calm, wise indulgence of a mother, and stroked the nearest cat. "Oh, no, George, not to you." (She had remembered his name at last.)

"Why do you smile like that?" said Robert Loo, almost with agitation. "What do you mean?"

"What could I write to you about, George?" Pleased at having remembered his name, she determined to insert it into every utterance now. But soon he must go: poor boy, he was a nice boy, but only a boy. She did not feel she was yet old enough to be worshipped by boys.

Robert Loo blushed. "I don't know," he said. "I just thought . . ."

"You shouldn't follow me to school," she said. "And you shouldn't really come here. What are people going to think?" Then she added: "George."

"They'll think that I love you," he mumbled. Then, louder, he said: "I love you."

"Oh, George," she smiled, not above simpering.

"My name isn't George," he said, mumbling again. "It's Robert."

"You're only a boy," she said. "I'm older than you. Some day soon you'll find some nice Chinese girl. Robert," she added, "I thought your name was George. It must have been somebody else I was thinking about."

"There've been others," he said jealously. "I know. Lots of others."

"Oh, yes. Lots of men have said they loved me. But all the time I was waiting for Mr. Right." She looked dreamily into air, still stroking the cat.

"Mr. Wright? Who's Mr. Wright?" Then he remembered a ginger tubby man in shorts, a P.W.D. official who had run up a large account in their shop. "I know the man," he said with bitterness. "He's old and fat. A European." He had the faint beginnings of an understanding of why people disliked Europeans: they took things away from the Asians.

"Oh, no," said Rosemary, her eyes still smiling absently. "You don't know who it is. But perhaps you soon will know." It would, of course, be a Christian ceremony, perhaps in Penang. "You could play the organ," she said. "I remember now. You're fond of music. Victor Crabbe told me."

"I love you," he said. "Marry me." Saying the words, he felt horror and excitement equally. Marriage meant becoming, almost overnight, like his father, an old man with responsibilities. But it also meant that delicious, that unspeakable, that dizzying crowd of sensations over and over again. His flesh responded to the image. He clumsily sought Rosemary's right hand, the one that was not absently stroking, and tried to kiss it. His lips smacked against it inexpertly: it was neither passion nor old-world courtesy that the cats saw.

"Oh, George," she said, "I mean, Robert. Don't be a silly boy."

"I'm not a boy," he said loudly. "I'm a man. I'm a composer. Could your Joe do what I've done? Could he write a string quartet and a symphony and a violin concerto? I'm a man, I tell you. I'll be a great man. Not just somebody like this Mr. Wright of yours in P.W.D. I'll be famous. You'll be proud . . ."

"Yes, yes," she soothed. "I know you're very clever. Victor Crabbe's always telling me that. But you're being silly, just the same. And if you stay here any longer your father will be angry. You shouldn't leave your work like that, just to come and see me."

"I'll do what I like," he said. "I'm a man."

"Yes," she said. "But I must write this letter. Please go now."

"I won't go! I'm going to kiss you, I'm going . . ."

At the door appeared masses of flowers and, behind them, the wheezing Jalil.

"Oh, Jalil," she shouted. "You shouldn't have come, you know you shouldn't." And then, with relief: "Oh, come in, Jalil, do come in. Oooooh, what lovely flowers." In relief she got up from the chair, taking the bright and scentless bunches from Jalil's arms. Jalil was now fully disclosed, wheezing hard, noticing Robert Loo, nodding pleasantly, humming gently down a chromatic scale, then, as he lowered himself into an arm-chair, saying: "Chinese boy. Crabbe's Chinese boy. Boys I not like." He was unabashed, relaxed, only his chest working.

"Oh, lovely, lovely," said Rosemary, briskly seeking jars for the flowers. "Robert," she said, "be an angel and fill these with water. The amah's gone to the market." Robert Loo noted bitterly the mature approach, the gift of flowers.

All he had been able to think of was to wear a tie. He sullenly took the jar that Rosemary proffered and went to the kitchen. As the water drummed in he heard Jalil say: "You have boy now. How much you pay him?" and Rosemary's reply: "Oh, Jalil, what a filthy, what a cruel, unforgivable thing to say." And then Robert Loo came out swiftly with the half-filled jar lest more be said. Cats milled round the table where Rosemary was arranging her flowers, and over one of these cats Robert Loo nearly stumbled. He recovered in time but splashed his shirt and tie. Rosemary said kindly: "Oh, you silly boy. You've made yourself all wet." He blushed. The cat he had come up against crouched by a table leg with its ears back, its fur stiff.

"I suppose," said Robert Loo lamely, "I'd better be going."

"Oh, no ," said Rosemary swiftly. "Do stay. Have a glass of lemon squash or something."

"No, I must go." His eyes tried to speak to her, but he was not one of those Chinese who have great liquid expressive eyes; his eyes were small, black, unable to convey much.

"Perhaps you'd better go too, Jalil. Thank you so much for bringing the flowers." But Jalil put one leg over the other, settling his shoulders more comfortably against the chair. He was going to stay. "Come drink," he said. "Come make jolly time."

"Oh, Jalil!" Then Rosemary remembered that she was supposed to be ill. "My head," she cried dramatically, both hands on her brow like a neuralgia advertisement. "Oh, it's splitting."

At the door Robert Loo hesitated, thinking: 'She's a liar. She lies about everything,' but feeling strong pangs of thwarted desire more painful than any headache. He would not go back to work: he would go and brood in a coffee-shop not his father's.

"You no headache," said Jalil. "I see amah on street. She say you want be lazy today." He smiled, nodding his head and then wagging his foot in a different rhythm.

"I'm going," said Robert Loo.

"Yes, yes, all right," said Rosemary. Then, to Jalil: "I haven't forgotten about yesterday, you know. You're a pig." She kicked the leg of his chair. "A nasty, horrible pig." Jalil laughed quietly. Shamed and frustrated, Robert Loo had gone.

"We go in car," said Jalil, "to Lotong. Drink and make jolly in Rest House."

Rosemary hesitated. It was not, she thought, a bad idea. Thirty miles, a chance to be away from the town. She had not expected these declarations from Robert Loo: she was somewhat embarrassed by the thought that it was perhaps all her fault. She did not want him coming back later in the day, more passionate, perhaps—in a boyish way—violent. And she did not want to be seen in the town here by people ready to report her healthy appearance to the headmaster. And what was the use of a day off if you couldn't have a couple of drinks and a blow in a car?

"I must write this letter first," she said. "It's important."

Jalil laughed, coughed, laughed again. "No use you write," he said. "I tell you he not marry. He not love. Only me love."

"That's just where you're wrong," said Rosemary haughtily and triumphantly. "I've got his proposal here." She waved it. "And I'm going to write to him accepting. To-morrow," she added.

"He never marry," said Jalil. "Only me marry."

. . . . .

Robert Loo walked gloomily down the avenue, his hands in his pockets. As he approached the main street of the town he remembered that he was wearing a tie, so he removed his hands from his pockets to tear it off and open up the neck-buttons of his shirt. What did he want with wearing a tie? He came to the shop-window of Chung the dentist. In that window was a ghastly gilt picture of a cross-section of the human mouth and also a mirror. Above the mirror was written in Chinese: "Take a good look at your teeth. They are undoubtedly rotten. Come inside and I will make all well again." And from within came the noise of all being made well again—groans and the practitioner's encouraging laughter. Robert Loo looked at his face, not his teeth, and saw the smooth face of a boy, a thin neck, slim shoulders. Behind his image passed real boys, schoolboys on their way home from school, none of them wearing ties. Boy, boy, boy. Chinese boy. Portrait of the composer as a young boy. Then into the mirror flashed the face of another boy, brown, splay-nosed, his hair long, showing teeth in greeting. The greeting made Robert Loo turn to meet a shy hand ready for shaking. It was Syed Hassan.

"Where you go now?" asked Syed Hassan.

"I don't know. Just walking, just eating the wind," said Robert Loo in Malay.

"Tomorrow," said Hassan with pride, "is the day of the trial. A big day."

"What will happen to you?"

"Oh, prison, perhaps for many years. With hard labour, perhaps. Perhaps today is my last day of freedom." He smiled proudly. "I have committed a terrible crime."

"Not so terrible."

"Oh, yes," insisted Hassan. "Very terrible. Violence, attempted murder. Don't say it's not terrible."

178

"Terrible," agreed Robert Loo.

"Tonight we will celebrate," suggested Hassan. "Have you any money?"

"My father gave me ten dollars." It was true. Inexplicably, when Robert Loo came down from his breakfast, washed and neck-tied, his father had put his fist in the till and brought out a note, saying: "There, my son, take this. Buy yourself a little something. Life should not be all work."

"I," said Hassan, "have five dollars. I cleaned the car of a P.W.D. man called Mr. Wright."

"Oh," said Robert Loo. And then: "What are we going to do?"

"I'll call for you this evening." Syed Hassan winked. "At about ten o'clock. Then you'll see what we're going to do. But," he remembered, "I forgot. There is the question of your beloved. When do you see her again?"

"Not for a long time," said Robert Loo. "She's busy."

They parted. Robert Loo went back to his father's shop. His father was out, gambling somewhere, his mother greeted him with three raw eggs beaten up in brandy.

"Take this, son. You look very pale. And for lunch I am giving you fried pork. That makes blood." This new solicitude was very puzzling.

But Robert Loo could eat little. After lunch he sat in his accustomed place behind the counter, totting up bills mechanically, before him the few scored pages of the violin concerto, beneath them the many blank lined pages still to be filled. It was very hot. Dust swirled outside, a few listless coffee-drinkers lounged at the tables, the day slept. The great music-god was silent, the hours were propitious for the welling-up of theme and development from a subconscious the more lively because of the torpor of the mind's surfaces. And nothing came. The solo violinist seemed to have vanished. Robert Loo took from the till a ten-cent piece and fed it to the sleeping god. It awoke languidly, searched with insolent slowness for the record Robert Loo's random hand had chosen, and then the afternoon exploded into a larger-than-life dance orchestra crying false emotions. His chin on his fist, Robert Loo sat and listened behind his counter, his heart aching, his eyes staring at nothing, while his brothers cheerfully clopped around, occasionally calling to the kitchen, as customers drifted somnambulistically in:

"Kopi O!"

"Kopi O ping!"

But he could not call for anything so simple as black coffee, hot or iced, to soothe this thirst which had no name. It was not a thirst for Rosemary, it was not that great thirst which, so Paul Claudel once said, is excited by woman but can only be slaked by God. And art seemed to give no solace. But when the record had ended and the machine dozed again, Robert Loo took a small piece of manuscript paper suitable for piano compositions and idly wrote a few bars of lush but near-astringent Debussyish chords. Hearing these with his mind's ear, he felt comforted, as though his self-pity were somehow connected with a great unseen plan organised by a god who was all soft lips and huge melting eyes, a god expertly invoked by Tchaikowski or Rachmaninoff or the early works of the French impressionistic composers. He glanced over the first bars of his violin concerto and, taking their scores from his dispatch-case under the counter, the string quartet and the symphony (whose last pages his father had torn up). Clever, he thought, all that counterpoint. The work of a clever boy who was top in maths. But what did it say to him now? Where was the yearning, the heart-break, to be comforted by the easy message of the single flowing tune and the big chords? That music was not him; it was the work of somebody else, somebody he did not like very much.

Vythilingam sat, sweating and breathing hard, in one of Rosemary's arm-chairs. She was out, the amah had said, she had gone out for the day with the Turkish gentleman. Round Vythilingam were ranged the cats, a soft army, knowing him, not disliking him despite his sharp needles and his strong medicine-feeding hands, half-attracted by the mysterious scents that his clothes had brought from the surgery. Vythilingam did not see them. Rosemary was out. Rosemary was out. The amah did not know when she would be back.

This at least was not dreaming. The wood of the chair-arms was solid beneath his nails. And now he could hear the whirr of the ceiling-fan which Rosemary, careless of electricity bills, had not turned off. That was real enough, and so now were the twitching muzzles, the yawns, the washings of furry legs like turkey drum-sticks, the panther-glidings all about him. What was dream, untrue, not to be thought of more, was his standing there in the surgery, delicately inserting the hypodermic nozzle into the anus of the ailing pet honey-bear, and then the inanely smiling herald-face of Arumugam, and then the fat hand-some woman in the *sari*, and then the nervously grinning girl behind, plump, prettyish, dumb, and then the greet-ings . . .

One of his assistants had taken over the honey-bear, smiling whitely, aware of what was happening, hearing the words "My boy!" and Arumugam's stupid squeal about a lovely surprise.

Oh, God, a beast, that wants discourse of reason . . . The beasts, the beasts, he had to go and see about the beasts. Work would not wait. Yes, yes, Arumugam would take them to his house in the car. He would meet them later. But now, suffering another kiss from the handsome black woman, he had to go. Half an hour, no more. They would go out for lunch somewhere. But he had to see to the beasts.

The furry beasts grew tired of watching and nosing around one so still, limp and sweating in an arm-chair. They went about their business, to licking saucers, to washing, to blinking in the sun. It would have been easy, thought Vythilingam, easy if they had been married. Even now, if she accepted him. But he could not pretend to his mother: she would see through all disguises, pull down his dusty curtains, that strong woman, that woman whose name was frailty. But still, of course, it wasn't true. After a brief breathing spell he would go back to empty bachelor quarters and, in the afternoon, to the cool aseptic quiet of the Veterinary Department, the whole vision exorcised by an hour or so of calm and deep breathing.

But the cats twitched and stirred, hearing with sharper ears than his the approach of a car. The amah came out, saying that perhaps *Missi* had returned. But Vythilingam knew it was not that. They were after him, the leisurely following feet. Hide? But the Veterinary Department Land-Rover was outside, twenty yards down the street. If he could get into that, rush off, shouting, if they saw and hailed him, that there was more urgent work to be done, that he couldn't stop. But he would stutter out the words, waste time, they would be on to him. This was the work of Sundralingam and Arumugam. 'Hale him out, keep him away from that woman, that corrupting unclean Christian woman. We told you we'd find him here, Mrs. Smith. He comes here, but there is really nothing in it, ha ha. Just friends. He looks after her cats, that's all. You will hear as much from his own lips. But now somebody else can look after the cats, for he will have much else to occupy him.'

No! Vythilingam, hearing already known voices, the slam of the car door, saw a way out through the kitchen, through the servants' quarters, a way out that Rosemary herself had, so little time ago, sought blindly. Now there was knocking at the front door. Vythilingam nodded vigorously, with shaking nerves, to the amah, miming that she should open the door, let in the visitors. The amah, a not very bright Malay girl, looked at Vythilingam with frowning brows of no comprehension.

"He *must* be here." Arumugam's voice, outside the door. Vythilingam rushed through to the kitchen, the quarters beyond, as the amah at last caught his drift, went to open. He was out, stumbling over servants' litter, an overflow of cats from the house itself, under the sun. He saw known backs at the front door as he sought his own car. Let them take the Land-Rover, with its space at the back for animals of some bulk. Let them, beasts that want discourse of reason. The visitors—Arumugam, Sundralingam, the fat handsome woman, but not the grinning girl—turned in surprise as they saw him there, already in the driver's seat, switching on the ignition. His face twitched in a grin of agony as he called: "Urgent!" And then he wrestled with the word 'must' but abandoned it, shrugging his shoulders at them, pantomiming swiftly "Duty, duty, duty. What can I do? I'll be back later." They called, they began to come down to him, but the engine responded, he was in gear, he was off.

He did not know where he was driving. It was too late now, he thought. If he could have asked Rosemary, if he could have pleaded with her to say yes. And he felt that she would, for this Joe business was all over, he was sure of that, for the Turkish gentleman had told somebody and somebody had told Vythilingam. If only he could have confronted her, that handsome fat woman, together, both of them, Rosemary saying: "He is mine. We're going to be married," or better still, not lying but just stating proleptically: "We are married. He's my husband first. He's your son second." A woman to meet a woman, black eyes flashing opposing swords. "Leave us alone. Let us be happy together. You have no power over him any longer, no rights of any kind." But it was too late.

Where should he go? He could see no following Land-Rover in the driver's mirror. He had to hide. No. He slowed down, parked for an instant at the side of the road —it was the long empty road leading out of town—to think that it was no longer merely a question of hiding. She had come for him. She would not rest till she got him. And he knew he would yield all too easily.

And now what about Chou En Lai and the Communist Manifesto? Eh? Were they over, then, the days of doctrinaire musings, the mere dreaming of action? Was it at last time to act?

But there were the animals to think of, there was his duty to the animals.

How about duty to mankind?

These things must be thought about later, at leisure, if there was ever to be leisure for thinking again. In the meantime, on, on. He was, he noticed, on the road to Anjing. Anjing to Mawas. By railway. His car could, or could not, be sent on later. It could, or could not, be left in the station yard to be picked up on his return. And, anyway, it was time he went to Mawas. In the routine of tending sick buffaloes and goats he could slowly arrive at some kind of decision. The train to Mawas went sometime in the evening. But where was his black bag? Of course, there it was, on the car floor beside him. That had made them suspicious, seeing it there when they drove to his house, wondering why he should plead urgent duty and yet forget to take his black bag. Why couldn't they leave him alone? But he wasn't really running away from them. It was time he went to Mawas, wasn't it? There was, in a sense, always urgent duty.

Duty, duty, duty. The car sped down the hot road, its horn, as it warned a careless old man, hesitant at the roadside, calling: "Duty, duty."

"It's down this street you see most of them," said Syed Hassan. "Now that they've closed down the Park."

"Yes," said Robert Loo. He did not care much one way or the other. It was dark, dark that enclosed in one big coat Crabbe in Mawas, groaning with his scorpion bite, Vythilingam in the gently ambling train, Rosemary home at last, with the door shut on Jalil, Syed Omar cursing his lot in a coffee-shop over cadged brandy and ginger ale. And the dark brought out the prostitutes, Malay divorcées mostly, quietly moving from light to light, gaudy and graceful, like other of night's creatures.

Hassan could not hide either his fear or his excitement. He did not try to pose as a young man of the world: Robert Loo's experience stood between the two of them like another person, a person Hassan had deliberately sought as a dragoman. At one point, breathless, he said: "What shall we do? Shall we speak to two of them?"

"I think," said Robert Loo, "the best thing is just to stand somewhere and wait." And now he too felt excitement stirring: he was to know that complex of sensations again, that piece of music which was all crescendo. But was it right just to seek it blindly, in a void, with no reference to what they called love? Last night he had not looked for it at all; it had just happened. Let the same thing happen again now, let the moment arrive. And so they waited, and Hassan took from his shirt pocket a packet of Rough Rider cigarettes and offered one to Robert Loo. Robert Loo refused: he had no vices. Hassan puffed till the end glowed bright and the tube itself grew almost too hot to hold. And they waited.

They did not have long to wait. The two girls were clean, though they reeked of 'Himalayan Bouquet' perfume. They were tiny though well-developed. Their costumes proclaimed modest submission to custom and religion while at the same time suggesting untold treasures beneath for the asking, or buying. They went off with their young customers, arms linked warmly, chattering in soft dark Malay, Malay of the night, off to the same house. Robert Loo's girl was called Asma binte Ismail, and she lived a floor above her colleague. It was not hard to make love to her.

At the blinding moment of climax Robert Loo saw quite clearly the kind of music he wanted to write: his vision confirmed those shafts, those bursting fragments, of last night. The claims of the body, the claims of the emotions —some fine soaring melody above the lush piano chords of the soloist. The violinist had disappeared. When his body had quietened, Robert Loo saw an unbidden picture of rows of tins on his father's shelves. He frowned at first, wondering what this could mean, and then smiled faintly. He had conquered those giants—harmony, counterpoint, orchestration—long ago. And now he had conquered love.

She asked for five dollars and he gave her six.

9

"Are you sure you can make it?" asked Temple Haynes, not without anxiety. He helped Crabbe along to the rough landing-stage, a groaning Crabbe sorry for himself, a Crabbe with a bandaged foot, looking like a gouty uncle, a Crabbe whose luggage was heavier by a single shoe, who carried a walking-stick donated by a well-equipped and resourceful American.

"Got to," clenched Crabbe. "Won't stay there any longer with that insulting bastard."

Haynes tut-tutted at the strong language but said: "He did pile it on. I failed to see any connection between your laughing at butterflies and being stung by a scorpion, but then perhaps my particular line of study has made me too rational-minded."

It was a mid-morning of huge heat, a vast river sky above, the reek and shimmer of the river below, the green jaws of the jungle opening on either hand, the launch waiting. Crabbe, through his pain, noticed a man he knew sitting alone and silent in the bows: Vythilingam of the State Veterinary Department. Boatmen and passengers— a Chinese assistant manager and a Tamil hospital dresser whom Crabbe had met before, two Malays of occupation undefined—helped Crabbe into the launch, but Vythilingam did not move, did not even seem to see.

Temple Haynes looked down into the hot, rocking, oil-smelling boat, the river dancing on his spotless shirt.

"Take it easy," he warned. "Don't try and do too much. And I hope to be seeing you in a week or so."

"When you move to the capital."

"That's right. There's so much to be done."

"Yes." Crabbe winced, closing his eyes in the full sunlight that made them water, and opening them again to the shining river, to the waving Haynes as the launch throbbed and bounced and made ready to move off.

Nobody spoke to anybody. Crabbe's greeting to Vythilingam met a stare of more than recognition, not friendly, not hostile, rather a stare of distracted interest as though seeing in Crabbe more than the man who had given the party a few days ago, more than the Education Officer who was slowly handing over his burden to one of the new masters. Meanwhile foot and engine and sky and river throbbed, and they moved towards the *hulu*. '*Hulu*,' thought Crabbe, trying to grasp at anything to take his mind off his foot. '*Hulu*, the head. Head of my stick. Head of the river. *Penghulu*, head of the village, head of a religion. *Hulu*, really the desolate cry of some bird up-river, an ululation of a mouth finally going under. *Hulu*.'

The river was broad and silver, and the sunlight was merry on it. But to port and starboard jungle exerted an influence more powerful than the sun, its smell as strong as the smell of warmed wood in the boat or of the sun-warmed river. And it was finally to the jungle-gods that the Malays would be most faithful. The sun of Islam, disguising itself cunningly as a sickle moon, was appropriate only to the clearings, which meant the towns with their refrigerators and mosques, where the muezzin's call mingled well with the music of the bars. Now the towns were beginning to entertain their vain dream of realised independence—the bright fresh paint for the visitors, the new stadium and the luxury hotel. Some Arab theologian-philosopher had said that Islam decayed in the towns. Only when the decay of Islam brought the decay of the cities, when the desert, with its frail tented communities, reasserted itself, only then could the faith be renewed. But there was no desert here, no dominion of sun and oasis. There was nothing to believe in except the jungle. That was home, that was reality. Crabbe gazed in a kind of horror mixed with peace at the endless vista of soaring trunks, lianas, garish flowers. They were chugging towards the *hulu,* the head or fount of everything, where there was no pretence or deception.

Settled to the river life, the transiently permanent, a fragile community was possible. The Chinese assistant manager spoke, with a wide smile of insincere teeth, to Crabbe, asking: "Did you have the bad luck to fall down when you were drunk, Mr. Crabbe?" It was not an insolent question, it was Chinese and clinical. The Tamil hospital dresser bubbled away, showing teeth as good: "The monsoon drains are very treacherous. It is possible to break a leg when one is not walking straight." They smiled and smiled, waiting for confirmation.

"I was struck by a scorpion," said Crabbe, "when I was perfectly sober." There was polite laughter of sixty-four teeth. "I am now Club-foot the Tyrant." The teeth disappeared in sympathy. "But I didn't kill my father and I didn't marry my mother."

"Marry your mother," laughed the Chinese. "That is very good."

"Marry my mother," suddenly said Vythilingam. Those were his first words of the voyage, and they were spoken with unstuttered labials. He provoked a fresh silence. "Kill my father," he added, for good measure.

"The Japanese killed my father," smiled the Chinese. "They poured petrol on him and then threw a lighted match." He laughed modestly. "They made me watch. They were not very good people."

"History," said Crabbe, battering his pain with words at random. "The best thing to do is to put all that in books and forget about it. A book is a kind of lavatory. We've got to throw up the past, otherwise we can't live in the present. The past has got to be killed." But, in saying that, off his guard with the pain in his foot, he reverted to his own past, and pronounced the very word in the Northern style, the style of his childhood.

"Excuse me," said the Tamil dresser. "To which pest do you refer? Surely all pests have to be killed? I do not quite understand the drift of your statement."

"It was only talk," said Crabbe. "It didn't mean anything."

And now the colour changed to brown, the soft brown of Malay, for one of the Malays of undefined occupation spoke, sitting on a bench by the gunwale, his brown arms stretched out, gripping the boat's side. "Allah," he said, "disposes all things. The tea-cup I broke as a child, and the lottery my father failed to win by only one number. That was only two years after I broke the tea-cup. I blamed the breaking of the tea-cup on my younger brother, and this, as it turned out, was not unjust, for four years later, two years after my father failed to win the lottery, he broke a tea-cup on his own account. Then we had more tea-cups than formerly, and my mother was never very clever at counting. So he escaped punishment, which in a sense was just, for he had already been wrongly punished." He now gave an exhibition of Malay teeth, bits of gold glinting in the sun and river, teeth not so good as the others' teeth.

"But the lottery ticket," said the Tamil in Malay. "I am not able to see the drift."

"Allah disposes all things," repeated the Malay, his teeth hidden in solemnity. "If my father had been predestined to win he would have won. It was of no use for him to prate about injustice." He smiled around and then closed up his mouth for the rest of the voyage, leaving his boat-mates with much to think about. The broken tea-cup tinkled in their brains and the number by which this man's father had failed to win glowed dimly and faded. Meanwhile the river narrowed somewhat, and the green bodies and arms and legs of the twin jungles shambled nearer.

"But, despite your father's failure to become rich," said the Chinese assistant manager, "you still had more tea-cups than you could count."

The Malay nodded, smiling, saying nothing. Ahead, on the starboard side, the jungle began to thin out to scrub, and then came a regular forest of rubber trees. Crabbe remembered an English politician of a mystical frame of mind who, having spent two days in Malaya, wrote in a Sunday paper that the very jungles were symmetrical, neat as the trim garden of British rule. Crabbe thought of many other palm-beach-suited visitors who, through pink mists of hospitable whisky, had mistaken Malays for Chinese, mosques for Anglican churches, plantations for jungles, neat dishes of canapés for calm and happy order. But at the *hulu* or head of the river the two halves of the jungle joined up and became one, and there there was no mistaking one thing for another. The jungle called "OM", like the Malay showman of the shadow-play, one and indivisible, ultimate numen.

The launch moved into the landing-stage of Rambutan Estate, and here the Chinese and the Tamil disembarked, with smiles and waves. Beyond was a pleasance of lawn, a company bungalow magnificent in shining glass, beyond again the rubber and the coolie lines. The launch moved out to mid-river, Crabbe and Vythilingam silent, the Malays silent with cigarettes, the boatmen chattering. Next stop was Durian Estate.

After a mile of further narrowing river Crabbe celebrated the slight easing of his pain by saying a few polite words to Vythilingam, asking him why he was going to the upriver plantation. Vythilingam jerked out, with throbbing larynx, the one word: "Beasts."

"To examine the cattle?" Vythilingam did not nod; Crabbe said: "I'm going to see the family of this Tamil schoolmaster who was murdered. Perhaps you knew him. He ran the estate school."

Vythilingam turned to look at Crabbe, nodding that he thought he knew the man. He uttered the name "Yogam." He added: "Not a good man. A drunkard."

"He'll never drink again."

Vythilingam said nothing more. It was not long before they arrived at the final river outpost of industry and civilisation. Here were even wider lawns than at Rambutan Estate, with Tamil gardeners at work with hoses on flower-beds. The planter's house was no mere bungalow. It stood on high pillars, shading under its belly an armoured car for running round the many square miles of rubber, and soaring up in two storeys to a roof garden with striped umbrellas. Here the lonely manager had to drink desperately of whatever solace boat could bring and private power-station could drive. For few now would risk the holiday trip to huge curry tiffins, gin parties with dancing, moonlight swimming in the pool that stood, its water changed daily, surrounded by banyan and rain tree, bougainvillea and hibiscus, before the proud manor house. It was a nail-biting life for the exile, soothed inadequately by the hum of his refrigerators, the roar of his many fans, the high fidelity tone of his record-player. He drank much before dinner, and the dinner with its many courses appeared in the early hours of the morning, the fish and the mutton dried up, the tired cook forgetting about the coffee. Coombes, thought Crabbe, poor Coombes, despite his many thousands in the bank, the welcome of plush chairs and cigars on his rare trips to the London office.

The Malays smilingly helped Crabbe ashore, leaving him with his stick and his bag while they strolled off, waving, to their lines. Vythilingam stood hesitant, his black bag of medicine and instruments swinging in his right hand, smiling nervously, saying at length: "The cattle. Cancerous growths on the cattle."

"You'd better come and see Coombes first," said Crabbe, "and have a drink or something." Vythilingam shook his head. "My duty," he said without stuttering. Then he went off in the direction of the labourers' houses, the self-contained world of village shop, cows and chickens, school and first-aid post. Alone, Crabbe walked painfully towards the house, a long stretch from the riverside, hearing the boat throbbing finally, then the click-off of the engine as it was moored against the later afternoon's return journey.

As Crabbe approached the outer stairs of the house a man appeared in the doorway. He called: "Hello, hello, hello" in hearty welcome and then athletically began to run down the wooden steps. He was a stranger to Crabbe, and Crabbe said: "I was looking for Mr. Coombes."

"Just a day too late, old boy," said the man. "Here, you *are* in a bad way, aren't you? Let me give you a helping hand." He was a big chubby man, in his middle thirties, the muscle of his rugger days now settling placidly to reminiscent fat. He was not unhandsome. He had dark polished hair, a moustache, a plummy patrician voice, fine fat brown dimpled knees between blue shorts and football stockings. His shirt was of checked cotton, and within it a loose stomach and fleshy breasts bounced gently. "You're the education chap," he said, as he steered Crabbe strongly up the steps. He laughed, the loud laugh of rugger dinners. "There's a telegram about you inside. Coombes left it for me. Something about this chap getting murdered. But I don't see what you can do."

"It's quite usual," said Crabbe, as they reached the top of the steps and stood before the large open doorway among potted plants. "Condolences for the widow, find out what really happened for the records, assure her that she'll get a widow's and orphans' pension. We don't know how many orphans there are." He panted, standing there, waiting to be asked in.

"This telegram," said the man. He picked it up from the hall table. The hall was wide, magnificent with inlays of imported oak, heads of African beasts on the walls, flowers, a suite of rattan furniture. "It says: 'Murder regretted. Am sending my assistant as I must stay in the office.' And it's signed Something bin Somebody. Never could read these Malay names. Tamil's my language." He laughed again, plummily. "Sounds as though he'd committed the murder himself. Well, come inside, Mr. Assistant. Damn cheek of that bloke calling you his assistant. You give him hell when you get back."

"It's true in a way, you know," said Crabbe. They went slowly, Crabbe limping, into the vast drawing-room. "I *am* an assistant. I'm assisting this chap to take over my job." The drawing-room seemed an acre of polished floor-boards, with complete units for sitting or lounging—drink-table, settee, arm-chairs—placed at intervals along the walls, by the windows that looked down at river and jungle beyond, in the body of the echoing room. It was monstrous and pathetic, this lavishness, a child's tongue put out at the great green giant. On the walls were square patches unfaded by sun, where pictures had been and would be again. On the floor were treasures of this new man—gramophone records, books, papers, group photographs of rugger clubs—half unpacked. A radio-gramophone stood in the middle of the floor, a voice in the wilderness at present silent, though it was already plugged into a light socket high above. "Where," asked Crabbe, "is Coombes?"

"He's been moved. Apparently this place has been getting on his nerves." The man made a swigging motion and winked. "He's gone to a place in Johore. Demotion really. And this is promotion for me." He looked round with satisfaction at the vast anonymous room. "I was in Negri Duabelas," he said. "I ran the Union Jack Society in Timbang. And a music club. I wasn't so isolated there as I'm going to be here. But I don't mind isolation. I've got my records and my books. I read a lot of poetry. My name's George Costard. I don't think I quite caught yours."

Crabbe thought for an instant and then said: "Victor." If this man read poetry it was just possible he might have read some of Fenella's. After all, Crabbe was his name before it was hers; why should she usurp it and make it well known on her own behalf? "Victor," he said.

"So you're Mr. Victor," said Costard, "assistant to Whoisit bin Whatshisname. Sit down, Victor, and take a load off that foot. You been playing soccer in your bare feet or something? I never did care for soccer. I'll get some beer from the fridge." He went off, briskly walking the half-mile or so to the kitchen, and then called a Tamil name and Tamil orders. He walked the half-mile back again, saying: "I've asked Tambi to bring a large bottle every twenty minutes. Is that all right with you? It saves the trouble of going to the kitchen and shouting. This is a hell of a big place." He sat down, one big bare knee over the other, and looked at Crabbe complacently. "Music," he said. "Do you care for music?" Crabbe said he did. The Tamil boy came with beer. "Watch this," said Costard with pride. "This lad can do anything." He gave Tamil orders and the Tamil boy, lean, black, sly-looking, took a random pile of thick smeared records (old style: seventy-eight revolutions per minute) and carried them over to the radio-gramophone. With practised skill he set the machine working: the first of the skewered pile submitted to the needle and, through loud scratch noises, the opening theme of Beethoven's Ninth Symphony began to emerge. "I like it that way," said Costard. "I never know what I'm going to get. After this you'll probably get a bit of Schubert or Brahms or a Hebridean folk-song. I just leave it to him. I've got catholic tastes. Catholic with a small 'c', of course. The family's always been Church of England. There was an Archbishop George Costard in the eighteenth century. You may have heard of him."

Crabbe settled as comfortably as he could with his beer. 'Here we go again,' he thought. 'Drink and reminiscence. Another day of wasted time. They're right when they say we drink too much out here. And we slobber too much over ourselves. "Did you ever hear how I came out here? It's rather an interesting story, really. Have another drink and I'll tell you about it." We're all sorry for ourselves because we're not big executives or artists or happily married men in a civilised temperate climate.' Crabbe noted that the pain in his foot was going, to be followed by a numbness as though the foot were not really there.

"Some people make fun of the name," said Costard. "Ignorant people. Although at school I didn't suffer too much because most of the kids had heard of Custard's last stand. I don't think he'd anything to do with our family, though. I think the two names are different in origin. Costard means an apple, you know."

Over in a flash, Beethoven's first theme having been just about stated, the record was replaced mechanically by part of the music for King George VI's Coronation, Parry's 'I was glad when they said unto me'. Costard said happily: "You just never know what you're going to get." Crabbe was glad Costard said that to him, changing the subject, for, off his guard, he had very nearly begun to say that his own name meant a kind of apple. "Have a cigarette, Victor," said Costard. The table was full of half-empty Capstan tins, and Crabbe helped himself. Again off his guard, warmed by the sound of his Christian name, he said automatically: "Thank you, George." Then he blushed.

"Funny," said Costard. "You're a Christian name man. I shouldn't have thought that. I've never found it easy to call a man by his Christian name, except my brothers, of course. It's public school training, I suppose." He looked at Crabbe suspiciously. "What was your school, if I may ask?"

"You wouldn't know it," said Crabbe. "It was a rather obscure grammar school in the north of England."

"You a 'Varsity man?"

"Oh yes." And he named his red-brick university.

"Oxford, me," said Costard. "The House. I took a first in Greats. You wouldn't think that to look at me, would you? Perhaps you wonder why I came out here at all. It's rather an interesting story, really. Look," he said urgently, "twenty minutes is nearly up, and you haven't finished your beer. That boy of mine's a walking clock." He examined his watch narrowly. "One minute to go. Time." Sure enough, the Tamil boy smugly reappeared, bearing another large bottle. And then Parry's anthem finished triumphantly. There was the muffled fall of a new record, a click, and the sound of Schubert's 'Trout' Quintet, half-buried under surface noise, swam sweetly forth. "We ought to have bets on it," suggested Costard. "I bet you five dollars the next record will be more Beethoven."

"I can't bet," said Crabbe. "I just don't know what records you've got."

"No more do I," said Costard cheerfully. "That's the fun of it. Some of these records down there on the floor—why, I haven't seen them for years. When we were packing up to leave Negri Duabelas my boy discovered stacks of them in the place under the stairs where I kept the Christmas decorations. What time would you like lunch?"

"Any time that suits you," said Crabbe.

"I thought you'd say that. I normally have lunch about four. Dinner at any time after midnight. Except when I have lady guests. You must stay for dinner."

"I really ought to go and see this woman," said Crabbe. "And then get back."

"Nonsense," said Costard warmly. "It's a real stroke of luck, you dropping in like this. You can tell me the set-up in this state, and who the important people are, and what the local Cold Storage is like. And I can tell you my story, which is pretty interesting, really."

"But I really came down to see this woman," said Crabbe.

"You can't speak Tamil, can you? No. Well, I can. I'll get the dope from her and send it on in an official letter. And I don't suppose you can walk very far with that foot of yours."

"It's not painful now. It's just a bit numb."

"Ah. Well, when I left Oxford, I wondered for a long time what to do. The family has money, of course, so there was no immediate urgency. Yes, I know what you're thinking. You want to know why I didn't go straight into the army. But, you see, I joined up in my first year at Oxford, and finished my degree after the war. Were you in the Forces, by any chance?"

"Army too?"

"What rank?" Crabbe told him. "I," said Costard, "didn't do too badly, all things considered. Captain at twenty-one isn't too bad, is it? No. I wasn't all that heroic, though they were good enough to mention me in dispatches. Anyway, after the war, I went back to Oxford and did pretty well, on the whole. A first in Greats and a Rugger Blue. Soccer's your game, I take it?"

"No."

"Ah," beamed Costard, as the record changed. "What did I tell you? Beethoven. That's the Hammerklavier. I knew a girl who played that marvellously. A fragile little thing, to look at, but the strength in those wrists." His face grew dark. "Poor, poor girl. Poor, poor, poor little thing. But I'll come to her in due course. She's part of the story."

"Not if it makes you sad," said Crabbe.

"Oh, it's life. We all get over these things. We've got to, else life just couldn't go on. But she meant a lot, a hell of a lot. Perhaps, really, I'd better not speak about her. I mean, to a stranger. And I'm used to keeping it bottled up. There was never really anybody I could tell. I just couldn't. My mother was always strait-laced. Don't get me wrong; I adore her, but there were some things she could never understand." He sighed. "Adultery." He sighed again. "That's a hard word. And yet it never seemed as though we were doing wrong. I don't know why I'm telling you these things. It seemed rather as though her marriage was all wrong. He was to blame, not us."

"On the whole," said Crabbe in swift embarrassment, "this isn't too bad a state to be in. The Sultan's go-ahead, modern in some of his views. There aren't so many British left now, of course, and the British Adviser's gone. But if you're a club man you'll find plenty of Asians to drink with, and there's even a sort of Rugger Club."

"What do you mean—'sort of'?"

"They don't find it easy to get anybody to play with. They just meet and drink beer and sing songs. But they talk about rugger: most of them were educated in England."

"Asians, you say?" Costard looked darkly. "No," he said. "That's not really my line. The Asians are all right in their place, I suppose, but I don't think they ought to do that sort of thing. After all, it is an English game. And you mean to say that they sing, 'If I were a marrying maid which thank the Lord I'm not, sir'? That's a kind of desecration. Oh, I know you'll probably think me stupidly conservative, and all that sort of rot, but that's the way I was brought up. I can't help it." The record changed. They were now treated to Clara Butt singing 'Land of Hope and Glory'. She sang through a thick mist of scratches. Costard began to swing his beer-mug gently in time. Then he looked at his watch. "I say," he said, "you *are* slow. Tambi will be here in . . ." He computed carefully. ". . . in exactly twenty seconds." And, lo, Tambi appeared at that very moment. "He's a bit too early," said Costard. "Still, it's a fault on the right side. I'm always punctual to a fault, personally. It's a family tradition. The old man used to knock hell out of me if I was ever late for anything. He was right, I see that now. I've always insisted on punctuality in my own underlings. It's no good their saying they haven't got watches or their watches stopped or something. Where there's a will there's a way." Beer was poured for Costard and his guest. His feet flapping gently on the parquet, Tambi returned to his kitchen. There was a silent space, during which Dame Clara Butt, with brass behind her, was able to boom her climax to two conventionally grave, lonely, moved, head-drooping exiles. The Edwardian expansionist prayer came to an end. "I suppose I am a bit old-fashioned, really," admitted Costard. "But I'm enough of a realist to know that those days are over. The Empire's cracking up, they say. Well, some of us must keep the traditions alive. That's the meaning of Conservatism, as I see it. Some of us have got to conserve."

"But you're not an Empire-builder," said Crabbe. "You're a rubber-planter. You're a commercial man." A new record started—a dance of clean dainty shep-herdesses by Edward German. Costard looked at Crabbe with beetled brows and a pout of distaste.

"That's where you're wrong," he said. "Do you think the money matters to me? I'm in this game to keep some-thing alive that's very, very beautiful. The feudal tradi-tion, the enlightened patriarchal principle. You people have been throwing it all away, educating them to revolt against us. They won't be happy, any of them. It's only on the estates now that the old ideas can be preserved. I'm the father of these people. They can look up to me, bring me their troubles and let me participate in their joys. Don't you think that's good and beautiful? They're my children, all of them. I correct them, I cherish them, I show them the way that they should go. Of course, you could say that it's more than just an ideological matter with me. I suppose I'm really the paternal type." He looked it, big and dark and comely, his large knees com-fortable stools for climbing brats lisping "Daddy."

"And yet you've never married," said Crabbe. "You've no children of your own."

"How about you?"

"Oh yes, married. No children, though. But I've been a schoolmaster for a long time. That's satisfied and finally cured any paternal instinct in me." The Tamil boy had entered again, without a tray. Crabbe said: "Something's gone wrong with your human clock."

Costard smiled with infinite complacency. "That boy's marvellous. He's counted the number of records. Now he's going to change them." And indeed the boy lifted the pile of worn discs tenderly from the turntable and, at random, picked up a new pile—dusty ten-inchers. And now for some reason Crabbe felt a strange uneasiness in his stomach.

"Good," said Costard, settling himself anew, listening to a boy soprano of the nineteen-thirties singing 'Oh, for the wings of a dove'. Crabbe's uneasiness passed: it was pure breakfastlessness, he decided, hearing a comforting rumble from the pit. Costard insisted on silence for the creamy Mendelssohn. And then, as the march from *Aida* struck up—Sunday school outing trumpets and a smell of orange-peel—he big-drummed the air with his fist, lalling the square tune vigorously. "Come on," he paused to invite, "join in. Grand stuff, this." Crabbe smiled with the corners of his lips, and then sought an alibi in his tankard. "Good man," said Costard. "You couldn't have timed that better." For there again was Tambi with beer. And then the record changed, a piano pinking high a Poulenc-like theme. Crabbe heard absently, then listened incredulously. And Costard also was listening in a kind of stupid horrified wonder. "No," he said. "No. That was lost. That was lost in Negri." The piano slid in grotesque arpeggio to the bass register: a comic fugato, the left hand occasionally leaping up to pink a discord in the high treble. Crabbe saw the hand doing it, the sweep of the bare arm.

He was on his feet. The stung foot, now quite nerveless, gave way under him, and he clung to the table. "Where did you get that?" he asked breathlessly. "Who gave you that? You bloody thief, you stole it."

The Tamil boy stood looking, bewildered, a dog prepared for a whipping for no crime he knew of. *"Utundu povay!"* cried Costard, also on his feet. "Where was it? Why didn't you tell me?" The boy cringed. *"Ni ennai vansiththup-podday!"* yelled Costard.

"What's going on?" cried Crabbe. "Where did you get it? Who gave you that?"

Costard made a hitting gesture. The boy, understanding nothing of this wrath, this agitation, shambled off like an ape. The two Englishmen faced each other, breathing heavily.

"There was only one of those," said Crabbe. "She only made one. She said she'd lost it." The music tinkled on, a gay brief satire on Scarlatti or Galuppi. "You stole it, you stole it from her!"

Costard gazed at Crabbe, his plump English face a mask of loathing. "So it was you, was it?" he said. "You were the man. You the bloody murderer."

"What do you know about it? What's it to do with you?"

"You saved your own bloody skin, didn't you? You let her drown. I know it all, I know the whole filthy story. You wanted to be rid of her, didn't you? Why couldn't you tell her like a man? I wanted her. I wanted her, do you hear?"

"No," said Crabbe. "No, no, no. It's not true. It can't be true. She would have told me. There weren't any secrets."

"Oh yes, there was one. That she loathed your guts. That she was going to be with me. With me. For ever, do you hear? Only a week after that happened. I know it

all, you bloody murderer. You came home once a fortnight. You'd no particular wish to be with her, but you
wouldn't let her go."

"There was no room there. It was after the war. The
housing shortage. I had to be where my job was. It was
the only thing I could do. I didn't mean it. God knows
I didn't mean it. I tried to save her."

"Driving like a bloody lunatic on an icy road."

"I know, I know, I know. It was an accident. An accident. I lost control, the car went over, into the river. I
tried to save her. I've suffered enough. Christ, I've suffered
enough."

"Only a week after that we were going to go away. We
were going to be together." The merry piano tinklings
were gone. Scratchings, a soft click, then the 'Hebrides'
Overture started. Costard sat down lumpily. "Oh, I know
it's all over," he said. "Nearly ten years."

"I never knew. She never told me."

"We kept our secret well. I never even came for her in
the car. We always met in town." He sat, his pudgy hands
clasped, tears in his eyes, the corners of his mouth droop-
ing, the large brown schoolboy knees grotesquely irrele-
vant, almost indecent in this context of mature anguish.
"I loved her." Then Costard murmured her name.

"How dare you!" cried Crabbe. Feebly, tottering on his
numb foot, he made for Costard, a hand up for slapping.
Costard gripped Crabbe's wrist powerfully. "No, you
don't," said Costard. "You're a liar and a coward and a
murderer. You wouldn't even tell me your real name."
His grip loosened and his hand dropped. "Yes, that was
his name. She always said Victor. And she said she
wouldn't have to change her monogram. Poor girl. Poor,
poor little girl."

"You," said Crabbe, standing with limp arms at his

sides. "It's all lies. She loved me. There was never any-body else. You're making it all up. You've dreamed it all. None of it's true."

Costard looked up gravely. "It's true," he said. "And to think that it had to be here, eight thousand miles away. Eight thousand miles and the first man I meet in this bloody place. You've poisoned it for me. Poisoned it for me on my first day. My second day," he amended, then put his heavy head into cupped hands. "Oh, God, God."

Crabbe stood limp, his numb foot somehow bearing him. The blood of realisation of what all this meant had not yet flowed into his arteries. "I'd better go," he said.

"Yes, go, go!"

"But I still can't understand."

"Get out, go on, get out!"

"I mean, I was bound to have suspected. She just didn't do that sort of thing. And with a man like you."

Costard looked up. "A man like me," he said slowly. "What do you mean?"

"She couldn't. It's just impossible."

Costard rose. "A man who could give her a bit of love. A man who was straight and honest. Not a dithering bloody would-be intellectual. You're cheap. Cheap educa-tion, cheap ideas, a half-baked bloody nobody. You didn't deserve her. Go on, get out before I throw you out. Get back to bloody town." Crabbe picked up his stick from the side of the chair. His bag was in the hall. "A man with a body. A man with blood. A man with something to give. Get out." Slowly Crabbe traversed the half-acre of parquet floor. "A man with an education. A man with a bloody family background," Costard was shouting. "Go on. Get to that bloody launch. They'll take you back. Tambi! Tambi!" he called. "I'll get those bloody boat-men." Crabbe moved on, still many yards from the door.

"You don't know what love means!" called Costard, in a voice like a loud-hailer. "Your type never do!" Crabbe reached the hall. With some difficulty he inched down the steps, hearing Costard calling still and, feeble behind the manly voice, the voice of the pack-leader, a hundred wind and strings playing the *Tannhäuser* Overture.

In the open air, under the afternoon blast furnace in the empty blue, Crabbe stood, saying quietly: "She just couldn't do that. It's all a trick. He's mad, that's it. That wasn't her piece on the gramophone. It was something like it. We're talking of two different people. I'll go back and we'll talk quietly and everything will come right." He turned, thought of the weary stairs, the miles of parquet. It was too far. Too far for this foot. He moved on over lawn, past swimming-pool, orderly trees and flower-beds. Tamil gardeners showed him friendly teeth. The path turned, past wilder trees, towards the landing-stage.

Vythilingam saw a white man coming and hid himself. There were plenty of bushes. He had not been to see the cattle and the goats and the chickens. He had been sitting, his black bag at his side, trying to think, looking at the river, wondering if that jungle beyond could really take him, wondering if that jungle really held his duty. With only the mildest interest he saw Crabbe approach the waiting launch. There was nobody else about. Crabbe looked left and right, leaning on his stick. Jungle, river and sky.

Vythilingam saw Crabbe try to board the launch. He put his foot clumsily on the gunwale. The foot seemed to crumple underneath him. Still carrying his stick and his bag, he faltered in the air for an instant and fell. Vythilingam saw water, green and white, shoot up long fingers of protest as a weight crashed the surface. He heard faint human noises, and then animal noises, and, hearing the animal noises, he rose to his feet in compassion. He stood undecided. And then, as noise subsided and the river settled and the launch moved in again, he sat down on the grass once more. Human lives were not his professional concern. Humanity? Yes, humanity, but humanity was altogether a different matter. He sat for a time thinking about humanity, seeing the great abstractions move and wave in the fronds of the jungle over the river.

10

Mr. Liversedge always chewed gum quietly and imperceptibly on the bench. If anyone in court did perceive that gentle rolling of the jaws, they might well take it for an easing-in of new dentures or a symptom of mild tropical neurasthenia. In any case, it didn't matter. This was the East, where much was allowed that would be inadmissible in the Antipodes. Mr. Liversedge, born in Toowoomba, educated in Brisbane, was a tough common-sensical Queenslander who saw the whole ridiculous Oriental *susah* in true proportion. Here men would murder for five dollars, here men would seek divorce because their wives sighed at the handsomeness of the film star P. Ramlee, here the very night-roaming dogs screamed blue murder if another dog bit their little toe. Mr. Liversedge chewed, nodding at the lucid exposition of Mr. Lim from Penang, though contemning inwardly the Pommie accent, chewing more roundly with a twitch of the nose at the rhetoric of the Tamils, especially that Tamil with a voice like a bloody sheila, and the clipped incoherencies of the police. He gave swift judgment.

"A lot of fuss about nothing. Here you have a few boys who want a bit of adventure. Where are they going to get it? At least, they're not mooning in the cinema every night, hanging round the coffee-shops. They showed initiative. They meant no real harm. Look at these knives, which the police call deadly weapons." Mr. Liversedge took one of the rusting exhibits. "This wouldn't cut butter when it's hot. Look at the point. You couldn't harm a fly with it." The four defendants hated Mr. Liversedge for these words. This, then, was British justice. "They stole nothing. The pair of trousers was recovered. If boys want to steal, they'll steal more than a dirty baggy pair of trousers." Maniam blushed. He had not been able to obtain a change of clothes from Pahang. "In this state there's real villainy going on, in the jungle, in the villages, and a lot of people who should know better are aiding and abetting it. But don't pick on a handful of harmless boys who are looking for an innocent bit of amusement. Don't waste our time. We've bigger things to do." The four boys pumped up their hate to hissing steam. Harmless, quotha. Innocent, forsooth. "The case is dismissed. But I'd like to warn these boys." Warning, warn. They were being warned; that was better. "Like to warn them to find a better outlet for their spare energy and love of adventure. Join some bigger organisation. The Boy Scouts, for instance." The four young Malays froze in horror. "And I'd like to add that it's really the responsibility of this State to provide some kind of spare-time activity for young men of energy and initiative who otherwise might be tempted into adventure which, however harmless, might be construed by people old enough to know better as . . ." He read from the sheet ironically ". . . attempted murder, theft, assault with battery and heaven knows what. All right, hurry up with the next case."

The Malay interpreter worked swiftly, condensing Mr. Liversedge's already condensed judgment into a few packed, flavoursome idioms. Mr. Liversedge chewed gum amiably, looking round at the gay spectators, the protagonists making ready to go, Maniam and Lim both watching the time anxiously, both having planes to catch.

Outside the court Syed Omar, in collar, tie and jacket, clapped his son hard on the back. "You heard what he said," he said. "He said that the Tamils only got what was coming to them. He said, in effect, that it is time the Malays chewed up the Tamils, and, by implication of course, the Chinese. For many years I have inveighed against British justice. Now I feel that there is something in it after all. Though, of course, this *hakim* is an Australian, which makes some difference. They have suffered under the yoke of the English. Perhaps that division ought to be made clear."

"He never said that about the Tamils," protested Syed Hassan. "I can understand some English."

"You have to read between the lines," said his father. "They are not so direct as us. They say a lot by implication. You saw the look he flashed on the Tamils, rolling his jaws in dislike. However, thank God, it is over. Now we can concentrate on our normal worries. Getting jobs, for instance. Borrowing money, for instance. Wait, the bail. That money will now go back to Crabbe. There is definitely one man I can borrow off."

"There he goes now," said Hamzah. "The Tamil, off to the airport. His nose is still swollen, but he has been a long time away from Pahang. He has to go back some-time."

Syed Omar grinned viciously at the sight of the dis-comfited Arumugam, Sundralingam and Maniam getting into Sundralingam's car. Then he opened his mouth in the shock of remembering that he had forgotten some-thing. "My God," he said. "Yusof. There he is. There is Yusof." He saw 'Che Yusof, his former colleague, most clerkly in horn-rims and neat receding hair, getting into a small Austin car with his daughter, the daughter that, so Syed Omar had definitely at last learned, though only indirectly, having many times been ejected from the office where he had formerly worked, where he had given to the Department his blood and sweat for many years, was now occupying his desk, showing smiling teeth and a brown bosom to the C.P.O. in the intervals of typing reports, letters and memoranda. "My God," said Syed Omar. He saw Mr. Lim from Penang, Anglicanly elegant, climbing into the Hillman that the firm used on this side of the peninsula, a Malay driver closing the door smartly after him. "Stop!" called Syed Omar. "Stop! I am coming with you!"

"Don't be a fool, Father."

"He has already made me a fool, that bastard. Wait!" called Syed Omar. He was at the car window, saying to the astonished Mr. Lim: "Follow that car, that Austin. Quick, it is a matter of urgency."

"Really," said Lim Cheng Po. "Really. I have to get to the airport. I have a plane to catch."

"That's where he is going," said Syed Omar. "I know. He is going to drink beer at the bar. It will be bitter beer for him."

"No," said Mr. Lim. "If you're going to start any more of your nonsense, you can't expect me to help you. Find your own way."

"It is all one can expect from a Chinese," called Syed Omar after the departing car. "The Chinese are our enemies. Curse you, you yellow-skinned bastard." Then he called: "Taxi!" Ashamed, Syed Hassan shepherded his friends away. "To Loo's place," he said. "He invited us all to go there for a drink if we got off."

"He? A Chinese?"

"He's all right."

Syed Omar, though unable to pay the fare, gave the driver of the taxi lordly instructions. 'Che Yusof's car, like Sundralingam's and Lim Cheng Po's, was already long away, churning up dust in the rainless weather. The taxi coughed and shook at the tail of the procession. But, realised Syed Omar, as he sat back against a naked cushion spring and took off his tie and opened his shirt for action, there was no hurry. Nobody could get away. He hoped there would be a fair-sized crowd at the airport, enough people to justify the expense of all his dramatic talents, the energy of his blows. Cool air blew in from the open window. They cruised gently along, the road to themselves. Then the driver said, as they approached an attap coffee-stand on the outskirts of the village midway between town and airport:

"I need cigarettes. Pay me half my fare now and I can buy them." He was a sly, hard, thin man of Syed Omar's age, a man who had suffered much in his time from wives and no money. He had been already five years paying for his taxi.

"When we arrive," said Syed Omar. "Not before. Come on, we have little time to lose."

"Half the fare. A dollar."

"You will have the whole fare when we arrive."

"Show me your money. I suspect that you haven't any." A hard life had taught him much.

"Insolence," said Syed Omar. "It's your job to drive me to wherever I say. Who are you to start inquiring insolently into the financial position of your betters?"

The taxi was now parked by the attap coffee-stand. The driver looked forward to a leisurely altercation. "What do you mean, betters? I have a job and you haven't. I don't believe you have two cents to rub together." He leaned an arm comfortably over the driver's seat. The heat beat in, the breeze of motion gone.

"Allah most high," swore Syed Omar. "I will argue with

you another time. Your job now is not to argue but to get me to the airport. That's what I am paying you for."

"I doubt if I'll see many signs of paying."

"I am of the line of the Prophet. That's what my name Syed means, though probably you're too ignorant to know that. I have my honour, and you are impugning my honour. When I take a thing I always pay for it. Now, come on, quickly. The airport."

"Let's see the colour of your money."

"You'll see the colour of my fist if you don't do what I say."

"Fighting words, eh? Well, now, I'm really frightened." The driver grinned, showing few teeth, but those golden. "You must have a lot of muscle hidden underneath that flab."

"I refuse to argue further with you. Do your job and you will be paid at the end of it. But you've been so insolent that you certainly won't get a tip."

"Ha, that's a good one. No tip, he says. No fare either."

"Look," said Syed Omar, "I'll go over there and get you cigarettes with my own hands. Will that satisfy you?"

"You won't get any credit here. They know your kind."

"My kind. By God!" Syed Omar began to beat the hard shoulder of the driver. "Go on. Do what I say. If you don't, I'll report you. I'll report you to the police, to the Town Board, to the Mentri Besar. Do your job, damn you."

At the sound of the hard word *chelaka*, the driver said: "Out. Go on, out. You can walk the rest of the way. You can be thankful that I've taken you half of the way for nothing."

"Take me back to town, then."

"Not likely. Go on, out." The man got out of his own seat and opened the door for Syed Omar. "The airport's

213

in that direction," he said, "if you don't already know."

"By God," said Syed Omar, "you'll suffer for this." He got out, and squared up to the driver, but the driver laughed gaily and skipped back to his seat. He switched on, put the groaning vehicle into gear, turned it round skilfully and sped dustily townwards. Syed Omar shook his fist repeatedly. Meanwhile, the old woman who kept the coffee-stand sucked her gums and shook her head at the follies of the modern world.

Syed Omar began to walk to the airport. Sweat pearled his tough brown skin, his fat bounced in rhythm. No car passed for him to flag. Nay, but a car did, coming from the airport, an Austin with a known and hated number— PP 197—and in the car 'Che Yusof and his daughter. The daughter waved and smiled. Syed Omar danced on the hot road. He had now passed the point of no return: the airport was a mile away, the town nearly three miles. He walked on, reaching an airport silver with sun on the waiting plane's body, silver glancing from the glass of the control tower, cars parked. The plane, whose tortuous route accommodated both Pahang and Penang passengers, was late taking off. Perhaps the Sultan's name was on the manifest and His Highness, aware that he was above schedules and the law, was still dawdling over early curry in the Istana. But no, there were instructions to passengers now crackling through the loudspeakers and, as Syed Omar came near to the airfield, he could see the thin string of people, turning often to smile and wave, already filing towards the air-hostess in the hole in the huge silver body. And here, as Syed Omar limped into the waiting-hall, were two Tamils saying good-bye to one other, embracing, slapping, hand-pumping, one with a girl's voice piping high in most cordial valedictory emotion. Then Maniam, his nose not too red or swollen, almost, in fact, presentable to his masters in Pahang, joined the waving file, smiling back sadly. Syed Omar broke through the gentle cordon of white-clad Chinese officials. "A last-minute message," he improvised. "From the police. Very urgent." Maniam was the last of the embarking line. Syed Omar dived at him, bowled him over on the asphalt in view of the smiling wavers, the shining plane, the hot indifferent sun, and said:

"It was all your fault." He knelt on Maniam and hit various parts of his face. Maniam wailed. "You started it all." One on the chest. "We were happy till you came." But now the officials were timidly interfering, and others were coming languidly to the scene, and even the police discussed this violence as possibly coming within the scope of their terms of reference. Syed Omar gave Maniam one good knuckling in the eye and was led off, not unsatisfied, saying: "He started it all. He put the idea of treachery into everybody's head." Meanwhile Maniam, disfigured, wailed forlornly.

"This time," sighed Sundralingam, "he had better stay in your house. I've done my share. You'd better get a bed made up for him."

"No room," squealed Arumugam. "You know there's no room."

"Vythilingam, then. It's time Vythilingam did something. Dear, dear, what a mess."

But days passed, and Vythilingam did not return. In any case, Sundralingam had forgotten that Mrs. Smith and the wealthy orphan called Chelvanajaky were already installed in Vythilingam's quarters (his predecessor had been a married man: there were rooms enough, though not now room for Maniam), Mrs. Smith herself sweeping out the corners, ordering the Siamese servant to scrub (whereupon he gave in his notice), planning tasty meals for her son's return. And then mysterious news about Crabbe began to leak through many crevices and, in the manner of the East, news about Vythilingam was inferred from the external accidents of Vythilingam and Crabbe's being in the same boat, going to the same place, both disappearing at the same time. More, there were signatures left in river and on river-bank, or near it—a black bag nearly empty of medicaments, a floating stick and overnight satchel containing, among other things, a shoe. The lizards, before fleeting off, had left their tails in the clutching hand of the upper air. Bodies, it was well-known, were near-irrecoverable in that river of deep-set weeds. Nobody felt inclined to give orders to drag: let the river keep them.

"It is clear what happened," said Sundralingam, while Mrs. Smith sat dumbly but not over-sadly, for this was the East. "Your son was heroic. He dived in after this Mr. Crabbe, and Mr. Crabbe himself dragged him to his death, or else both were caught in the weeds. It is sad, but life has to go on. And, for us Hindus, death is not an end but a fresh beginning. I do not need to remind you of that, Mrs. Smith. Your son is already reincarnated. We do not know, of course, in what form. It would be pleasant to think that he was now one of the little animals being treated at this moment in his own dispensary, though, of course, his assistant will not be treating it very well. Or perhaps he is born again as some great future politician, some saviour of his people. But he always said there was more virtue in dumb animals than in some human beings. And he was, you will remember, himself very nearly dumb."

"All my plans disarranged," said Mrs. Smith. Her voice was curiously deep and compelling, unlike the pretty bird-song of so many of the women of her race. Her voice was the voice of some competent chairman of a ladies' social guild, as her handsome and bulky person, with its rich *sari*, was apt for the heart of a group photograph in a local Ceylon newspaper. "I had hoped so much," she said. "Perhaps I am very deeply to blame for being out of touch with him for so long. But I wrote letters, I tried to arrange marriages. I had my own commitments, you see. One cannot do everything. But," she sighed, "perhaps I can make amends in another life. He needed his mother, perhaps, more than we shall ever know. I do not think he was too happy. Men only do brave and desperate things when they are not too happy, and this thing was brave and desperate. What was this Englishman to him, anyway?"

"He was just an Englishman," shrugged Sundralingam. "But your son would save the life of a rat or a toad if he could. I think it quite likely that he would try to save an Englishman."

To those who doubted that Crabbe and Vythilingam— one or other or both—were dead, Sundralingam said: "Look at the facts. Both have disappeared. People have to disappear somewhere. The river is the obvious place."

"There is the jungle. They could both have taken to the jungle."

"Well, yes," Sundralingam would say. "I think Crabbe possibly might go and join the Communists. A Tamil gentleman named Jaganathan—a gentleman who worked with Crabbe in Dahaga, whom I met in Kuala Lumpur— said that he had strong Communist leanings. Again, he may have embezzled cash or taken many bribes and now be over the border in Thailand with his ill-gotten gains. One cannot be sure. But Vythilingam is certainly dead. You can be quite sure of that." And then Sundralingam would spend a cosy evening with Mrs. Smith and Chelvanajaky, while Arumugam fretted jealously, aware of what Sundralingam was after, aware, as Sundralingam was aware, that, owing to the economic recession, fathers were cutting dowries by as much as fifty per cent and that here was a pleasingly shy and not unpersonable girl whose dowry could never be cut.

But there were men, white, whose word could naturally be relied on, who were prepared to ease the work of the police so far as Crabbe's disappearance was concerned. The Independence celebrations were coming, contingents of police had to be drilled and blancoed and starched before proceeding to Kuala Lumpur to represent the state. Crabbe's disappearance, if pursued to the point of river-dredging or keeping a file open till the body bobbed up down-stream, would mean overmuch trouble at this busy time. And so the Malay C.P.O. listened, with a Tertullian willingness to believe, to the white men's stories.

George Costard said that the boatmen, reporting to their launch for the afternoon down-stream voyage, found a stick and a bag floating, and one said he saw bubbles, and the other could not swear to it but thought he saw a hand come up and grasp at air for the last time. Costard had no doubt that Crabbe had accidentally or, for all he knew, not so accidentally drowned. He added that he had been forced to tell his coolies that this white man had deliberately taken his own life to compensate, by obscure logic, for the death of Yogam the Tamil schoolmaster—a white for a black, a restoration of the balance of life. Otherwise there would be a tendency for them to think that a sudden and unexpected death was a bad augury for the prosperity of the estate under its new manager. Small shrines were already in existence in the coolie lines, dedicated to the spirit of the man with the strange name, and offerings of crayfish (in default of saltier crustaceans) were already being made. This would not last long, however. The tiny cult would be swallowed up in the bigger ones, probably on the next Hindu feast-day. The point was that Costard's first duty, as the C.P.O. would realise, had to be to the estate and the company that owned it. Thank you, Mr. Costard.

"A nice chap," said Tommy Jones, promoting thirst in the State capital, "but a bit queer. Didn't know his name at the time, of course, but met him on the train going to Tikus, and we had a sort of night out together, though neither of us did anything really. He said he'd been told that it was up-river that he'd conk out sometime or other, and I got the idea that he wasn't all that keen on carrying on, he wouldn't mind snuffing it all that much. But I didn't pay too much attention because you don't really when a bloke talks that way. Met too many of them in my line of business. Still, he was a bit low because his wife was a bit too brainy for him or something. Anyway, she'd been writing poetry about him in some paper or other, a paper that didn't much go for putting flowers on dogs' graves, I do at least remember that bit. That made him a bit down in the mouth. He didn't seem himself the next morning either, kept talking about the Prophet Mohammed inventing beer or some such story. A bit crackers, I thought. He travelled with a pig in a Land-Rover."

The C.P.O., sophisticated by an education at a British Police College, pretended to be scandalised. He tut-tutted at the crimes: self-murder, blasphemy, perversion.

Moneypenny's simple testimony was much appreciated at Police Headquarters. "I knew something like that would happen to him. He laughed at a butterfly."

Anyway, there was little trouble about writing Crabbe off. Crabbe was dead. His death, though little mourned, was resented by a few. Rosemary felt that he might have, sooner or later, introduced her to somebody eligible, or, perhaps in an ultimate weariness matching hers, have been tossed legitimately to her breast. Robert Loo felt, in a way, let down, for Crabbe had promised much and fulfilled little. And Syed Omar remembered something about the possibility of a situation in the Education Department, now not likely to be realised. The white man lies, or dies, or goes away, or forgets. Moreover, money cannot be borrowed from a dead man. Crabbe's cook-boy had some weeks of unemployment, which was rather a nuisance. Lim Cheng Po said an Anglican prayer or two, not too perfunctorily. The Malay whom Crabbe had been training to take over his job now took over his job with trumpets and cocktails, finding it convenient to blame missing letters and mislaid files on a defunct infidel. And the great golden day of Independence approached.

Flowers and Jalil in Rosemary's house. And on Rosemary's desk a letter hardly begun, the two words 'My dear' becoming blurred in the damp heat.

"Now," wheezed Jalil in asthmatic triumph, "who you marry? I tell you nobody left. Only me marry."

"Oooooh, go away, Jalil, you're filthy, you're horrible, I wouldn't marry you if you were the last man on earth. And I told the amah not to let you in. Oh, what lovely flowers." Cats stalked, sniffed, inspected.

"I last man on earth. You marry me."

Rosemary looked at him. "I've too much respect for myself. You with three wives already and me sleeping in the spare room."

"I sleep there too."

"Horrible, horrible pig of a man."

"You want marry European? I European, I sick man of Europe. You want marry Asian? I Asian too. I anything you want."

"I don't want a man with three wives."

"I divorce other wives. Divorce one every day. In three days I bachelor."

"And then it'll start all over again. I know. Me thrown out on the streets, a divorced woman. You're horrible."

"We go Istanbul. My brother part shares in hotel in Beyoglu. Make jolly time."

"Where's Istanbul?"

"Old name Constantinople." Jalil managed the many syllables with surprising smoothness. He was really no fool. "Big town, very big. Bazaars, many shops, hotels big too. Can eat, drink, make jolly time."

"Oh, I don't know," said Rosemary. "I don't know what I want. It can't be like London, can it? I mean, it's neither one thing nor the other, is it? I mean, London's every-thing, isn't it?" Jalil did not understand, but he smiled with faint encouragement and a heaving chest. And now Rosemary saw films unwind swiftly in her head, a montage of the mysterious Orient which she had never visited, an Orient purged of hoicking Chinese in underpants, an Orient without a Public Works Department, an Orient visited by Europeans wearing white tuxedos not bought on an initial outfit allowance. Glamour, romance, cock-tails by a shining evening river. Could Jalil sustain the part?

"You're not a Christian," she said.

"I be anything," said Jalil. "In Turkey can be anything. Kemal Ataturk he make that happen."

"Oh, I don't know, I don't know."

"We go K.L. for *Merdeka*," said Jalil. "I book room in hotel."

"Oh yes, yes," enthused Rosemary. "Oh, yes, that *is* a good idea. Rooms," she amended primly.

"Room. Rooms. It same thing." Jalil was above accidence.

But room it had to be. Kuala Hantu, clean and freshly made-up, the dirtier natives, like skin blemishes, hidden from the eyes of visitors, Kuala Hantu, self-consciously prancing and crowing in its new-found metropolitan glory, Kuala Hantu could only find them one room in a hotel on Batu Road. That, anyway, was Jalil's story. "It ɔɔ good go anywhere else," he said, as the taxi-driver pulled their luggage from the boot. "No good to look. I know. We stay here." A ragged Malay child greeted them as they made for the hotel entrance, begging for the odd ten cents. His eyes were intelligent, and he had the im- memorial Malay curiosity about prices and relationships. "He your father," he announced. Jalil chuckled ironically.

But it was worth it—the double bed, Jalil's deep wheezy sleep—for the sake of those few glamour-brimming days. In a shower of rain the tape to a shining-new free land was cut, the keys of authority handed over. And the full- throated cries of *"Merdeka!"* Even Rosemary joined in, though her woman's eyes were really on the so-sweet clothes of the Duchess of Gloucester. Nobody said what Crabbe had once ironically said: that Karl Marx's real name was Mordeca and might well carry the same Arabic transliteration as the slogan that had brought the Alliance to power (without, which so many thought a good sign, opposition). One cynic, a Malay trumpet-player who had once played in a Singapore orchestra under a French leader, would only shout the first syllable. Rosemary heard him quite distinctly and wondered why.

And the men, oh, the men. So many strong and hand- some Europeans, impeccably dressed. To Rosemary's sur- prise, Jalil turned out to be a member of the Selangor Club, and he took her there twice to dine and drink. He merely chuckled to himself when the men flocked round, much taken with her dark beauty, standing her drinks and showing fine teeth in social laughter, for it was Jalil who took her back to the double bed.

"Oooooh, wasn't he wonderful, Jalil, that man with the little moustache, Alan, and the other man, the fair one, called Geoffrey, and that very nice elderly man, Peter or Paul or something? He said he'd take me away with him any time for a week-end and he's got pots and pots of money. And that man standing just by you, the fat one, that was Sir Ronald Somebody-or-other. Oooooh, Jalil, it was just like London."

"You go sleep. I tired now."

Independence achieved and celebrated, everybody went back to work. "Many people," said the Chinese leader-writer in the *Singapore Bugle,* "many people seem to con-sider independence as licensed irresponsibility. Nothing could be further from the truth. We must all, the Malays especially, put our shoulders to the wheel and prove our-selves worthy of the great gift of freedom and self-determination. The clerks in the offices, the coolies on the rubber estates, tin-miners, fisher-folk and paddy-planters, have had their brief hour of rejoicing and now must buckle down to the hard tasks ahead. There have been too many false promises made by politicians to ignorant members of the *ra'ayat,* promises about there being no further need to work once the British disgorged the wealth they had stolen from the sons of the soil. Now perhaps those promises are being seen for what they are—mere straws and bubbles in the wind of self-advancement." And so on. But few people read the leaders. Nobody worked any harder, though few worked (which a cynic might allege to be impossible) less hard.

But the Communists in the jungle buckled to and put their shoulders to the wheel. Independence meant little:

the capitalists had been at their tricks again. In at least one state the Communists redoubled their attacks on villages, their ambushings of motorists, their decapitations and guttings of the jackals of the rubber-sucking white parasites, and sometimes of the parasites themselves. It was grossly unfair to suggest, however, as Syed Omar once suggested, that this was because Vythilingam had gone over to the rebels. But the independent Government of the Federation of Malaya acted promptly. *"Il faut en finir,"* said a Malay minister. So into at least one state troops poured, a battalion of decent National Service lads, to continue to carry, posthumously as it must be supposed, the White Man's Burden. The more subtle warfare of ideas was carried on by the Information Department and by certain American organisations which did heroic—and voluntary—work. There was more to it than just ideas, of course. The library of the United States Information Service contained plenty of good clean non-ideological books, in Chinese, English and Malay, and—better still— provided an air-conditioned refuge from the day's heat, much appreciated by workless illiterates. Temple Haynes knew a good deal about the organic processes of speech and gave to Arumugam virtually a new voice. It happened this way: Arumugam inveighed against British injustice (retrospectively, it should be presumed) at a drunken farewell dinner for somebody or other. Temple Haynes, enjoying a cool lager at a table away from the party, heard him and was clinically interested. Arumugam sped homewards from the party, drunk, on his new motor-cycle and crashed rather badly. It was by fortunate chance that Temple Haynes was cruising in his van shortly after the crash and found Arumugam moaning in his blood. Temple Haynes got Malay assistance from a near-by attap house and took Arumugam to hospital. All the time that

Arumugam lay under harsh lights on the table in the casualty ward he moaned: "I am dying. I did not mean what I said about the British. You are an Englishman. I am sorry," in a high voice that seemed to Haynes proleptically cherubic.

"I'm not an Englishman," said Haynes. "Take it easy now. You'll be all right soon." A fierce-looking Malay hospital assistant was stitching away at Arumugam's scalp; another Malay, gentler but less efficient, was swabbing Arumugam's body-wounds with dirty water.

"Forgive me just the same," said Arumugam. "Forgive me before I die."

"You're not going to die."

"Oh yes, I must, I must." Arumugam rolled large eyes under the lights. "I have spoken against the British. A British motor-cycle has had its revenge." He was still very drunk.

"Take it easy now. I've spoken against the British myself."

While Arumugam was convalescing in a Division Two Officers' ward, Haynes came often with gifts of candy and copies of *Life* and *Time*. Arumugam was enchanted to learn that the Americans had once actually fought the British and defeated them. He told Haynes about the sufferings of the Jaffna Tamils under the British yoke and Haynes told him about the Boston Tea Party. And then Haynes quietly insinuated certain therapeutic measures into their chatty intercourse, asking Arumugam to read aloud and suggesting certain approaches to the use of the voice. Soon, surprisingly soon, the articles in *Life* and the waspish biographies of *Time* were rolled out in a manly music which Arumugam at first refused to believe his own.

"I see now," boomed Arumugam. "It was psychological.

The British forced me to be a slave, and that voice was the voice of a slave. A slave," he added, "whose birthright had been cut off. We have both suffered," he said, "you and I, our two nations. Now we are men, not slaves. You have made a man of me." His devotion to Haynes became considerable, and Haynes's work in certain quarters was made easy. And at Sundralingam's wedding Arumugam, as best man, could hardly be persuaded to stop making speeches. He even sang a song called 'In Cellar Cool' from the *Indian Students' Song-book*.

One evening Syed Hassan and Idris and Azman and Hamzah were sitting in Loo's shop. All wore a costume suggestive of a more tranquil and prosperous age than this —Dame Clara Butt singing, in a voice not quite so deep as Arumugam's, 'Land of Hope and Glory', the gold squeezed from tropical helots enhancing the upper-class comforts of a cold climate. Their costumes were not suitable for Malayan heat, but they were stoics prepared to suffer for smartness and conformity. To their interest and joy three soldiers of the Royal Barsets came in, and they were wearing this identical uniform of drainpipe trousers and serge waisted jacket and boot-lace tie.

They strutted to the bar, bringing their plentiful back-hair behind them. "Here, John," said one of the new-comers to Robert Loo. "Give us three beers." Robert Loo looked up distractedly from his music. "And stand to attention when a corporal's talkin' to yer," added the man jocularly. This disguised corporal then turned lordly to survey the other customers and caught sight of Syed Hassan and his friends. "Cor," he said. "Ted's 'ere too. Oo'd 'ave thought we'd meet nigger Teds?" He greeted the four Malay boys cordially and, without invitation, brought his fresh-faced party of two to their table. "More chairs, John," he called to one of Robert Loo's brothers. "We're goin' ter sit 'ere."

"What is a Ted?" asked Hamzah shyly.

"Speak English, do yer? A Ted's what you are. Teds is what we are. Teddy boys. Edwardian strutters was what they used to call 'em in the old days. Cor, flamin' 'ot in 'ere. Turn up that fan, John, will yer?"

"Why do they call you that?" asked Hassan. He found difficulty in following much of the corporal's English, but, not doubting that this was *echt* English, began to feel resentment towards those English masters of his who had taught him English. It was colonial English they had taught him, that was it. But he would soon learn this new, free, democratic English.

"Why? Because we go back to the good old days, see, when there was none of this bleedin' nonsense. No wars and what not. Beer a penny a gallon and that. Bleedin' sight more than that 'ere. 'Ere, gizza bit er music, John. What you lads goin' to 'ave?"

The Malay boys now drank beer for the first time in their lives. It was itself, as Crabbe had once said, a language. Robert Loo, at his father's behest, gave the new customers a free gift of juke-box music. He himself listened to the brave harmonics of saxophones and brass, the sedative drum-beat, not without a minimal physical tingling. Syed Hassan winked at him; he winked back—stiffly, however, not being used to such social gestures.

But there now started a sodality that was to prove more fruitful in promoting inter-racial harmony than any of Crabbe's vague dreams. Wandering down the street one night, the seven of them, they came across a Tamil youth in Edwardian costume. "Wotcher, Sambo," said the corporal. "You doin' anythin'?" And later there were two

Chinese boys who joined the gang, and one of these, whose name was Philip Aloysius Tan, swiftly became the gang-leader. The corporal was good-humoured about it, glad to see it: after all, the days of British rule were over.

For Rosemary the days of glorious expectation had returned. There was a lieutenant-colonel in the town, majors, captains, raw conscript lieutenants. Jalil? "The unspeakable Turk should be immediately struck out of the question." (Letter from Carlyle to Howard, 24th November, 1876, as Crabbe might have verified from his books had Crabbe still been alive and his books not on their way home to his widow.) Jalil was not a gentleman. Colonel Richman was, so was Major Anstruther, so were Captains Tickell and Forsyth. Lieutenants Creek, Looker, Jones, Dwyer? Callow, guffawish, no longer her meat. Major Anstruther was unmarried, a good dancer, skilled in the arts of love. He had a neat square face, hair greying neatly, a neat broad body, a voice and accent like Lim Cheng Po's. To Rosemary he was England—fog, primroses, Shaftesbury Avenue, South Kensington Tube Station, the Antelope and the Captain's Cabin, the downstairs bar of the Café Royal, Kew in lilac-time; only occasionally Crewe at 3 a.m., Stoke-on-Trent on a Sunday, the smells of Warrington. She was, you might say, in love again.

There was something for everybody in the new dispensation. Syed Omar was given a van with a left-hand drive and a salary of two hundred dollars a month. (Malayan dollars, not American dollars, though at the end of his first month he had sworn to his employers that he had thought it would be American dollars, else he would not have taken the job on. He was promised an increase in the near future.) On this van was painted a picture of an eagle shaking claws with a tiger, symbolic of new friendship between two free peoples. In this van were stacked, weekly, copies of a newspaper printed in the most beautiful Arabic script, called *Suara Amerika* (The Voice of America.) This newspaper had to be delivered to humble kampong folk who else would know nothing of events in the great world outside. Few of them could read, however. Still, they welcomed Syed Omar's appearances and treated him to fresh toddy and simple curries, and they never tired of laughing at the picture of the eagle shaking claws with the tiger.

Syed Omar did quite a profitable side-line selling *Suara Amerika* to various shops in the towns as wrapping-paper. But, to do justice to his loyalty, he always took a copy of the paper home with him and read extracts to his wives about the private affairs of film stars. They liked this. In the evenings too, when he was in, Syed Hassan gave his father English lessons. The two got on quite well together now, especially as Syed Hassan had a job with prospects: he was fifth driver to the Sultan and occasionally had the thrill of running the new Cadillac round town.

Robert Loo was one day summoned to the United States Information Service building. This had formerly been the British Residency: the Americans paid a generous rent to the Sultan for its use. Robert Loo was cordially greeted by two youngish American gentlemen who expressed interest in his music. He was taken to a music-room whose air-conditioning made him shiver, and he was asked to sit down at the tropicalised Bechstein and play some of his works. Robert Loo smiled.

"I'm not a pianist," he said. "I'm a composer."

"You can't play the piano at all?"

"No."

"Well, how do you know what your music sounds like?"

"I hear it in my head."

"Well, then, perhaps you'd be good enough to leave some of your manuscripts with us."

"I've not very much," said Robert Loo. "I destroyed a lot of my early work. There was a symphony and a string quartet. They were immature, so I destroyed them."

"What have you, then?"

"This." Robert Loo took from his case the score of a brief work. "This," he said, "is a Legend for Piano and Orchestra."

"Legend, eh?"

"I call it that. I don't know why." Robert Loo smiled nervously.

"Well, leave it with us, and we'll call you back in a couple of days."

Robert Loo was duly called back and treated kindly. "You know all the tricks," they said. "It's very competent. You've obviously heard a lot of the better class of film music."

"I never go to the films," said Robert Loo.

"Well, it's a very neat pastiche of the sort of Rachmaninoff film-piano-concerto stuff you used to hear a lot of just after the war."

"Pastiche?" Robert Loo did not know the word.

"Yes. It's funny that you haven't absorbed much of the local musical idioms. Very rich possibilities there. Look what Bartok did, for instance."

"I want to write music from the heart," said Robert Loo.

"Yes? Well, very commendable, I suppose, in its way. Thank you, Mr. Loo. It was very kind of you to give us the opportunity to look at your music." And Robert Loo was kindly dismissed.

Mr. Roget, one of these two gentlemen, wrote a friendly

note to Temple Haynes, who was at the time running a course in the Phonetics of Anglo–American in Kuala Hantu.

Dear Temple,

Joe and I had a look at the music of this Chinese boy that the Englishman told you about before he died. Frankly, I don't think there's much we can do. He's got past the stage of elementary harmony and counterpoint and so on: in fact, he's technically very competent. But it's not technique we're after. We can soon give them the technique. What we want is the indigenous stuff—folk-song and dance, six-tone scales and the rest of it. Our assignment is to study indigenous music and find out some of the real native artists. This Chinese boy has sort of rejected the native stuff (for instance, there's not a trace of the Chinese pentatonic in his work) and turns out very competent imitations of imitations—second-rate cinematic romantic stuff, complete with big Rachmaninoff tunes on the violins and chords banging out on the solo piano. We've heard it all before. We can do it far better ourselves. In fact, we didn't come out these thousands of miles to see a distorted image of ourselves in a mirror. So there it is. Hope the course is going well. Joe and I hope soon to do a bit of travelling round the remoter villages, complete with recording apparatus, of course. A Malay here is proving helpful— Syed Omar, who says he's descended from Mohammed —and he's going to take us around. For a consideration, of course, but what the hell!

Be seeing you,

Harry.

There was a dance in the Officers' Mess. Rosemary sat in her underwear under the fan of the living-room, her bright red dress ready waiting over a chair, wondering whether she ought to go. Tom would be coming round to fetch her in an hour's time (she needed a full hour for her make-up), but, perhaps for the first time in her life, she was in the position of wondering whether she would be doing the right thing in accepting a pleasure. On the floor lay four of her cats ill, definitely ill, and of the other cats some were restless, some listless. She had tried to give the sick cats milk, but they could not keep it down. She had been wiping the floor all day. The amah was frightened and would not come near them. The cats' noses were hot. Tigger, the great malevolent striped creature that normally spent so much time brooding evil and acting evil, lay on his side, his coat matted, his breathing shallow. Rosemary had phoned the Veterinary Department, asking for someone to come, but nobody had come. "Transport," they had said. "No transport. Land-Rover broken down."

"Well, get a taxi, borrow a car, anything. It's urgent."

"Better you bring cats here."

"I can't, I can't. There are too many of them. They're too ill. Please, please come."

"I try."

But nobody had come. Rosemary wondered what to do. Tigger feebly tried to crawl to a corner, there to retch on an empty stomach. Rosemary knew how precarious was the life of any domestic animal in this country, any human animal, for that matter: death came so easily, hardly announced, without apparent cause, often greeted with smiles. It was a fall of rain or of coconuts, part of the pattern. Here there were no myths of struggle between life and death, perhaps because there were no spring and winter myths. But Rosemary, having absorbed so much of the North, wrung her hands and cried and blamed herself. She became superstitious, she half remembered old prayers; she said:

"I know I've done wrong, I know I've sinned, but I've never done any harm to anyone. Please, God, let them get well. I won't drink again, I won't go to dances. I'll be good, honestly I will. I'll never sleep with anyone again, I promise. Please, please let them get well."

Rosemary said a 'Hail Mary' in English and a few words of the 'Confiteor' in Latin. She prayed to St. Anthony—knocking, in her ignorance, at the wrong door—and to the Little Flower. But there was no stir of life from the torpid bodies, and the restless cats mewed and sniffed at the listless cats.

And now a car was heard approaching and now the grinding of brakes. "Oh no," said Rosemary, crossing her arms over her nakedness, "oh no. He's early, he's much too early." And then: "I'll have to fly. I'd better go, I'll have to go, I promised. And that Brigadier's coming to the dance. A gala night. Oh, I'll have to hurry. Perhaps they'll be better when I come back. Oh, God, please make them better, and I won't have more than two drinks. Three," she amended. She rushed into her bedroom to make up. In the bedroom she heard a perfunctory knock and then the front door open. "You're early, Tom," she called. "Get yourself a drink. I shan't be long." And then: "Look at all my poor pussies. I'm worried to death about them." There was no hearty English reply from the living-room, no clink of glass and bottle. "Is that you, Jalil?" she called suspiciously. "I told the amah not to let you in. There's no point in your staying, because I'm going out. So there." But there was no asthmatic wheeze, no invitation to a jolly time. More suspicious still, she put on a wrap and peered round the door. Someone was busy on the floor, leaning tenderly over the sick beasts.

"Oh, Vy," called Rosemary, coming out—un-made-up, hair anyhow—in relief. "Oh, Vy, thank **God** you've come. They heard my prayer. God heard it, St. Anthony heard it. Oh, thank God they heard it. I'll never drink again. I'll say fifteen decades of the Rosary. I'll be good, I promise."

Vythilingam said nothing. Expert with phial and plunger, he worked busily. But once he broke silence to say: "Feline. Feline. Feline enteritis. Kampong cats had it. Disease spreads."

"Oh, bless you, bless you, Vy. While you're doing that, I'll get ready. I'll be late. Tom will be here soon." And she dashed back to her cream-pots and mascara and lipstick. "I knew," she said between lipstick strokes, "that you wouldn't—let me—down." There was no reply. And soon there was a rat-tat-tat and the front door burst heartily open and there was a hearty greeting. "Hello, girl. Where are you, Rosie?" And then: "Oh, I beg your pardon. Didn't see you. Oh, I suppose you're the vet."

"Shan't be a minute, Tom dear," sang Rosemary. "Just doing my hair. Bring my dress in, there's a dear."

"Not sure I can trust myself, ha-ha. You and me alone in a bedroom, eh?"

"You are *naughty*, Tom."

But Major Anstruther, a gentleman, was soon back in the living-room, watching politely the deft hands of the shy brown man on the floor. Major Anstruther did not care much for cats: he was a dog-man himself. "Will they be all right now?" he asked politely.

Vythilingam said: "Injection every day. Perhaps all right then."

Anstruther had not been long in Malaya. He attributed this wog's clipped telegraphese to the shyness of one who meets socially a racial superior. He tried to put the poor man at his ease.

"Hot for the time of the year," he said.

Vythilingam nodded, got up, put away his instruments. "Hot," he agreed.

"I have a Golden Labrador," said Anstruther. "Back in England. You fond of dogs?"

"Some."

"It amuses some of us that the Chinese call us 'running dogs'," said Anstruther. "They don't seem to realise that it's really a kind of compliment." He laughed. "A dog's a noble beast."

"Yes."

"We'll be glad when it's over," said Anstruther. "This war's been going on too long. It's not a clean war, somehow. You can't get at the devils. That jungle's a nightmare."

"Nightmare."

"Here we are, Tom. You finished, Vy? I'm so, so grateful. I'm so glad you're back. We all wondered what had happened to you. Your mother was worried, I believe. She's gone back now. She'll be so pleased you're alive. There's *so* much news, Vy. Will you be in tomorrow? Bless you. Now we've got to fly. We mustn't keep the Brigadier waiting."

"Oh, the Brig's always late," said Anstruther. "Still, we'd better go. Get ginned up a bit before the fun starts. Good-bye, Mr. er—I hope we meet again."

"Good-bye, Vy," said the magnificent Rosemary, a vision of warm brown skin and rustling red silk. "You're a dear."

They were gone. The door slammed, Anstruther's cigarette smoke and Rosemary's perfume still faintly riding the air. Their laugher could be heard as they got in the car, fading as the car started and they moved off to the Mess. Vythilingam tenderly stroked Tigger, wiping with a bit of paper tissue the defiled mouth of the beast. He would get well. They would all get well. There was a medicine for everything. If one failed, you could try another. Vythilingam sighed, packed his State Veterinary Department bag, and left the cats lying there, confident that the healing juices would soon start their work. In the meantime there was bound to be a big back-log of correspondence in the office.

His car started quite well. That station-master had looked after it. And, moving gently down the avenue, Vythilingam thought that he had better pay a brief visit to his friends, the staid bachelor Sundralingam, and Arumugam of the high voice, before he returned to the office. They, at least, unchanged and yearning for better things, might welcome him back. He smiled slightly as he drove on the wrong side of the road.

It was a lovely night for Rosemary. The lights, the music, the attention. White-coated National Servicemen brought her pink gins (many, many: she forgot her promise to God and St. Anthony and the Little Flower and the rest of the baroque pantheon) and occasionally winked at her appreciatively. At so many levels did she appeal. So many officers with cummerbunds round slim waists, smelling of sweet young dewy manhood, asked her to dance. And she danced so well. She told a group, graduated from one star to three and a crown, about her London experiences and decorations-will-be-worn and television appearances and Oooooh, the proposals. Everybody was very gay.

The refreshments were excellent. Canapés of many kinds, galantines to be scooped or carved, cheese and onions, no Worcestershire sauce. But you could not have everything. The mousse of crab was most tasty. At the fifth mouthful something smote Rosemary hard. It was a memory of a poetry lesson in her training college in Liverpool: an earnest Empsonian young man, not really attractive. Tears began to smudge her mascara. "Poor Victor," she said to an empty space by the white-clothed table, "poor, poor Victor."

"He came, he saw, he conquered," said a quite handsome subaltern. "Victor ludorum."

"Poor Victor." And then somebody asked her to dance.

Also available by
ANTHONY BURGESS

NOVELS
Time for a Tiger
The Enemy in the Blanket
The Right to an Answer
The Doctor is Sick
The Worm and the Ring
Devil of a State
A Clockwork Orange
The Wanting Seed
Honey for the Bears
Nothing like the Sun
Tremor of Intent

(originally published as Joseph Kell)
Inside Mr Enderby

MINE OWN EXECUTIONER